PARADISE BOUND

Rafaële Désiré

Clear Source Publishing

To Raquel and Roxanne:

May you live your wildest dreams!

ACKNOWLEDGMENTS

My deep appreciation goes to my very first readers, Richard and Gabrielle. Thank you for your encouragement and support. You are a part of this and I'm eternally grateful for your contribution.

To David, Veronique, Charlayne, Nygel, Debra, Ben, Charla, Patrick, Jeff and Mark: Thank you for your precious feedback. James, seeing you realizing your dream was an inspiration. Thank you.

To my wonderful daughters Raquel and Roxanne: My heartfelt thanks for your precious suggestions and insights.

Thank you to Mike Sirota, who edited the first draft, and to Trai Cartwright, who edited and copy-edited the final draft: Trai, your input was invaluable and I owe you the title.

To the late Rachelle Benveniste, poet and writing teacher extraordinaire: I miss you. Thank you for giving me the confidence to write in my second language.

To my mother Gabrielle: Thank you for your unwavering support and for gifting me with the love of reading.

To my father Rodolphe, my brothers, Patrick, Mehdy, and Arjuna, and my aunts, uncles, cousins, nephews and nieces: Thank you for your love and encouragement.

And to my beloved late grandmother, Bonne-Maman: Thank you for watching over me.

CHAPTER ONE

I can't take this anymore. If somebody else dies on me today, I'm going to lose my mind. A heavy feeling of dread sliced through Natalie's heart and she put one hand on the wall to steady herself.

"*Dr. Dorel? Ça va?*"

"*Ça va, merci.*" Natalie had no choice but to turn toward the nurse behind her and force a smile. But Lucile's usually jovial face showed concern. "Really Lucile, I'm okay." Natalie took her hand off the wall and made an effort to stand up straight. "I haven't eaten this morning, that's all." Lucile had been her ally these past years, but Natalie wouldn't admit to anyone how frazzled she felt in that moment. Death was a daily occurrence at the hospital, so by now she should have developed a thick skin like most of her colleagues.

Lucile offered to get her something to eat and Natalie accepted, grateful to get a few moments to herself. She took refuge in the restrooms. A look in the mirror was enough to understand why the nurse had looked worried. The face that looked back was pale, almost haggard, the sad dark brown eyes nearly too large above the high cheekbones, the full heart-shaped lips pursed tight. A few strands of the straight jet-black hair had fallen out of her work ponytail and made her look even wearier.

She should have known that the last day of her residency at

the Val-Dieu Hospital in Paris would be brutal. She rubbed her face in her hands, trying to erase the memory of the failed CPR attempt on Mme Maurice, her favorite patient, a witty old lady, so precious and full of life in spite of a weak heart. The resuscitation team had tried to revive her for almost forty-five minutes.

Crying felt like an act of weakness, but it relieved Natalie's tension and she found herself calmer afterwards. Rolling her shoulders back and forth, she wondered if any of the other resident surgeons ever felt as drained as she did right now; if they did no one would know. Most of them projected an image of confidence and poise. None of them would ever admit feeling overwhelmed. Not at this point. But for Natalie the load had felt heavier these past months.

What was happening to her? What had happened to the strength and enthusiasm of the early years, when fighting to save lives seemed such a noble concept? Her stomach tightened. She used to feel so confident, so strong. All her life she had heard her mother telling family members, friends, whoever, how strong her daughter Natalie was; it almost sounded like criticism. It had to be the lack of sleep. She hadn't slept more than four hours a night in months.

"It's the last day," she chanted until she felt calmer. Then she washed her face, fixed her hair and exited the restrooms.

Lucile was waiting outside with a banana and a steaming cup of coffee, which Natalie accepted gratefully.

"Dr. Dorel," Lucile said with an apologetic smile while Natalie ate her banana, "I'm sorry but Dr. Bertrand was delayed. We have an emergency appendectomy and he asked for you to replace him."

Dr. Bertrand, the attending surgeon, was often late, and he always asked for Natalie to start without him, which was against hospital rules. It usually didn't bother her too much because she took it as a sign of trust, but this time, after witnessing the passing of a patient she had befriended, she would've preferred Bertrand there with her. However, there was no point in protesting.

Natalie took a few moments to gulp down her coffee and flew down the stairs to the operating room.

Her heart was beating fast as she scrubbed and slipped on her gown, hat, and gloves while her patient, a teenager of about seventeen years old, was getting prepped for the anesthesia. Natalie took a few deep breaths until she felt a cloud of calm descend on her.

Her hand was assured when she made a neat two-and-a-half inch incision through creamy pale skin and muscle layers. She brought up the red and swollen appendix through the opened wounds, separating it from the adjacent tissues, then ligated it and cut it off. The girl's abdomen rose up and down with the rhythm of her breathing.

So far, so good. Vital signs held steady. Appendectomies were usually easy surgical acts and Natalie felt in control.

She closed the site the appendix used to occupy and checked twice that no sponge had been left in the wounds before she finished suturing. She was starting to relax when an alarming beep went off, signaling a sudden drop in the young girl's blood pressure. The patient's heartbeat accelerated to a dangerous high. Jacques, the anesthesiologist, immediately injected her with beta-blockers, but the medication didn't have the expected effect.

"She going into cardiac arrest," he stated with an astonishing calm.

Natalie's own heart seemed to plunge in her chest before thumping loudly. She managed to keep her voice steady. "Ready to start CPR."

A defibrillator was immediately plugged to the girl's chest. The first charge brought no result. Natalie felt desperate. *No! Not again! Please God!* There was a second charge.

At the third, the patient's heart was restarted.

The whole team took a collective breath. Natalie took off her gloves and grabbed a clean towel to wipe her forehead, now wet with sweat. Her whole body was damp and her knees wobbly.

Jacques took over again and woke up the patient before she was wheeled to the recovery room. The team cheered and Natalie gave a silent prayer of thanks, but the truth was, she would have given anything to be able to go home right then, take a leisurely bath and crawl into bed.

Minutes later Dr. Bertrand showed up, offering no apologies for his lateness, but Natalie couldn't care less. She was finally dismissed and it was time to say *au revoir*.

"We are going to miss you Dr. Dorel," Lucile said, as they awkwardly kissed on both cheeks. "The patients will miss you, too. You were great." Lucile eyes seemed a little red and Natalie was touched. She would miss Lucile, Jacques and a few other staff members, but she was so glad her residency was officially over, she almost wanted to skip.

Natalie changed into her street clothes and left through the front doors. It was hard to believe that this stage of her life was finally over. She thought she should feel happy, but all she felt was emptiness and an immense fatigue. She had no idea what she would be doing next. She hadn't yet applied for work anywhere.

Val-Dieu Hospital wanted to keep her, but she hadn't given them an answer. Truth was, when she was in the vicinity of the icy hospital director, she wanted to flee. All she wanted was time to recharge her batteries, and maybe then she'd be able to think clearly and apply to various hospitals in town.

The sun was still high in the sky when Natalie hopped on a bus for a ten-minute ride to the *Faculté de Mèdecine*. She knew that the events of the day wouldn't allow her to rest, so she spent the next few hours at the medical library, putting the final touches to her upcoming thesis.

Satisfied with the final draft, she ran down the squeaky stairs of the moldy old school of medicine, feeling relieved. This was the moment she had prayed for. She exhaled and stepped out into the paved courtyard where the sunlight blinded her for an instant.

Summer was the only season she enjoyed in Paris, when winter boots were traded for open-toed sandals, and smiling tourists replaced the usual grumpy natives. Gone were the cold rains and depressing grayish sky. Sunrays poured on old stone buildings, making them look brand new and revealing their architectural splendor. Cafés spilled out on the sidewalk and life seemed more vibrant.

Natalie had envied those with enough free time to hang out in cafés and enjoy the city, but her hospital pager had enslaved her. If she hadn't been so tired, she would've enjoyed walking down the boulevard Saint-Michel to check out the many clothing stores.

She thought about Jean-Marc. His flight was scheduled to arrive later in the evening and he'd said that he wanted to take her out to celebrate, but where would she find the energy to go out? She felt guilty not to be more excited to see him.

Jean-Marc was an airline pilot for Air France and between his flight schedule and the hospital calling her at any time of the day or night, spending time together was often a challenge. To Natalie's surprise and relief, Jean-Marc hadn't complained too much about her crazy schedule, and she was grateful for his understanding. She had to make an effort to forget her day and enjoy the evening with him.

Natalie dozed off during the thirty-minute bus ride to her apartment and almost missed her stop. Stumbling on the last step, she lost her footing and nearly fell. Disheveled and clutching her heavy shoulder bag under her arm, she buzzed herself into her building, rode the tiny squeaky elevator to the fifth floor, and with a sigh of relief, let herself into her one-bedroom apartment.

Besides a few dishes in the sink and the unmade bed, the place was almost in order, so Natalie decided to spend the next hour in the bathroom. She shampooed her hair and sat for the longest time in a warm bubbly bath, but she still couldn't shake the tension. Her feet, her legs and her whole body ached. She finally got out of the bathroom in her bathrobe, a towel wrapped around her head, to retrieve an unopened bottle of coconut liquor from the fridge. She usually didn't drink, but she hoped alcohol would help her finally relax.

Pouring herself a small glass, she looked at the clock. Jean-Marc had promised he would call as soon as he landed around 6 p.m., but it was already past 7. His flight was probably delayed. That often happened during summer.

With a loud sigh she plopped onto her couch. Her body relaxed a little as she sipped the sweet liquor, but her mind stayed restless.

Was she fit for the profession she had chosen? Was it normal to feel dread before going to work every day? She wished she had a friend to talk to right now. The few friends she had in Paris were all in the medical field, but Natalie didn't think they'd really understand. Simone, her best friend, who now lived in Los Angeles, came to her mind.

Simone had been her roommate years ago at the Foyer International, a place that welcomed students coming from different parts of the country and abroad. While Natalie came from Martinique to start her medical studies, Simone, whose father was French and mother American, traveled to France from L.A. to study art history. They became close friends despite their different backgrounds and temperaments, and Natalie never regretted when she neglected her studies to follow her friend to lively parties or art exhibitions. At the end of the year, Simone decided art history was boring, and returned to the United States to study acting. Despite the distance, they never lost contact.

Natalie grabbed her address book by the phone and dialed the number in Los Angeles. Simone rarely went to bed before 3 a.m.

"Natalie! What's up girl?" Simone's voice was perky even at 2 a.m., L.A. time. "I'm so glad to hear your voice."

Natalie smiled, genuinely happy to hear her friend. "Same here. How are you?"

"Well, I'm just going through the motions. You know, auditioning and all. I shot a national commercial last month, so that was cool. What about you, *doctor*?"

Natalie smiled. "I'm finally done with the residency, if you can believe it. Today was my last day."

"Yay!" Simone gasped. "I'm so excited for you. Are you

celebrating?"

"Well, Jean-Marc is taking me to dinner…"

"Dinner and that's it? Seems boring. What about real party-ing? I mean, going to clubs, dancing, getting drunk. You know what I'm talking about."

Natalie laughed. "That's not Jean-Marc's style. And anyway, I'm too exhausted to party. As it is, I'll have to drag my feet to the restaurant."

"Girl, you forgot how to have fun. Don't worry, I'll remind you. *I* know you're a party girl at heart."

Natalie sighed. "The party girl is no more. It's all work and responsibilities now."

"Uh-oh! You don't sound too good. You actually sound a lit-tle depressed." Simone paused. "Hey, you've been promising for years to come visit me in L.A. Maybe now is the time."

Natalie stayed silent for a while. Simone had invited her to come to L.A. several times, but she never had a chance to seriously consider it. However, this time, the idea of going far away from Paris to an exciting place like Los Angeles made her mind feel clearer and her body lighter. The corners of her mouth turned up a little. God knew how much she needed a vacation. But could she go on her own, without Jean-Marc? He had no days off planned in the near future. And what about her job search? Natalie sighed. "I don't know if it's possible right now."

"Why not?"

"I still have so many things to figure out…"

"Figure them out in L.A. then," Simone argued. "Nat, you're thinking too much. Just come and have some fun. Do you remem-ber how much fun we had last time in Martinique?" Simone's voice was so full of enthusiasm that Natalie found herself smiling wildly. A vacation in Los Angeles could be just what she needed. "You're tempting me," she finally said.

"Yay! I'll take that as a yes," Simone said, laughing.

The air smelled of the sugary crepes sold by street vendors. Herds of backpackers and youngsters sat around the fountain St-Michel to enjoy the sweetness of the early evening. Natalie hurried through the restaurant district, the kingdom of mostly Greek and Moroccan eateries. She hoped that she would be at Chez Momo before Jean-Marc because she needed some time to think about how she would break the news to him. So far, she couldn't think of anything to say. The elation she felt at her rash decision was mixed with a heavy dose of guilt.

She arrived at the busy restaurant before Jean-Marc and ordered the house cocktail while she waited for him. How would she approach the subject? There was no way around it. She had to come to terms with the fact that Jean-Marc would be upset.

He appeared a few minutes later, a handsome young man still dressed in his navy blue pilot's uniform. Jean-Marc had a big smile as he approached the table.

"Is this a new dress? You look very pretty tonight," he said as he sat down.

Natalie smiled and pulled him toward her for a kiss. "You're too kind. Thank you." In his light brown eyes she could see an appreciative spark. Jean-Marc always liked it when she wore a dress, a rare event these past months.

"So you've made it. Congratulations, Dr. Dorel." He raised his hand for a high-five. Natalie returned the gesture and Jean-

Marc was about to pull her for a kiss when the waiter came to take their order. As usual, Jean-Marc asked for couscous merguez and Natalie chose the lamb.

The restaurant buzzed with the hum of conversation, the clicking of forks, and the jovial voices of the waiters. The aroma of sausages, chicken, and stewed meat spread across the small dining room. Natalie observed Jean-Marc as he smiled at her. There were many things she liked about him. He was always thoughtful and attentive. Those who didn't know him would sometimes consider him to be smug because he often stated his point of view with authority, but Natalie liked his self-confidence.

The way he looked at her made her feel desirable. When she had so much in her head that she forgot that she was a woman, Jean-Marc made her feel sexy anyway. And he looked good. She cared about him and she felt proud of him. It was just that she needed to figure out her life right now.

"You know what I'm thinking about?" he said just as she was about to speak. He reached out to caress her cheek. "We should move in together." He caught her legs between his and squeezed them.

"Oh… you think so?" Natalie felt her cheeks heat up. Jean-Marc had already made several allusions to living together, but this was the most direct one. "But my place is too small for the both of us, and yours is too far outside Paris," she said, knowing that her excuse wouldn't be enough for Jean-Marc.

"We could look for a new place together," Jean-Marc answered as if he had anticipated Natalie's response. "What do you say?" The smile on his face made Natalie's heart sink. She loved spending time with him, but the truth was she enjoyed their arrangement living apart.

"That's something I'll have to consider," she said after a pause. Jean-Marc raised an eyebrow. She couldn't delay any longer what she had in mind.

"Jean-Marc, there's something I need to tell you." She took a deep breath. "I'm going to Los Angeles for a month."

There, she'd let it out. Natalie braced herself for Jean-Marc's reaction.

Jean-Marc's jaw dropped open. "What?"

"Simone invited me to visit her in L.A. and I accepted," Natalie said quickly. "I just need time away from the hospital. It has nothing to do with us."

"To Los Angeles? For a month?" Jean-Marc repeated. His tone was calm but incredulous.

"It just felt like what I needed," Natalie said, crossing her hands in front of her as she pleaded for Jean-Marc's understanding. "I need to leave Paris and the hospital for a while. I had the shittiest day ever and I really want to get away from it all." Jean-Marc's silence suggested that there was more she needed to say and Natalie started to feel some irritation at his reaction. She wanted him to understand her decision, but she didn't like having to defend it. Wasn't she a free woman? Did she need anyone's permission to take a month vacation?

"What do you think?" she asked with some exasperation when the silence became too long.

"What do you want me to think?" Jean-Marc spoke slowly, as if he was trying to stay calm. "I've been waiting for you to finish your residency so that we can spend more time together, and now as soon as you're done, you're going away for a month... on your own?" He was trying to keep his voice level, but his frown gave away his anger.

Natalie couldn't apologize for what she felt was necessary to her survival. How could no one see that she was close to a nervous breakdown?

"We can't spend that much more time together anyway," she said, louder and more defiantly than she had wanted. "You're always gone! You want me to stay in Paris the whole summer so I can see you once or twice on the weekends?" She rubbed her temples in an attempt to erase the beginnings of a headache. Jean-Marc sighed and took both of her hands in his.

"I just asked you to live with me," he said, his tone softening. "Maybe you don't have to go away for a month. Or maybe you can postpone your trip? Paris is the most beautiful city in the world. Why go anywhere else?" Jean-Marc's voice grew more desperate. "We can have dinner on the Eiffel Tower, hang out in Montmartre, and do what the tourists do. You have a lot going on here. We could look for an apartment in August and be settled by September."

Natalie lifted her eyes to meet his. She was aware that most women would have sacrificed a vacation for him without hesitation. She couldn't say this to Jean-Marc without hurting his feelings, but she didn't want to spend her summer looking for an apartment. Her relationship with Jean-Marc so far had been uncomplicated. The sex was good and they rarely argued about anything. Jean-Marc had always been cool and understanding. She understood that her last-minute decision was a shock for him, but could he really deny her this much-needed time off?

Her chest tightened and she considered taking an anti-anxiety pill from the little bottle she carried in her handbag. She'd been relying on those pills to relieve her of her anxiety for a year now.

Natalie sighed. "Today I lost my favorite patient and had to resuscitate someone. I haven't had a full night's sleep in months. I am exhausted. I know that if I stay in Paris the hospital will keep calling me since they're understaffed. They may even give me a full-time position there. But I need a real vacation. I can't even think straight right now. Please understand that."

Jean-Marc looked dejected. "I'm sorry you had a terrible day. Believe me, I understand your frustration, but I really want you to stay, Natalie."

She removed her hands from his. "Why?"

"I was planning to take you to Rome next weekend."

Natalie didn't expect this. "Rome?" Italy was her favorite country in Europe. Did he just make that up? "Next weekend?"

Jean-Marc flashed a crooked smile. "Yeah! We can fly first thing Saturday morning."

"And be back by Sunday night?" How could she exchange a whole month away for the promise of an ultra-short weekend– even if it was in Italy? And then she would have to return to the threat of being called back to the hospital as well as the daunting task of looking for an apartment.

A surge of indignation rose through her. She'd worked hard and she deserved some down time.

"Why are you doing this to me?" she demanded. "If you were the one going away, I would be happy that you would get to relax. Even if I'm not there."

"I agree that you need a break and, of course, I'm happy

that you can finally have some downtime," Jean-Marc answered quickly. Then he paused. "But I don't know about you hanging out in Hollywood with your actress girlfriend."

Natalie thought for a moment, then understood what he meant. "I'm not going there to do anything wild. If you can't trust me then what's the point of us living together?" The expression in his eyes confirmed that she was right. He was afraid of losing her.

Natalie softened. "A month will go by fast. Then I'll be rested, in a much better mood, and ready to start again. Maybe we can still take a few days off together when you're free?" She was pleading again, but the guilt she felt creeping inside her head wasn't strong enough to change her mind. She leaned forward and placed her hand on top of his.

"I guess I can look for the apartment by myself," he conceded reluctantly.

"Just wait for me," Natalie said. "We'll find the perfect place together."

The thought made her vaguely queasy. It wasn't that she didn't love Jean-Marc; she was sure she did, but agreeing to live with him only so he would let her go on her vacation was wrong. It felt like she was a prisoner trying to escape a jail she had built for herself.

Jean-Marc sighed in resignation and forced a smile.

At that moment, two waiters appeared and, with the grace of dancers, placed tureens of heavenly smelling lamb, sausages, and couscous in front of them. Natalie and Jean-Marc ate without any more references to Natalie's upcoming trip. Jean-Marc talked about the crazy air traffic that often forced him to fly above Paris for an hour before he could land his plane and Natalie just listened.

She didn't want to talk about her day. Her flash of anger toward him dissolved as she watched him talk. She liked the way his eyebrows would knit together, making him look intense. She liked how tall and broad-shouldered he was, and she liked the crooked smile that hadn't changed from the time they were both teenagers.

He was the perfect man for her, smart and handsome. They both came from the same tiny Caribbean island and their parents used to be neighbors. There was a feeling of comfort and security in their relationship that Natalie appreciated.

But if everything is so perfect with him, why is it so urgent for me to get away? She rubbed her forehead with both hands, but it did little to erase her headache. Jean-Marc didn't seem to notice anything.

After they ordered coffee, Jean-Marc retrieved a long velvet box from his pocket.

"I bought you something to celebrate the end of your ordeal and the beginning of our new life." With a mysterious smile he pushed the box in front of her and Natalie's mouth opened in surprise. Inside the box, on a black satin pillow, sat a gold necklace with an exquisite house-shaped gold locket. Its roof and door were finely chiseled and made of white gold. Natalie swung the tiny door open. Inside was an engraved heart with Natalie and Jean-Marc's initials on each side.

"Oh! It is beautiful. How sweet..." Jean-Marc's thoughtfulness brought tears to her eyes. She leaned over the table to give him a long, tender kiss. Then, she removed the necklace from its box so that she could put it on.

"Let me help you with it." Jean-Marc slid from his chair to sit next to her. She moved her hair to the side as he attached the striking jewel onto her neck. Looking into Jean-Marc's eyes, Natalie saw his hopefulness about their relationship.

But then the necklace felt heavy on her chest, as if it were binding her to him like a weight keeping a helium balloon from flying away.

Natalie's pager buzzed in her handbag and they both froze, knowing what it meant. Jean-Marc shook his head and looked away.

Dr. Dorel, call Lucile at the hospital ASAP, the text said.

Her hands shaking, Natalie dialed the number.

"Dr. Dorel!" Lucile's voice sounded urgent. "I'm really sorry. I know that your residency is over, but we are swamped and Dr. Bertrand requested you. Can you be here as soon as possible?"

Natalie sighed and agreed to be there within an hour. After she hung up, she didn't speak for a while. In that moment, she remembered her patient Mme Maurice. "Life is precious and each moment is a gift. Make sure that you enjoy every second of it," the old lady had told her the day before she died. Natalie knew she couldn't keep going like this. If she was to listen to Mme Maurice's advice, she *had* to escape from Paris.

CHAPTER TWO

Natalie exited Los Angeles International Airport with her two pieces of luggage, and smiled when she looked up at the blue sky. She registered the activity outside the terminal with curiosity mixed with a bit of apprehension. There she was, on her own, in this mega metropolis, and her friend was nowhere in sight. Natalie didn't mind taking a cab, but Simone had insisted on picking her up. As Natalie debated her options, Simone finally sent a text message announcing that she was on her way.

Natalie sat on a bench outside the terminal to wait, cheerfully at first. As the time passed she started to wonder if Simone had really meant her invitation. Then she recalled that her friend was always late.

Simone's black Jeep pulled up an hour later. The beautiful creature that ran out of the car with open arms looked like a much blonder, curvier, and sexier version of the Simone Natalie remembered.

"You've made it. I'm so happy." Simone gave Natalie a bear hug. "Sorry I'm late. I had a last-minute audition I couldn't cancel. And the traffic at this time of day is terrible."

Natalie relaxed. Simone, like everyone, had a busy life. She was there, and a last-minute audition was an important matter—or at least a good excuse to be late.

"That's okay, don't worry about it," Natalie said. "I should have arranged to take a cab anyway. How did your audition go?"

Simone dismissed the question with a flip of her hand. "It was bull. I only went there because my agent insisted that I show up. He loves to submit me for those low-paying bimbo roles. I can't wait to be in a position to fire him."

Natalie smiled. Her friend hadn't changed much. She'd always said what was on her mind.

Simone ran her hand through Natalie's smooth shoulder-length hair. "I love your haircut. You look great."

"Thank you, Sims. You look wonderful," Natalie said, hugging her friend again.

They stuffed Natalie's luggage in the back seat of the Jeep and hopped in. Natalie grinned. Here she was, finally in Los Angeles. She couldn't believe it. The sight of gigantic palm trees swaying in the blue sky filled her with delight.

"So you have a new boyfriend?" she asked Simone as they merged into the traffic exiting the airport.

"Yeah! Ted. He's so cute. Did I tell you that he's a movie director? And guess what, he's been slowly moving in with me. He's already brought over his toothbrush. That's a sign, right?" Her smile widened.

In Paris it wouldn't mean anything but maybe it means something in L.A., Natalie thought. "You think he's moving in?" she said, squirming. "I need to find a hotel then."

"Oh don't worry. My parents are off to Hawaii. They'll be gone for the month. You can stay in their guesthouse. It's only a block from the beach."

"Are you sure they're okay with that?"

"They are totally fine with it, don't worry. Anyway, Ted's

busy working on a new project. We'll have plenty of time to-gether."

"Well, okay then." Again, Natalie pushed away her concerns. If things didn't work out, she would just shorten her trip. Jean-Marc would be delighted.

She observed her new environment with acute interest. The roads were so large, with so many lanes; they felt like freeways. Noticing some stretch limousines, Natalie chuckled, wondering if a movie star was hiding in one of them. In Paris, the truly wealthy often enjoyed the discretion of regular cars. This world was quite remote from the one she lived in.

"Where are the skyscrapers?" Natalie asked. "It's very different from what I'd imagined."

"We have skyscrapers in downtown L.A.," Simone answered, "but the Westside is a whole different vibe. I'll take you through Venice Beach. It's my favorite place in the city. My parents live not too far away, in Santa Monica."

Natalie caught glimpses of the ocean sparkling between the small buildings. Pedestrians in shorts and bathing suits crossed the street in front of them. Pacific Avenue became Ocean Avenue, bordered by tall palm trees, chic hotels, and restaurants. An immense white sandy beach stretched below in the distance, a truly beautiful sight that reminded Natalie of the South of France. She hadn't expected Los Angeles to be so cheerful. There was a sort of nonchalance in the way people walked down the street. *Oh, I'm going to enjoy this vacation,* she thought as a big smile stretched her lips.

Then Ocean Avenue became narrow and residential, turning into a sinuous road flanked by beautiful houses.

Simone slowed down in front of an entrance bordered by high hedges. She turned into an alley leading to a semi-circular driveway, and then stopped in front of a handsome two-story Italian villa whose front lawn was beautifully landscaped with banana trees, red cannas, and birds of paradise–the same kind of flora that could be found in Martinique. Natalie instantly fell in love with the house and its salmon color, red brick roof, and iron rod balconies.

"Wow! Is this where you grew up?" she asked.

"No, unfortunately! My parents bought this house four years ago. I lived most of my life in an apartment building in Manhattan Beach across from their restaurant. But believe me, I visit them as often as I can." She unlocked the heavy wooden gate, leading into a backyard with a large blue-bottom pool, a gazebo and a small grassy yard. The guesthouse, with the same cheerful salmon stucco and red brick roof, stood on the other side of the pool.

"Do you come here with Ted?" Natalie asked.

"I don't talk to him about my parents. I'm a struggling actress so I don't want him to think that I have it easy."

"But he'll have to meet your parents at some point, right?"

"Well yes, but not now. Anyway, it's complicated. When I first met him, I told him that I was born and raised in New York to impress him. You know, New York actresses are taken much more seriously. It's a small lie; I did study in New York, but I can't tell him now that my parents have a restaurant in Manhattan Beach. I think I'll wait until I'm sure he's hopelessly in love, and then I'll break the news of my bourgeois roots." Simone opened the door of the guesthouse. "*Et voila!*"

The guesthouse was a bright one-bedroom with shiny wood floors under a large skylight. It had a small kitchen and even a fireplace. Natalie couldn't believe her good fortune.

She took a quick shower and changed clothes before jumping in the Jeep with Simone. Just riding to an unknown destination was more fun than she'd had in months. Jean-Marc's face popped up in her thoughts. She touched her little house-shaped locket, which hadn't left her neck since he had given it to her. Their last night had been spoiled by his disapproval of her vacation. They had made love but it had felt a little awkward, and she had faked an orgasm to make him feel better.

"Be good," was the last thing he'd said to her before kissing her goodbye.

During the long time spent in traffic, Natalie told Simone about her life with Jean-Marc. They finally exited a crowded avenue to turn onto a quiet street with big trees and small buildings. They parked in front of an apartment complex of several two-story buildings grouped around a flowery courtyard.

"That's where I live," Simone said.

Natalie found the place charming. Simone had a corner apartment on the ground level. It had a small porch with an arcade and a patch of roses and gardenias under her windows.

Natalie followed her friend into a nicely decorated small living room with hardwood floors, Spanish red walls, and white moldings. Pictures of Simone in various poses and theater posters with her name in big letters hung on the walls.

"It's so cute," Natalie said.

"Yes! But it's too small. If Ted really moves in, we'll have to get a bigger place."

"I thought he was moving in for sure."

Simone frowned. "He's here most of the time but his work

stuff is still at his house, and he has a lot of that. We'll see."

There was a small kitchen off the living room, a tiny bathroom and a spacious bedroom. On the wall above the bed hung a remarkable painting of a naked woman with long black hair, sitting at the top of a cliff above a sparkling midnight blue ocean. Her face was turned toward a blue moon and her skin had a pale blue shade. Her hair seemed to meld with the dark ocean. The painting reminded Natalie of Salvador Dali's surrealistic style. It was signed *Jerry McDane*.

"I like this painting," Natalie said.

"That's by my cousin Jerry. We're going to see an exhibition of his work tonight."

"When? Now? Why didn't you tell me? I'm not dressed enough." She wore jeans, high heel sandals and a curve-hugging white top.

"You look great. Don't worry, it's pretty casual. Nobody dresses much in L.A. I've got to change, though. Make yourself comfortable, you're at home."

Natalie was grateful to have a spacious guesthouse for herself. It would have been difficult to share such a small space, even one as cute as Simone's apartment, for a whole month. You should never plan to stay a month at someone's house. What was she thinking? She sat on the bed and stared at the painting.

Simone emerged from the bathroom naked and rummaged in her dresser for panties. She had never been shy with her body. She stopped to admire herself in the mirror.

"I'm very happy with my implants," she said, holding her breasts in each hand.

"Oh, I thought there was something different from the last

time I saw you. You didn't need that," Natalie said.

"Girl, in Hollywood you need all the help you can get. I started to get work as soon as I got my big boobs. You should see those casting directors drooling over my cleavage," Simone laughed. "Best money I ever spent. The unwanted side effect is that nobody looks at me in the eye anymore."

"Can't have it all," Natalie said, chuckling.

After trying several outfits, Simone finally slipped into a tiny and revealing black dress that Natalie thought looked rather fancy. Natalie checked her own reflection in the mirror and felt fine with it. What she had on fit her well. As a teenager growing up in Martinique, she loved to dress in shorts and tank tops. Her bikinis were nothing short of scandalous. She started to favor a more classic style in Paris, when her high heels and colorful skirts were looked upon with raised eyebrows by the academia. Her integration from her island to Paris had been slow. In med school, she learned to stop smiling brightly each time someone said hello. She also learned to play down her looks by cutting her long hair to shoulder length, keeping her nails short, and eliminating bright colors from her wardrobe. While at school, she wore glasses that made her look more bookish. But she kept her toenails brightly painted, and wore the gold jewels typical to her island. On her wrist she kept a shell bracelet bought on the beach of Sainte-Anne on a particularly blissful day. She sighed at the memory.

An hour later, Simone pulled in front of a white one-story building on Melrose Avenue. Valets in red jackets and black pants rushed to the Jeep and helped them out.

Through the gallery's glass walls, Natalie could see a hip young crowd moving around with glasses in hand between huge paintings hung on the gallery's white walls. It wasn't the kind of art exhibition she had attended in Paris, where people did their best to appear chic and cultured. This looked more like a party, with loud Techno music competing with the hum of a rather casual crowd. Simone smiled brightly, offering greetings and air kisses.

To Natalie's surprise, she got compliments on her accent when all she said was *Nice to meet you*. That was different. Parisians had the lowest tolerance for accents.

Simone sometimes forgot to introduce Natalie, who didn't mind. She understood that her friend was somehow working. She decided to wander around and explore the place on her own.

The surrealistic artwork was intriguing with its choice of blatant colors and the incorporation of abstract elements. Most of the paintings represented frail human figures surrounded by apocalyptic landscapes. After she toured the gallery she came back to her favorite piece, a three-by-four-foot painting of a small brown-skinned boy fishing from his little canoe in a sea of blood and flames. The calm attitude of the boy and the innocence of his face contrasted sharply with the violence of the crimson waves. Natalie was hypnotized. Someone tapped her on the shoulder. She spun around to see Simone.

"Hey Nat, let me introduce you to my cousin Jerry. He painted all these masterpieces."

Jerry was so handsome that when their eyes met, Natalie felt a stab in the middle of her chest. She had imagined a nice-looking blond guy, but in front of her was a man no doubt of African descent, with wild, wooly hair and skin the same copper shade as hers. His pupils, very dark, glistened. Somehow he looked familiar. If he was Simone's cousin, his mother or father must be black.

"*Enchantée*," Natalie said in French. In her confusion, she spontaneously used her native language.

"*Moi de même,*" he answered with a faint smile. So he spoke French. *He must know the effect he has on women,* Natalie thought. She indicated the painting of the boy. "I love it." She wanted to add something meaningful but nothing came out. There was an awkward moment of silence. Jerry seemed to wait for the rest of her sentence.

"Thank you," he finally said, then excused himself and walked away. Admirers, likely with more original comments than hers, surrounded him immediately.

Puzzled, Natalie turned toward Simone.

"Don't worry," Simone laughed. "He acts like a weirdo before he gets to know people, but it's because he's kind of shy."

"He doesn't seem shy," Natalie said as she kept looking at him. He wore black slacks and a crisp white shirt, untucked and unbuttoned at the sleeves and collar. Jerry looked like the kind of man that drove women crazy and turned them into fools. Blinking danger signs flashed in front of her eyes. She decided in a split second to steer clear from him.

"How come you never mentioned your cousin?" she asked Simone.

Her friend giggled. "I told you that I had a cousin who was a painter. That's why I dragged you to all those art exhibitions in Paris. That's even why I studied art history. You didn't pay attention."

"You never mentioned he was that good-looking," Natalie said.

Simone rolled her eyes. "If you knew how many of my girlfriends fall for him… it's ridiculous. Please don't be one of them."

"Don't worry, I won't. I already have a man. Besides, I don't think I made a big impression on him."

"Don't bet on it," Simone said with a sneer.

Natalie saw her friend's eyes light up when a blond man made his way toward her. They kissed on the lips, and she looked at Natalie, beaming.

"Nat, this is Ted. Ted, meet my friend Natalie."

"Natalie, it's a pleasure to meet you," Ted said with a pleasant smile.

Ted was cute in a California surfer kind of way. His appearance didn't surprise Natalie. Simone generally fell for this type of pretty boy. Ted wasn't tall, but he had a beautiful smile with perfectly white straight teeth. He asked Natalie questions about Paris, his favorite place in the world ever since he had shot a movie there.

"What movie was that?" Natalie asked.

"*Graveyard Shifters*," Simone answered. "Ted wrote and directed it."

"Oh, yes! I remember. It was a horror movie. It did really well in Paris." Natalie disliked horror movies. Fortunately, nobody asked her if she had seen it. Ted looked pleased that she knew about it. He did smile a lot. Natalie forbade herself to judge him. It was another of her bad habits, thinking that she could figure people out at first sight. She thought about Jerry and unconsciously surveyed the crowd, looking for him.

It was such a young crowd; she doubted that any of them could afford these paintings. Natalie wished she could buy the painting of the little boy in the sea of red flames, but it cost $10,000. Even if she had the money, it would be complicated to ship the painting to Paris.

As she finished her second glass of white wine, she felt ex-hausted. Her watch, still on Paris time, indicated 7 a.m.

"How can I get a taxi from here?" she asked Simone, whose eyes sparkled as if the night had just started. "I can't keep my eyes open anymore. I have to go to bed."

"You don't need a cab; we'll drive you back home," Simone said. She turned to Ted. "Nat wants to leave, let's go."

As they made their way toward the exit, Simone suddenly stopped. "One second, I have to go to the bathroom," she told Ted. "Nat, you want to come, too?" She dragged Natalie by her arm be-fore she could answer.

"Shoot, I told Ted you were staying in a hotel," she whis-pered in Natalie's ear as soon as they were out of sight. "I don't want him to see my parents' house; he's going to ask questions."

"I'll take a cab, that's all," Natalie said. All she wanted was to be able close her eyes.

"I don't want you to take a cab. Let me think... Okay, I'll just ask Ted to wait here while I drive you back."

Simone marched back to Ted before Natalie could say any-thing. From a distance, Natalie saw Jerry and Ted talking. A couple interrupted them and cornered Jerry. Ted stepped back and took a sip from his drink. Natalie watched him drop his glass and clutch his throat, a look of absolute terror on his face.

"What's wrong?" Simone shouted. Ted, trying desperately to breathe, was panicking. He was choking on something. *Oh no!* Natalie thought. She ran behind him and circled him with her arms. Her fists clenched, she gave an upward thrust under his solar plexus but nothing happened. Natalie felt her own fear weakening her knees. Repositioning herself behind him, she gave the biggest thrust she could muster, almost lifting him off his feet. Something that looked like a big black olive flew out of his mouth. He took a big gulp of air, which triggered a coughing fit, and then tripped, taking Natalie down with him. Simone dramatically fell on the floor to hug him.

Natalie had fallen awkwardly on her folded leg and had some difficulty getting up, but someone caught her under the armpits and lifted her. She turned to see Jerry.

"Are you okay?" he asked, with a look of concern. Natalie put her left foot on the floor with caution. It hurt a little, but she was fine. She nodded and thanked Jerry for his help.

Ted stood with Simone's assistance and looked at Natalie with obvious emotion, grasping her in a hug that seemed to last several minutes. Natalie patted him gently on the back, but broke away from him soon, worrying that Simone might take offense.

"It was awful! I couldn't breathe. I couldn't say a word. Oh my God! You saved my life," Ted said, his blue eyes wide open. He placed his arms around Natalie's shoulders and kissed her cheeks several times. His breath smelled of alcohol. "How can I ever pay you back?"

"Don't worry about it. I'm happy I could help," Natalie said. Ted gave her another big hug and kept hanging on to her. Simone grimaced. She separated them and hugged Natalie herself. "Wow, Nat," she said. "Thank you so much."

A few people who had witnessed the scene asked Ted how he felt and patted Natalie on the back. But her brain seemed to have shut off for the night; now she couldn't understand a word of the conversations taking place around her. She just wanted to drop on the floor and fall asleep right there. She turned to Jerry, who still stood close by, observing everything with interest.

"Could you please call me a cab? I need to go to bed."

"I can give you a ride," he said.

"Oh! No, Jerry, it's okay, I'll take her," Simone said. But Natalie didn't want Simone to leave Ted at the party by himself. He looked like he needed to go to bed himself. Nor did she want to complicate their relationship.

"You should take him home," she told Simone. "He needs rest."

"Don't worry, Sims," Jerry said quickly. "I can drive her home." He turned back to Natalie. "Besides, I owe you big time. You saved the night."

"It's your party," Natalie insisted. "You can't leave now."

"Nobody can stop me," Jerry said with a smile. "That's the beauty of being a free man."

"Are you sure?" Simone asked. Natalie wondered why Simone looked so worried when she should be relieved.

"I flew in this afternoon from Paris," Natalie said as they drove off in Jerry's car. It was a black SUV with its backseat filled with several oversized cans of paint. "I can hardly keep my eyes open." Her voice sounded foreign even to herself. She'd had quite a day; flying thirteen hours, attending an art exhibition, rescuing Simone's boyfriend, and now riding home with a man who looked like he came straight out of a fashion magazine. This was a far cry from her regular Paris routine.

"It's the jet lag, *le décalage horaire*," Jerry said.

"So you speak French?" Natalie asked.

"A little. I lived in Paris for almost a year, but that was a long time ago. What's the address of your hotel?"

"I'm staying at Simone's parents' guesthouse in Santa Monica. You know where it is, right?"

"Sure." Jerry kept his eyes on the road but occasionally gave her a piercing look that triggered a strange sensation in her body. Her skin seemed to tingle. She attributed this to her fatigue.

"Where did you learn the Heimlich maneuver?" Jerry asked, breaking the silence.

"I'm a surgeon. I just finished my residency." Jerry glanced at her and raised his eyebrows. She was used to the look of surprise on people's face when they learned her occupation—a reaction she usually savored.

"We were lucky to have a doctor at the party tonight. I don't want to think about what could have happened if you hadn't been there to rescue Simone's new flame." Jerry gave her another troubling, intense look through his thick eyelashes.

Natalie nodded, but was eager to change the conversation. "Are you pleased with tonight's outcome?" Images of emergencies and CPR rescues that didn't get happy endings started to pop into her inner vision, and she had come to L.A. to forget about it all for a while.

"It was going well before the incident," Jerry said. "We sold a few paintings and some reviewers showed up. Hopefully, they'll write something good. That's pretty much all we can hope for."

"I enjoyed your exhibition," she said. "The subjects in your paintings look like innocent victims, unaware of the danger surrounding them."

Jerry mumbled a thank you and his lips curled up in an ambiguous smile.

Natalie wondered what was on his mind. Did he think that she was flirting with him? She hadn't said anything inappropriate, but he was glancing at her with the confidence of a man sure he could get any girl he wanted. Well, unlike the subjects of his paintings, she wasn't an innocent victim. If he thought that she would fall into his arms, he was mistaken.

Still, just sitting next to him stirred something inside of her. His paintings were like a mysterious and fascinating language, but they made sense to her.

For some reason, she thought about her mother and the pain she'd gone through when her handsome father abandoned them for a young woman from Venezuela. Natalie was five years old and her brother Roger was twelve. When she grew older, she made a conscious effort to avoid playboys. Jerry was the kind of man she instinctively distrusted, but his talent made him intriguing.

She forced herself to think of something else. Looking through the window, she noticed how the streetlights were installed differently than in France, on the other side of the crossing instead of at the closest corner of the street. She observed the boutiques, tried to memorize the names of the streets and avenues, and noted how complicated it was to make a left turn with the way the traffic lights were set up. She had no real sense of where she was going. And her fatigue gave the whole experience a dreamy feeling.

"How long are you staying in L.A.?" Jerry asked, breaking the short silence.

"I plan to stay a month," she said. It sounded like she was talking about a year. The day that had just gone by felt like a week. "I have to rent a car tomorrow morning."

They finally reached their destination. Lanterns lit the house and its front yard, casting a beautiful glow on the many palm trees. Jerry got out of the car to open Natalie's door. She couldn't move. When he took her hand to help her out, his touch caused a sensation that shot all the way up her arm. He let go of her hand and walked her to the guesthouse. The pool and the backyard were also lit, giving the whole house the look of an exotic resort. Jerry waited for Natalie to open the door.

"Thank you for the ride," she said, her speech slurred.

"It was my pleasure. Welcome to L.A.," he said before disappearing into the night.

CHAPTER THREE

In the morning light, the guesthouse looked bright and cheerful with its lemon yellow walls. The pine furniture in the bedroom was simple and solid, reminding her of the bedroom of the three bears in the *Goldilocks* story. She had slept comfortably in the large bed, but her recurrent operating room nightmare had disrupted her sleep.

In her dream, her grandfather, Papa Eugene, was a surgery patient. His chest was opened and his arteries clamped, but Natalie stood frozen, her scalpel in her hand, with no idea of what to do next. At the beginning of her residency, she attributed the dreams to her fear of making mistakes. She thought that it would disappear as she gained experience, but the dream kept recurring, usually triggered by a stressful event, this time probably the choking incident with Ted.

Natalie opened all the kitchen cabinets in search of caffeine and felt a surge of love for Simone when she discovered a fragrant pack of Italian breakfast blend in the refrigerator. She put the coffee and water in the espresso machine on the kitchen counter, turned it on, and sat at the kitchen table.

Stretching her toes, she exhaled. A whole month in front of her to do whatever she pleased, to discover a new city, new people, and a new way of life! It didn't get any better than this. Jerry came to her mind. He was striking, but he looked liked the kind of man who collected women. She promised herself to keep away from him.

Her thoughts went to Simone. Natalie remembered her as being funny and earnest. Her enthusiasm now seemed a little less sincere, but everybody changed with time and circumstances. Simone was fun to be with, and Nathalie felt very grateful for her hospitality.

After finishing her coffee, she showered and got dressed. The day before, she had spotted several hotels not too far from the house on Ocean Avenue. One of them was bound to have a car rental service.

An hour later, Natalie had rented a cute silver American car whose name she had never heard before. She felt a short burst of apprehension driving off the lot. Driving in Los Angeles was intimidating but she told herself that after driving in Paris, she could drive anywhere. Paris' map was a nightmare with its complicated design. She had gotten lost many times just driving around the block. Natalie remembered her terror the first time she drove Place de l'Etoile, a giant roundabout around the *Arc de Triomphe,* the epicenter of twelve avenues. Los Angeles' street map was a piece of cake in comparison.

It felt great to have wheels. Now she was free to roam the city. She even discovered a French bakery and stopped to buy croissants and *pains au chocolat.*

Satisfied with her first outing on her own, she returned to the Millers' house. The property looked lovely in the morning light with its beautiful landscaping. Natalie was delighted to see hummingbirds and white butterflies flirting with the flowers. She sat down by the pool to enjoy her pastries, but just as she bit into a croissant, her cell phone rang.

Simone's voice boomed through the receiver. "Get up, girl; we're going out for breakfast."

"I'm having breakfast now," Natalie answered. "But I can always come watch you eat yours. By the way, thank you for the groceries you left in the cupboard."

"Oh, that was my mom. She's like that."

"Well, that was really nice of her. Guess what? I rented a car this morning."

"Hey, look at you. I forgot that you were so resourceful. Okay, come by my place. I'll be ready soon. Do you want to try the freeway or do you prefer the streets?"

"Err, I'll stick with the streets." Natalie jotted down the directions and hung up. Simone wasn't quite ready, which gave Natalie plenty of time.

The reflection of the sun on the pool water reminded her of the scintillating sea of Sainte-Anne in Martinique. In her mind, no country ever equaled her island. No beach, not even the huge, majestic Santa Monica Beach, compared with the splendor and turquoise waters of Martinique's beaches. But she hadn't come to Los Angeles for the beaches. She had been waiting for an opportunity like this, a chance to pause and reflect on her life.

The pool, bathed by the sun, seemed to call her name, but she had forgotten to pack her bathing suit. Natalie looked around. Strategically planted trees ensured total privacy from neighbors. *Why not?* she thought.

Removing her clothes, and, after hesitating, her bra and panties, she stepped into the pool and gave a sigh of delight when she was fully immersed in the fresh water. She swam vigorously at first, then rolled around, laughing out loud. Water was her element. Her body relaxed as she floated on her back and gazed at the cloudless sky. She almost wanted to cry with relief. Life should only be made of moments like this one. Why did she deprive herself of the simplest pleasures all year long? From now on, she had to be attentive to her own needs.

The sudden squeaking of the front gate made her freeze. Somebody was coming. She had forgotten to lock the entry gate. Horrified, she watched as a silhouette approached in the distance. She cursed herself for taking off all her clothes, which were now out of reach. What if it was Simone's mom or dad returning unexpectedly? She would die of embarrassment. There was no time to run for her towel, so she swam to a corner of the deep end of the pool, hoping somehow that the water's distortion would help cover her. With her back against the wall and her legs twisted like a pretzel, she covered her breasts with one hand and held to the edge of the pool with the other, while praying that whoever was coming wouldn't notice her and would leave quickly.

She almost passed out when she recognized Jerry. And she hadn't become invisible, because he headed straight to her corner of the pool.

"Hey!" he said as he approached. She didn't answer; she couldn't even breathe. His eyebrows rose in surprise and an incredulous smile stretched his lips.

"Oh! You're naked?" He stopped and took a step backward. "Am I interrupting something?" He looked around, as if to see if there was anyone else.

Natalie felt hot and cold at the same time. "Nobody ever told you to announce yourself before you come in? I didn't hear you ring a bell!" Then her hand slipped from the edge of the pool and she sank. She had to use her hands and legs to swim back up, which meant that she was now totally exposed.

Of course Jerry hadn't turned around; he seemed to enjoy the situation. His eyes were crinkled as he tried not to laugh. "You said you wanted to rent a car and I came to offer you a ride to a car rental place," he said. "I'm sorry I caught you at a bad time."

There was no point to hide now. Natalie's humiliation turned into defiance. She made no attempt to cover herself anymore.

"Thank you, but I already rented a car. It's in the driveway," she said, her tone icy cold.

He was no GQ model today. His jeans were splattered with paint; his t-shirt, wrinkled and torn at the collar, could have been black in a previous life, and he was unshaven. Even so, he looked good. Something changed in his attitude as he looked at her, unashamed. His eyes softened as they followed the contours of her body. The embarrassment sent blood flowing to her face, but at the same time her body tingled. The stir angered her. She glared at him, her eyebrows raised in interrogation. What was he still doing there?

He raised his hands as if surrendering. "Sorry again. Let me know if you need anything."

"Right. Thank you." Her voice was low this time. She felt miserable.

"Oh, come on! You were skinny-dipping. So what?" His eyes were mischievous again. "Do you want me to join you?" he added in a more serious tone, stepping forward.

"Just go," she shouted.

Jerry laughed. "Okay, Doc, no need to get upset. I'm leaving." Without looking at her again, he removed a small notebook from the back pocket of his jeans, jotted something down, then tore the piece of paper from the pad and left it on the table by the lounge.

After he disappeared from her sight, Natalie swore loudly. This had to be the most embarrassing and awkward moment she'd ever experienced.

She climbed out of the pool, covered herself with the towel and hurried to the guesthouse. In the safety of the living room she walked around in circles. This trip was cursed. First, the incident with Ted, now this. Didn't she deserve a moment of peace and re-laxation? What was it about her that attracted problems? She had to admit that in spite of the shame of being caught naked, she had felt something... physical. She could still feel it. Jerry was no doubt a dangerous woman manipulator. She had met this type of guy be-fore and always managed to avoid getting caught in their nets. They were often addicted to sex and collected women to forget their existential angst. There was no way she'd ever have sex with him. It was out of question. Did he really think that she would let him join her in the pool? These men could be so full of themselves. Maybe she should shorten her trip to a week...

The idea of spending the summer in Paris looking for an apartment and working at the hospital brought back a wave of anxiety. She just had to forget about the incident. And stop think-ing.

Only after she had showered and dressed did she remember the note Jerry had left on the table by the pool. *"Don't feel bad. You looked lovely,"* it said. Below the words he had left a phone number and sketched a mermaid looking like her with a long, twisted fishtail, one hand covering her breasts. He certainly had talent to sketch this in a few seconds; Natalie had to give him that. She also had no doubt that he used his artistic abilities to get women, but none of that would work with her. Natalie ripped up the note and marched to her car. It was getting late and she was eager to discover L.A.

"You don't eat like this every morning, I hope," Natalie said as a waiter placed scrambled eggs, bacon, sausages, hash browns, and waffles with a banana-and-nut topping in front of Simone. "It smells delicious, though."

The diner buzzed with busy waiters balancing enormous amounts of food on their arms, quite different from the cafés in Paris, where breakfast was usually an espresso with a croissant or *tartine*. The smell of sausages and coffee filled the room. Natalie almost regretted that her stomach was full.

"Girl, I'm starving. I had a little too much exercise with Ted last night." Simone winked and attacked her eggs enthusiastically. "I'm going to spend a little more time on the Stairmaster, that's all."

"How is Ted doing?" Natalie asked, surprised somehow that Ted had enough energy for sex last night.

Simone waved her hand dismissively and shrugged as if the question were irrelevant. "He's fine. Don't worry about him." Natalie understood not to mention the incident again. "How did it go with Jerry last night?" Simone asked, her mouth full.

"It went okay. He stopped by this morning to ask if I wanted a lift to a car rental service." Natalie blushed as she remembered what had happened earlier. She made the decision not to tell Simone about it and prayed that Jerry would keep his mouth shut.

"Oh no!" Simone said. She stopped chewing, her fork still suspended in midair. "That's not good."

"What do you mean?"

"Jerry isn't the thoughtful type unless he's interested. And Nat, I have to tell you. As much as I love my cousin, he's trouble. A few of my girlfriends dated him and he messed up their brain. I wouldn't like the same thing to happen to you, so be very careful!"

"I have Jean-Marc. I'm not interested in Jerry," Natalie answered somewhat defensively.

"Good. Because the problem with Jerry is that he goes through beautiful women rather fast," Simone said attacking her food again.

"I'm not surprised," Natalie said. She experienced satisfaction in knowing that she'd made an accurate assessment of Jerry's character.

"My theory is that his issues with women come from the fact that he never got along with his mother," Simone offered.

"Oh yeah? Why is that?" Natalie couldn't help asking.

Simone took a big bite of her sausage, chewed it thoroughly, swallowed, and took a sip of her coffee, but said nothing.

Natalie laughed. Simone relished having a story to tell. "Oh come on!" Natalie said.

"Well, to make a long story short. Jerry's father died when he was twelve and his mother wasn't the most maternal person in the world. So he raised himself on his own. He had a difficult childhood. He would skip school often and disappear for days. He left home as soon as he was sixteen and lived with us for a while, until he finished high school. He was a very disturbed teenager;

fortunately, he had his art. He's still pretty unstable as far as his love life is concerned. He's definitely not a regular type of guy."

Natalie wondered if Jean-Marc would qualify as what Simone called a regular type of guy. "Does he have a girlfriend now?" She scolded herself for her curiosity.

"Well, he has Brenda, on and off. She's a Swedish model, absolutely gorgeous. They've been seeing each other for over a year. They break up, see other people, and get back together."

"I see." Natalie had never heard Simone call another woman gorgeous. She understood that her friend was trying to discourage her interest in Jerry, but it wasn't necessary. She wouldn't cheat on Jean-Marc, and she had no intention of ever seeing Jerry again.

"I have an audition this afternoon. After that we can go shopping or sightseeing if you want."

They went back to Simone's flat so she could get ready for her audition. Natalie enjoyed helping her rehearse her lines. Then she busied herself reading *People* magazine while Simone decided what to wear. When Simone emerged from the bedroom, she wore a black business suit and a silk pink blouse. The skirt was, of course, as short as business would allow.

"They have to give you that part, you look better than Scarlett Johansson," Natalie said.

Simone looked pensive. "Hmm! Maybe that's not such a good thing. It's just a supporting part. Do I look like a journalist?"

"A very sexy one," Natalie answered.

Simone shrugged. "The hell with it! This is how I want to dress."

They took Simone's car to the audition. Natalie had no idea where she was, and didn't really care. It was a beautiful, hot day, and for once she had nothing to do.

"I'll wait for you in the car," Natalie said when they reached the casting office, located in a small, ordinary-looking brown building.

"You'll be too hot. You should come inside. I've already been to this casting office. They have a big waiting room."

The waiting room was vast but crowded, with only one empty chair left. Simone signed in and picked up some pages of the script. The tension in that room, full of beautiful young women and sharp-looking guys, was thick. Most kept their heads buried in their scripts; others looked like they were in deep thought. Natalie wondered if they were all competing for the same role.

"I think I prefer to wait downstairs," she said. This time Simone didn't protest.

Natalie decided to wait in a coffee shop across the street. She ordered some chamomile tea and sat at a table with a view of the building's entrance. As usual, when she had some time, she removed her little organizer from her handbag to make a to-do list. Number two on her list, just after *Buy a bathing suit,* she wrote, *Call Jean-Marc.*

She reached for his necklace and opened the little house. She did love him, but something was missing in their relationship. She took a sip of her chamomile tea and burned her tongue. *Passion.* The word stumbled from her subconscious and took center stage in her thoughts. Where was the passion in her life? She loved Jean-Marc, but was she passionately in love with him? She felt satisfaction and a sense of duty at the hospital, but did she love her profession with a passion? Only now that she was away from it all could she ask herself these questions.

Her eyes fell upon an attractive young black man in jeans and a long-sleeved blue shirt emerging from the casting agent's building. He sat in the shade by the stairs leading to the building's entrance and leaned back. Natalie observed him for a while. His long legs were stretched in front of him, his arms crossed on his chest. He had the confidence of an athlete after a great physical performance. His head, with only a shadow of hair on his scalp, was slightly bowed, giving the impression that he was focused inward.

When Simone came out of the building, the young man stood up to greet her. There was certain ease in his demeanor that kept Natalie's attention. He hugged Simone, they talked for a few minutes, and then he left. Natalie picked up her tea and went outside to meet her friend.

"How did it go?" she asked. Some of her tea had spilled while she was crossing the street, and it burned her fingers.

"It went well on my side. Now it's out of my hands. Anyway, I have an audition for a commercial tomorrow to think about." Simone looked tired.

"Who was the black guy you just said hi to?" Natalie asked.

"Michael? He's a good friend of mine. We studied acting together at HB Studios in New York. He's good. He's starting to get noticed."

Natalie wasn't surprised. Michael had a charisma you could feel from a distance.

"You know what?" Simone said with a burst of energy. "Let's hit the beach! It's beautiful today."

They went back to Simone's place to get Natalie's car and they drove to the beach in separate vehicles. On Fridays Natalie usually gave consultations in a clinic in Champigny-Sur-Marne, an unattractive suburb of Paris. She liked the clinic and its easy pace, mostly first aid, stitches, and dealing with elderly patients. At the end of the day, she would climb in her Peugeot then dive into the heavy traffic, wondering if she wasn't living someone else's life.

This one Friday afternoon, Natalie grinned all the way to the beach.

CHAPTER FOUR

"This is where I come to unwind," Simone said. "Nothing ever changes here."

The street life that couldn't be seen while driving around Los Angeles was in full force on Venice Beach. The boardwalk swarmed with street performers, dreadlocked musicians, local artists, and onlookers.

"Wow! This is surreal," Natalie said. "It's like a humongous beach party."

Rap and reggae music blasted from the souvenir shops and clothing stores, while African drumbeats emanated from the beach. Green lawns with tall palm trees and bicycle lanes separated the walkway from a vast expanse of yellow sand running along the ocean.

Natalie and Simone bought huge hot dogs and smothered them with ketchup and relish. Then they separated from the crowd and walked toward the ocean, crossing the lawns and the busy bike path. They removed their shoes to make their way across the sand, and they sat as close as possible to the shoreline. The boardwalk and its dense crowd seemed far away. A troop of seagulls dawdled on the sand looking for crumbs.

Natalie took a deep breath and exhaled, stretching her arms behind her. She extended her legs and offered her face to the warmth of the sun. "I wish I could just sell art on the beach," she said. "That seems like such a simpler life."

"It may seem simple to you, but most of those artists are in survival mode, you know." Simone's tone was abrupt. Natalie understood that she might have hit a raw nerve.

"You're right," she said. "I wasn't trying to belittle the artists. In fact, I wish I had some artistic talent."

"Maybe you haven't let it emerge." Simone bit into her hot dog as if it were her first meal of the day. The depth of her remark surprised Natalie. She remembered taking violin lessons until she was fifteen and at some point she had played fairly well, but she thought about it mostly as a testament to her good education. Her family didn't encourage art as an occupation, and even though she enjoyed doodling figures and faces in her notebooks, she had never taken any art classes. Was it too late now?

The beach ran along the coast for miles. In that immensity there seemed a sense of suspended time. Natalie finished her hot dog while watching the seagulls glide above the water. She couldn't help but compare Venice Beach, so vast it seemed endless, to the intimate beaches of Martinique, all intimate aliveness.

After a while, they got up and walked slowly back to the street, where they had miraculously found two parking spaces close to each other. A man on roller skates clutching a guitar rolled toward them. He carried an amplifier strapped on his back.

"Don't look at him too much," Simone said, "unless you want to buy his CD."

The strip seemed full of characters like him. Natalie enjoyed the contrast between the fair atmosphere of the boardwalk and the calmer section closer to the water. She promised herself to come back often.

They reached a shady alley parallel to a quiet section of the boardwalk. Simone pointed her finger at a white building.

"This is Jerry's house and studio."

The house was a large cubic building facing the boardwalk, with huge tinted glass windows on each wall. It had a garage door and back entry down the alley.

"That's a big house. It looks like a commercial building," Natalie said, studying the place with a curiosity she couldn't disguise.

"Jerry bought it from a rich friend who died a few years ago. He's probably in there working. Let's go say hi!"

"No, no." Natalie felt her body temperature rise. "If he's working let's not bother him—" but Simone was already at the door, a finger on the doorbell.

"I can't help it. When I pass by, I have to say hi." She made a face at the camera of the intercom on the side. "When he doesn't want company, he doesn't answer the door."

"I'm not going in," Natalie said. Why was Simone taking her to Jerry's house, after all the comments she made about him? Was it a game?

There was a buzz. Simone pushed open the heavy metallic door. "Why not? Come on, Nat, we won't be long."

Natalie sighed and dragged her feet after Simone. The front door opened to an immense loft with cement floors. The place was illuminated by filtered sunlight pouring through the huge windows. A spiral staircase led to the floor above.

Jerry must have buzzed them in from his working station near the farthest window. He appeared from behind a huge canvas facing that window, wearing only his stained jeans from the morning. There was something too intimate in the sight of his bare chest. Natalie noticed tight muscles on his abdomen, with a line of hair from his navel disappearing into his jeans. She tensed; her anger from the morning came back to her.

"Hey cousin, we were hanging out on the beach. Hope we're not disturbing you," Simone shouted from the door.

"That's fine. I was about to take a break." He smiled at them. Natalie didn't smile back. Simone moved toward him to give him a kiss while Natalie stayed behind.

The immense room was sparsely furnished. In Jerry's work area Natalie noticed a crimson sofa, a few wooden chairs and a huge table holding brushes, knives, paint, and all kinds of art supplies. The painting Jerry worked on, propped on a huge easel, was taller than him. She could only see the back of it. Many other over-sized canvases leaned on the walls. There was a bar and a kitchen to her left, near the front door.

"How's it going?" Jerry asked Natalie.

"Very well, thank you." Her voice was snappier than she intended it to be.

"So, did you sell a lot of paintings yesterday?" Simone asked.

"From what my agent told me, we did fine."

"Way to go. I'm proud of you." After a pause she added, "So what do you think of Ted?"

Jerry gave Simone an amused sideways look. "Is that why you came to visit? So we can talk about Ted?" He motioned to the kitchen. "Do you want a drink? Beer, Coke, wine?"

"I'll have a beer," Simone answered.

"Same," Natalie said. Getting drunk seemed like an appropriate way to deal with this awkward situation. It might help her find some humor in the whole thing.

Jerry walked to the bar, retrieved two beers and a cola for him and placed them on the counter. Simone climbed on a bar stool while Natalie just stood.

"So?" Simone insisted.

"Oh yeah, Ted!" Jerry said, rolling his eyes but smiling. "He seems all right." Using one hand, Jerry propelled himself up to sit on the counter. Then he chuckled and added, "As long as he doesn't choke on his martini."

Simone punched his arm. "Be serious. Do you think that he's into me?"

Jerry laughed. Natalie noticed the deep dimples on his cheeks. "Okay, okay," he said. "Let's be serious. Ted seems hooked. I even saw steam coming out of his ears."

Natalie thought that Jerry was kidding, but Simone looked pleased with his answer. Jerry glanced at Natalie and winked. She didn't react, but instead took a big gulp of her beer.

"Ted's really talented. You need to check out his movie. I'm sure you would dig it." Simone sang Ted's praises for a few minutes, while Jerry seemed to listen, even though he often glanced at Natalie. She concentrated on her beer.

"Oh! Can we see what you are working on?" Simone finally said.

"Sure, it's done. I just applied the final varnish."

Simone jumped off the kitchen stool to look at the painting by the window. Natalie, who couldn't help her curiosity, followed. The beer seemed to have a mellowing effect on her, because she felt that her interest for art trumped her earlier embarrassment. The easel seemed miles away from the kitchen bar.

The blue painting evoked a tumultuous underwater land-scape. A man dressed in a black business suit seemed to be swimming toward the light above, while his attaché case rested on the ocean floor.

Simone frowned. "That's a little bit morbid, J.," she commented. "Why is the man dressed up? Did he try to commit suicide?"

"That's for you to decide," Jerry said.

Natalie wasn't sure if she liked the subject of this painting, but she could appreciate the mastery in the fluidity of the brush strokes and the handling of colors.

"Do you always work from your imagination or do you have models pose for you?" she finally asked, surprised by the sound of her own voice. She hadn't planned to say anything, but it seemed that they were waiting for her to comment.

"I use everything, models, photos, memories. I mix it all."

"It's like an inner landscape. Is he going back up?" Natalie added, wishing she would stop talking. It was probably the beer loosening her up.

"He hasn't made up his mind yet," Jerry said and he looked at her as if there was a hidden meaning to what he'd just said. Whatever he meant, she couldn't get it.

Simone looked at her watch. "I have to meet Ted. By the way, we're having a party next Friday. Mark your calendar."

Jerry pulled on a shirt and walked them outside. He looked at Simone in an amused, affectionate way as she chattered nonstop. Natalie trailed behind, enjoying the beauty of the day. She wasn't ready to leave the beach yet. The sun still floated high, and she wanted to explore the little shops on the boardwalk—maybe look for a bathing suit.

"Do you want to come back to Hollywood with me, Nat?" Simone asked as she opened her car door. "Ted and I are going to a sushi bar with a few other friends."

"No, it's okay. I'd like to spend more time on the beach. I'll be fine," Natalie said. She wasn't sure if Simone was just being polite, her invitation coming after they had already driven to the beach in two separate cars.

"Do you know how to get back home?" Simone asked.

"I think so; I just follow Pacific until it becomes Ocean Avenue, right?"

"Yeah! You're good. I'll call you later." They kissed *à la française,* on both cheeks, and Simone drove away while Natalie walked toward the beach without a look back at Jerry.

"Natalie, wait," he called. "How about a drink at the Boardwalk Café?"

She stopped and turned to look at him. "Thanks, but I have some shopping to do. Next time." Her tone was friendly enough but determined.

"The shops will be open for a while," he said, coming toward her. "Let's bury the hatchet. You're right. I should've announced myself this morning. I caught you in a private moment. Please accept my apology." He extended his hand as if to offer a peace handshake.

Maybe it was the effect of the beer or the sweetness of the late afternoon, or maybe she caught a glimpse of sincerity in Jerry's eyes, but Natalie's resolve faded. She hesitated but accepted his handshake.

They walked side by side a few feet from each other. From the corner of her eye she could see him observing her.

"What are you planning to do in L.A?" Jerry asked.

"Well, I intend to recuperate from a hard year," she said and Jerry just nodded. They left the backstreets to merge into the busier boardwalk. Natalie noticed the harmony between the roller skaters gliding on the bike path and the seagulls above, as if they were part of the same harmonious dance. This place was special. Artists of all genres and ethnicities displayed their talents side by side. A man with long gray hair played classical music on a real piano a few feet from a Native American band. Fortune tellers sat by jewel makers. The carnival atmosphere masked a heart that spoke of freedom. A sudden and unexpected joy lifted Natalie's own heart and made it skip. A wide grin appeared on her face. Jerry saw it and smiled as if he understood her sudden spark of enthusiasm.

"It's hard to believe that you're a doctor," he said.

"Why is that?" Natalie was still smiling at the beauty of the day.

"It doesn't really fit you. Not because you're very beautiful, but you don't look like the scientific type. There's some-thing…different about you."

Natalie acknowledged the compliment, but couldn't disregard the last part of his remark.

"What do you mean?"

"You seem guarded."

"Maybe it's because I'm in a foreign country and I'm not speaking my native language? I don't think that anybody who really knows me thinks about me like that. But what is the relation-ship between being guarded and not looking like a doctor?"

"You strike me as someone who has subtlety. There's an artistic essence about you. In my experience, most doctors act and speak like people who have all the answers. They see things in black or white."

"You don't seem to like doctors very much," Natalie said.

"I'm not impressed with titles," Jerry answered.

Natalie shrugged. "Physicians deal with life and death issues. With that come many responsibilities."

"Some of them may be concerned with saving lives, but a lot don't care; they're interested in making money. Which kind are you?" Jerry said, his eyebrows raised in curiosity.

"I'm the kind who feels good about her ethics and doesn't answer to provocations," Natalie answered quietly.

Jerry chuckled. "Fair enough. And to your credit, when you don't have your bathing suit handy you just go ahead and swim *au naturel*. I like that."

Caught by surprise, Natalie opened her mouth wide and Jerry burst out laughing. She wanted to get upset, but his laugh was infectious.

"Okay, you got me, I didn't see it coming. Can you please never mention that again?" Natalie laughed.

"I won't. Your secret is safe with me."

"That was so embarrassing, I'm not sure if I'll ever recover."

"Don't worry, I'm used to seeing naked women," Jerry said with a mischievous smile.

"I'm sure," Natalie retorted, rolling her eyes.

"I mean as an artist," Jerry added quickly. "I do a lot of figure drawing and painting. Being naked is no big deal. And you *were* a pleasant sight."

Natalie gave him an oblique look, and he opened his eyes wide, as if his remark were innocent. She decided to let the subject go.

The Boardwalk Café was packed. People sat under its covered patio, huge salads or burgers with tons of fries in front of them. Checkered red and white tablecloths gave the restaurant the look of a French *guinguette*.

"Are you hungry?" Jerry asked her after they sat down.

"I just ate a hot dog, I'm fine. I'll have a cappuccino."

Jerry ordered two cappuccinos. He seemed oblivious to the people, especially women, staring at him as if he were a celebrity. "How old are you?" he asked.

"Twenty-nine. Why?"

"Have you ever been married?" The question surprised her. Was this his way of finding out if there was somebody in her life?

"No, I haven't. What about you?"

"I was married once, for six months," he said.

"How long ago was that?" Natalie asked.

"Ten years ago. I was twenty-three years old. We got drunk and we decided to fly to Vegas and get married. When we finally got sober, we divorced. That's when I left for Europe."

"I thought these kind of things only happened in movies."

"Unfortunately that was real life," Jerry said. "You said that you finished your residency, so what's next?" he asked.

"I'll probably stay a few years in Paris and then I may go back to Martinique. I'm not sure yet."

"Martinique? When I lived in Paris, I had a friend from Martinique. He spoke about it all the time. He lived there when he was a kid and said he always wanted to go back. I wanted to go there with him, and we'd even picked a date to leave, but we never made it."

"Why is that?" Natalie asked.

The waitress came back with their order. As she placed the beverages on the table her ample breast almost brushed Jerry's face. Natalie couldn't repress a smile, but Jerry didn't seem to notice.

"I got a grant to work in New York, and my friend died from an overdose." Jerry spoke matter-of-factly, as if dying from an overdose was not much different from moving to another country. Natalie felt a pang in her stomach as if she had known the man he was talking about.

"That's terrible," she said. "What was his name?"

"Marcel... Damn! I forgot his last name. He was a good artist."

"I miss Martinique most of the time, but I'm not quite sure that I can go back now."

"It's hard to go back home once you've left," Jerry said softly.

Natalie looked straight into his eyes, but she wasn't able to read his expression. She redirected her attention to pouring honey in her coffee.

"Sometimes I really want to go back home for good, but only after I've seen it all," she said.

He smiled and surprised her when he reached out and gently moved a lock of hair away from her eye to tuck it behind her ear.

"Do you think that you'll ever see it all?" There was an emotion swelling between them that moved her. She felt her eyes mist. She looked away and took a sip of the hot beverage, thankful for the familiar bitter and sweet taste.

"Would you model for me?" Jerry asked.

"Me? I…don't know." She wondered what to make of his request. Was he coming on to her? Was it because he had seen her naked this morning? Could it be only professional interest?

"It won't take long. I really like your face. I'd like to paint it."

"My face? What about my body?"

"I like your body, too," Jerry said with a twinkle in his eyes.

"I was joking. I don't want to do any nude modeling."

"You'll keep your clothes on, I swear," Jerry promised. "It won't take long. I just want to make a few quick sketches and maybe take some shots."

Natalie could hear two sides battling in her mind. One of them flashed warning signals and red lights. *It's a trap! Don't go!* The other side spoke of freedom and curiosity and opening up to different experiences.

"Will you give me a copy of your sketches?" she asked.

"Sure."

"Okay then, when?"

"What about now?"

Her breathing felt difficult. "Now? Err, okay." She slowly finished her cappuccino and made a move to grab the bill, but he reached it before her. He shook his index finger, indicating that this was a no-no.

She knew it wasn't that innocent to go back to his house and pose for him, but she couldn't help herself. She was under some kind of spell. The adventurous part of her had won. They left the restaurant and strolled back to his place.

When he fumbled in his pockets for his keys, she became agitated. What if he had interpreted her agreement to pose for him as an acceptance to have sex? He seemed to sense her hesitation.

"You can relax," he said, letting her go in the house first. "You are safe with me."

"Okay," she said with a nervous laugh.

"Do you want something else to drink?"

"I'm fine." She shouldn't have accepted the first beer to begin with. Realizing her arms were crossed on her chest, she uncrossed them and tried to relax. She walked straight to his work area and sat on the red sofa. "What do you want me to do?"

Jerry looked at her intently. "Just get comfortable." He leaned back on his worktable, studying her face for a few moments, his gaze tearing through her. She looked straight back at him. Her heart was beating fast. She couldn't understand her emotion.

Jerry was looking at her lips and she felt that stir again. To break the spell, she looked toward the window. He grabbed a block of drawing paper and a piece of charcoal then, flipping the pages quickly, he made several rapid sketches.

The last one took longer. He looked at her as if he was seeing only the forms that composed her face. Ten minutes passed, but they seemed like an eternity. Natalie had also studied his face, framed by wild and uncombed hair. Now she knew by heart the shape of his eyebrows, with their upward curve, his straight nose, full lips and square jaws.

He smiled. "Thank you, that's it for today."

"For today? You don't expect me to pose for you again, I hope," Natalie said.

"I'd also like to do some photos whenever you have time."

She felt flattered. "Are you going to use me for a painting?"

"If it's okay with you."

"I'd be interested to see how you're going to fit me into one of your surrealistic scenes." She came toward him to look at his last sketch. The drawing made her inhale sharply. It seemed alive. She was seeing herself for the first time through his eyes.

Like magic, the strokes of charcoal had brought to life a woman who looked just like her, only more alive and sensual than she had ever felt. The corners of her mouth were pulled slightly upward, as if she were about to smile. He had caught a spark in her eyes that made her look vulnerable, but also passionate. She saw desire in those eyes and felt ashamed that she had revealed so much about herself.

How could he read her like that, and then be able to draw it? It was as if he had drawn her state of mind. This was real artistic talent. She would have been delighted if she'd possessed a tenth of his talent. Without saying a word, she nodded her approval.

They stood a few feet from each other, and as she became more aware of his proximity, the atmosphere between them shifted. She could feel the heat of his body. The undisguised desire that she read in his eyes made her feel weak. He looked at her lips, his face so close to hers she could smell his scent, agreeable and almost familiar. For a half-second she was hypnotized, unable to move, the impulsive part of her wanting to touch his skin. Then her ability to think finally took over. *I can't let this happen.*

She moved away from him in a fluid motion as if nothing had happened.

"I have to go," she said, collecting her handbag from the

sofa, her voice light.

"I'm taking you to your car," Jerry said.

"It's okay. It's not far."

He ignored her protest and walked her to her car. Natalie could still sense the electricity between them.

"Thank you for the coffee," she said as she fumbled in her handbag for her keys.

He smiled as if he was amused. "Thank you for posing for me." He stepped closer and touched her cheek. The gesture provoked another rush of longing in her body that made her legs wobbly. She opened the car door and got in, waving goodbye before speeding away.

Natalie drove down Pacific Avenue in the wrong direction for several minutes and made a dangerous left turn that was saluted by angry honks. Then she made a U-turn, wondering if she was on Pacific Avenue to start with. She let out a nervous laugh. *Natalie, get a grip!* What had just happened with Jerry? It was highly unusual for her to feel that hot and flushed. She was used to connecting intellectually with men. Something they would say or do would affect her and attract her. She looked for qualities like kindness or thoughtfulness. A charming smile could pull her in, but she wasn't used to the intense physical effect Jerry had on her.

All the clichés that described sexual attraction applied: the weakening of her knees, electric jolts running through her body. It was quite ridiculous. She would have to squash all that nonsense. First of all, she wasn't free, and even if she were, she should run away from a man like that. There was nothing he could bring her but trouble and regrets. She pushed away the memory of Jerry's eyes gazing at her lips and concentrated on driving back to the guesthouse in one piece.

When she finally parked in the circular driveway, the thought of Jean-Marc emerged at last, and she firmly held on to it.

CHAPTER FIVE

Natalie let herself slip into the pool. She swam vigorously for a few laps then floated on her back and went limp. She hadn't felt so relaxed in years.

Afterward, her mind clear, she sat on her lounge chair in full sun. A week had passed since she had arrived in Los Angeles. She'd visited Universal Studios with Simone, explored the Getty Museum on her own, strolled down Rodeo Drive, and sipped a cappuccino on Melrose Avenue. It was all wonderful, but most of all, she enjoyed her morning swims while alone in the fresh pool, listening to the conversation of birds. After a whole week of making tremendous efforts to stop thinking about her heated afternoon with Jerry, she thought she had finally succeeded. She hadn't seen him since he'd sketched her, and even though she was a bit disappointed by his silence, she was also relieved.

The notebook she'd brought from Paris to record her thoughts was almost full with her attempts at sketching everything that caught her attention: landscapes, flowers, trees and unsuspecting sun worshippers. Her secret activity gave her unexpected pleasure.

The ring of her cell phone from the guesthouse interrupted the flow of her thoughts. Natalie ran inside to get the call. *"Bonjour, ma chérie. Comment vas-tu?"*

Her mother's voice took her back to Martinique. Natalie asked about the family and her mother Ginette railed on about Natalie's sister-in-law Véronique, her brother Roger's Parisian wife, who hung up on her when Ginette asked if Roger ate enough. Natalie tried not to laugh. As a child, Roger was a finicky eater, and his mother had a tendency to forget that he was now a grown married man. She kept worrying loudly about his health and his lifestyle, which enraged Véronique. Ginette's troubles with her daughter-in-law were nothing new. They never could understand each other.

After the conversation was over, Natalie longed to be home in Martinique. She decided to call Jean-Marc. It hadn't always been easy to reach him this past week with the eight-hour difference between Paris and Los Angeles, but she'd managed to talk to him twice.

Jean-Marc sounded a little tired when he answered the phone this time. He had just landed from Guadeloupe, he explained.

"I can't wait until I get my break in October," he said. "I'm thinking about taking you back to Martinique. We could rent a boat and sail to Sainte-Lucia. What do you think?"

"That would be absolutely wonderful! I can't wait." A little bit of pride swelled in Natalie's chest. Jean-Marc could drive anything: plane, boat, motorcycles, fast cars–you name it. And not only was he handsome and smart, but like many men from Martinique, he was also suave and fun-loving. Going to Martinique with him in October would be another dream vacation, if she could free herself again of course.

"I miss you like crazy," he said, his mood changing completely. "It's not the same coming back from work and you're not here. You should have stayed with me."

Natalie sighed. He had to make her feel guilty. "I really miss you, too, but I needed a real break from the hospital, remember?"

"Sure, I remember. So what have you been doing?"

Careful not to sound too enthusiastic, she gave him an account of her last few days. She didn't mention meeting Jerry, nor did she tell him she was going to Ted's party later that evening.

"Just don't let anybody grab you," Jean-Marc said.

"You don't have to worry about that. Be good yourself."

She hung up, realizing how possessive Jean-Marc had become these days. It was an aspect of him that had emerged only with the subject of her trip to L.A. But if he really loved her, shouldn't he be happy that she had fun? *He's afraid of losing you*, a voice in her head answered. But she had no intention of leaving Jean-Marc for anyone or any reason. She had played the field before him. Jean-Marc stood way above of any of the other guys she'd been with. She remembered Yves, her previous boyfriend, who had threatened to break her legs when she'd broken up with him, even though they disagreed on almost everything. Jean-Marc had been a revelation after him. Yes, he was a little possessive, but he had plenty of great qualities. And she had plenty of flaws as well.

Ted's house in the Hollywood Hills wasn't that easy to find. Natalie followed Sunset Boulevard, enjoying her drive through Bel Air and Beverly Hills; then the rich mansions and imposing trees disappeared and were replaced by a strip of trendy restaurants and shops. She took a whirly road called Laurel Canyon to get to the Hills and finally found Ted's house atop a sinuous street, which looked too narrow for two-way traffic. The area reminded her of some regions in the north of Martinique, where houses clung to steep hillsides.

She had come early to help but parking was scarce, though it was only seven o'clock. As she found a small space five houses up the street, Natalie wondered if some of the guests would be able to park at all.

Built on stilts, Ted's house, a large wooden cabin, was suspended on a cliff overlooking a canyon. Cacti and rocks bordered the stone pathway leading to the front door. The sound of joyful chatter and music escaped from the opened windows.

When Natalie walked in, she saw a dozen young men and women rushing around. Everyone seemed to have a task, some pushing the furniture to the side, others carrying boxes. Someone told Natalie that Simone was in the kitchen. She followed the sound of laughter to find her friend standing in front of an island counter with three other girls, arranging slices of meat and cheese on aluminum platters. Everyone had a glass of wine at arm's reach.

"Hey Nat! You look smashing!"

Natalie wore a short white pencil dress and high-heeled sandals. She had accentuated her makeup with golden bronze powder on her face, dark eye shadow and coral lipstick.

"This is Amanda, Jodi and Kate," Simone said, introducing her friends. Natalie smiled and waved at them. The girls offered weak smiles in return. "We're running late and I haven't had time to change yet."

"Let me wash my hands so I can help," Natalie said as she went to the sink and searched in vain for hand soap. When she didn't find any she simply rinsed her hands. She wondered if anyone there had even bothered to do the same before touching the food.

"Nat is a doctor," she heard Simone tell the others, as if it explained everything.

"You don't say," the brunette named Amanda said in what sounded like a mocking tone. She had large blue eyes and big red lips.

"Get yourself a glass of wine; it'll put you in the mood," Simone said, taking a sip of her white chardonnay. Amanda rolled her eyes. Natalie disliked her immediately. The feeling seemed to be mutual, but she was not about to let Amanda spoil her evening. She decided to ignore her.

Hours later, it was standing room only throughout the house. A dense crowd flowed toward the kitchen in search of food and beverages.

Simone had now changed into a red dress baring most of her thighs and back. She looked euphoric, greeting people, laughing, chatting, and drinking heavily.

Natalie had met Ted's two other roommates, both of them good-looking actors. Lots of pretty girls orbited around them. "You're the Natalie that saved Ted's life?" one of the guys, named Jeff, asked her. He grabbed her around her waist. "Nice dress," he added, looking at her with appreciation. He had been talking to Amanda, and Natalie saw the red-lipped brunette grimace.

Natalie smiled politely and escaped Jeff's embrace. The man was a little too friendly. She didn't feel at ease here, maybe because she'd only had one glass of wine and was now drinking cranberry juice for fear of driving home with impaired faculties. She felt a little foreign in the middle of these new faces. Everyone seemed to be happy just drinking. There was hardly enough room to move and some of those men had wandering hands. Nobody danced. She had expected to see Jerry, but he hadn't shown up. She reminded herself it was much better that way. Maybe she could just leave now. No one would notice, certainly not Simone, who looked like she was having a wonderful time.

Natalie stepped out on the deck to breathe some fresh air and enjoy the view of the city lights below. There, leaning back against the wooden fence surrounding the deck, she recognized the tall black actor she'd first noticed outside of Simone's audition. He smiled when their eyes met. She smiled back, not knowing if she should keep moving. As if he understood her dilemma, he nonchalantly rolled off the fence and made his way toward her.

"Hi, I'm Michael," he said, with a slight bow. He had a deep, warm voice.

"I'm Natalie." Now she was not as ready to leave. Michael was handsome, with warm, intense black eyes and chiseled features. He looked even more impressive up close, with his tall and trim body outlined by a fitted black shirt.

"We have met before, haven't we?" He extended his hand.

"I don't think so." Wouldn't he have remembered? She would've.

"Where are you from?" he said. "I can hear an accent."

"I'm from Martinique," Natalie answered. "It's a French Caribbean island."

"I know where Martinique is; my father's from Jamaica," Michael said. "Martinique is famous for its beautiful women," he added with a wink. Natalie thanked him with a smile.

"Are you enjoying the party?" he asked.

"I'm not sure. I only had one glass of wine."

Michael chuckled. "Are you the designated driver?"

"I'm only driving myself, but I don't hold alcohol very well and I want to come back in one piece."

Simone appeared out of nowhere. "Mike, I'm glad you made it." She gave him a peck on the lips, a practice current in Hollywood, it seemed. Natalie had seen Simone kiss many male friends on the lips. Simone's speech was slurred, and she held onto Michael to keep from falling. Ted was nowhere to be seen. Natalie had spotted him once earlier, and he already looked drunk.

She excused herself to get another glass of juice. It took a while to reach the kitchen, and longer to return. By that time, Michael was in conversation with an older man sporting a gray ponytail, who looked like he could be a movie director or somebody an actor would want to speak with. She decided to go to the restroom before heading back to Santa Monica.

When she pushed open the door of the guest bathroom, she found herself eye to eye with Ted, peeing. He opened his mouth in feigned shock and then smiled lewdly. Natalie slammed the door shut in real shock. The door hadn't been locked, she was certain, and the toilet bowl was positioned oddly, so Ted had been facing her and she'd gotten a full view of his penis. Disoriented, she went looking for another bathroom, which she found off the lower level master bedroom.

She was washing her hands when she heard the voices of Simone and Amanda coming from outside. Someone jiggled the doorknob. Before Natalie had time to answer she heard Amanda's hysterical laugh.

"You have to work a little more on your accent," Simone

said.

"My name is *Nattalee*, I am a *doc-toer*, I come from *Marrrtinik*." Amanda spoke with a faux French accent.

"Stop it," Simone sputtered, laughing hard.

Natalie was horrified. Not only was Amanda mocking her, but Simone was laughing? Blood rose up to her face, as if she'd just been slapped. She stood there frozen, her mouth open.

"Why did you invite her?" Amanda continued. "She's so stuck up. And she's staying with you how long? A month?"

"Oh, she doesn't bother me too much. She's staying at my folks' guesthouse. She's cool most of the time," Simone answered, still laughing drunkenly. *Most of the time?* Natalie was too upset to move. She sat down on the toilet lid, petrified.

This couldn't be true. Simone? Her best friend Simone was belittling her and letting Amanda mock her?

Natalie wanted to disappear and get beamed into her car without having to ever see those girls again. She'd never liked confrontation, but she felt that her chest would explode if she didn't address this. A force she had no control over pushed her up to her feet and out of the bathroom. Both girls blanched when they saw her. Amanda froze, her tube of lipstick a few inches from her face.

Natalie looked at Amanda with utter disdain and then turned to Simone. "Coming from her, nothing would surprise me. But you?"

Simone looked blank. "Wh…what?" Natalie could smell alcohol on her breath from five feet away.

Amanda quipped, "We can't quite get what you say. It must be the accent. Can you repeat, please?"

"Maybe I should speak French then. *Tu es une vraie con-*

nasse. Do you want me to translate that?" Natalie shot back.

Simone burst out laughing and sank to the floor, as if her legs couldn't carry her anymore. Natalie took this as her way of getting out of the situation. Amanda stepped forward, and looking at her straight in the eyes, smeared the red lipstick she was holding on the front of Natalie's white dress. "Oops!" she said.

"Uh-oh!" Simone said, her eyes opening wide. She looked at Amanda, who burst out laughing.

Natalie felt her body tense as energy rose from her core. Adrenaline rushed through her, making her heart beat wildly. She grabbed Amanda's lipstick and crushed it on the girl's face. Amanda stepped back in shock.

Natalie waited for her, her hand raised ready to slap the drunken girl. She must have looked menacing because Amanda stopped herself short.

"French bitch!" she muttered, looking like a deranged clown with the lipstick all over her face.

"That's right! Now move!" Without a glance at Simone, still splayed on the floor, Natalie marched out of the room. Amanda stepped aside. Stumbling outside, Natalie followed the steps on the side of the house leading up to the front yard. A young man was vomiting on a cactus, while others drank and smoked without paying him any attention. A couple made out on a bench in front of everyone, the man's face buried in the girl's blouse, his hands clutching her butt. Natalie rushed to her car. Her heart thumped loudly in her chest, disappointment and hurt almost choking her. What else had been said behind her back? Now she felt betrayed, humiliated, and out of place like a stranger in a strange land. She hadn't been in such a catty confrontation since the sixth grade.

Now she knew that she didn't belong in Simone's world. In fact, she didn't feel like she belonged anywhere anymore.

CHAPTER SIX

Natalie was determined to stay in Los Angeles as planned. She had considered taking the first flight back to Paris, but the prospect made her queasy. If she went home, she would have to start looking for an apartment with Jean-Marc and bear his "I-told-you-so" attitude. And only God knew when she would be able to get any more time off. She decided she wouldn't let Amanda or Simone run her out of town, but she had to get out of the guesthouse immediately.

Early in the morning, she drove down Ocean Avenue with the intention of checking out an affordable hotel she'd found on the Internet. It would give her time to find a sublet or a studio to rent for the remaining weeks of her vacation. She wouldn't want to fall from a Santa Monica mansion to a sleazy motel where something terrible could happen to her, like in those American movies they loved to import in France.

She kept driving toward Venice until she recognized the area close to Jerry's house, near a small center with restaurants, vintage clothing stores, a post office, and a small hotel. The Pacific Blue Hotel was just what she was looking for. It was clean and well-maintained. Most of the rooms had an ocean view and were equipped with kitchenettes. More important, she could afford to spend a week there without overextending herself. *And it was a short walk from Jerry's house.* She silenced that little voice in her head immediately.

After making hotel reservations, she drove back to the Santa Monica guesthouse to pick up her bags. She couldn't help but feel regret when she rolled her luggage around the sparkling pool. Until the night before, everything had been perfect. But the hurtful laughs came back to her mind, and she closed the gate without a backward glance.

Her new room was equipped with the basics: a king-sized bed, table and chairs, a small sofa and an armoire hiding a TV, but there was also a kitchenette, which increased the comfort. The balcony offered an unobstructed view of the boardwalk and a glimpse of the ocean. If she leaned out, she could see a corner of Jerry's building.

Natalie sat on the bed, not knowing what to do next. She thought about calling Jerry, as they were neighbors now. Socializing would keep her from going crazy. But she would have to explain why she'd moved out of the Santa Monica guesthouse, and she didn't feel like talking about it. It was painful to think about Simone's betrayal, and each time she did so she could not help but wince.

The familiar loud thumping of her heart that had disappeared after her arrival in Los Angeles got her up on her feet. For the first time since her arrival, she felt the need to use her anti-anxiety pills. She looked for them in her carry-on bag, hesitated, and then buried the bottle in her luggage. A walk on the beach would be better to release the tension building up inside her.

She slipped on shorts, a sleeveless tee and the tennis shoes she'd been wise enough to pack, and went outside.

To avoid the crowded boardwalk, Natalie crossed the expanse of sand until she reached the shore. She walked for a while on the wet sand, grateful for the ocean breeze and the clear cerulean sky. In spite of her efforts, though, she couldn't push away the memories of her confrontation with Simone and Amanda. How could Simone behave that way? Natalie remembered when Simone came to Martinique one summer, years ago, and stayed with Natalie and her mother. She'd been welcomed like a family member. Her betrayal might be attributed to being drunk, but something irreversible had happened to their relationship. Underneath the anger, rejection weighed even heavier.

So why did she want to stay in Los Angeles? Was it because in spite of all the drama the day before, she felt more alive now than a week ago in Paris? She had reconnected with her younger, more enthusiastic self and wasn't ready to lose it again so soon.

Instead of going back to the hotel, her steps had taken her to Jerry's house. But as she came closer she realized that she couldn't muster up the courage to knock on his door.

Stopping a house away from his, she was about to turn around when a sexy blond woman stormed out of his house and slammed the door behind her. Thin and tall, she wore khaki shorts that showed off her long legs. She stomped away, looking furious, her perky breasts jumping with indignation under her white tee shirt. She hopped into a silver Mercedes Benz convertible parked in front of Jerry's garage. Natalie had to stop short of the driveway as the woman backed up and then sped away. Her tires screeched on the asphalt.

That must be Brenda. Thank God I didn't knock on the

door.

Natalie turned to leave, but the front door opened again, slowly this time. Jerry appeared at the door, with the unshaved look of somebody who hadn't slept in a while. Had he seen her through the tinted glass window? He looked at her as she stood there, not knowing what to do.

"Natalie? Hey, come on in." His tone sounded somewhat urgent.

Natalie felt her face flushing. "I…was just passing by. I'll see you another time."

"It's fine. Come on in." His voice was slightly softer now. He left the door open and walked back inside, as if sure she'd follow him.

Natalie walked in carefully, wishing that she had chosen another moment to pass by, but knowing she needed to see such a scene. Jerry's life, as she had imagined it, was full of women and drama like this. She'd always stayed away from these types of men because of it.

"I don't want to disturb you; I know you're busy… I moved to the hotel a few blocks down, the Pacific Blue," she blurted.

Jerry went to the fridge and retrieved two Cokes. He offered one to Natalie, but she declined. "Water is fine."

He got a glass from the cabinet and poured her some cold water, then invited her to take a seat at the kitchen table.

"What happened?" he finally said.

"What do you mean?" She didn't want to tell him the story.

"Why'd you move into a hotel? Something must've happened." His eyes moved from her bare legs all the way back up to her eyes. She felt uncomfortable as she noticed his bare feet, torn jeans and open crumpled shirt. A raw sensuality emanated from him. He contemplated her boldly. She returned his stare, but she stood.

"I think it's a bad moment to visit. You had company and all that. I'll see you another time," she said, moving toward the door.

Jerry grabbed her by the wrist, forcing her to turn back. "Wait." The contact of his hand felt electric. A jolt shot up her arm and pinched the middle of her chest. He stepped in front of her. By the way he looked at her, she understood that he wanted her. He wasn't even trying to hide it. She looked away. He let go of her hand. She took a few steps back.

"Why don't you tell me what's going on? Maybe I can help," he said.

"Yesterday, at Ted's party, I overheard Simone's friend Amanda making fun of me... and I almost got into a fight with her."

Jerry frowned. "Where was Simone?"

"She was there, laughing," Natalie said, this time tears pricking her eyes. She forbade herself to cry. She hadn't cried before and she wouldn't now, definitely not in front of Jerry.

Jerry looked upset. "Amanda's a catty, bitchy chick," he said, "but I can't believe that Simone let you down. I'm sorry you had to deal with their jealousy."

"Why would they be jealous? They are gorgeous girls."

Jerry looked at her, surprised. "Come on. You know it's not only about physical beauty. It's about freshness, sophistication, poise. Qualities they can't have because they're trying too hard, and they've lost touch with their true selves. The fact that you're completely unaware of how attractive you are probably upsets them even more."

Natalie didn't know what to say.

"Anyway," she stuttered, "after that I couldn't stay at Simone's folks' house anymore."

"Does she know you moved out?"

"Not yet."

"Simone had to be drunk to act like that. She loves you. I'm sure she doesn't want to lose your friendship. But her behavior is indefensible."

Natalie didn't answer. She didn't know if Simone was really her friend anymore, and she sure didn't feel loved. At least Jerry's apparent indignation made her feel a little better.

"It seems that you went through some drama yourself," she said. "You look like somebody who hasn't slept in a while."

"I've been painting," he said, caressing his unshaved face.

"Can I see?" She headed toward his work area.

"Wait. I'm not sure you're going to like it." He grabbed her by her wrist again. She hesitated, but her curiosity was aroused. She shook her hand free and went to see what he had painted.

Some sketches of Natalie were spread out on the table. The large canvas on the easel faced the window, and she circled around it.

She gasped when she saw herself lying on the red sofa, semi-naked, covered only by a pearly piece of cloth on her lower abdomen, one arm folded on her chest, the other stretched back in abandon. Her legs were crossed high, and a sensual smile parted her lips. The sofa stood on a beach of white sand, in front of an apocalyptic background of tropical jungle, waterfalls and exotic flowers. The colors were vibrant; the rich reds of the sofa and her lips looking like fresh blood.

"Oh my God!" She was flattered but at the same time felt panicked. Anybody seeing this painting would think that she and Jerry were lovers. He had seen her naked in the pool and had re-produced her body in his painting. Turning away from the canvas, she faced Jerry.

"Are you upset?" he asked.

"I... don't know. People may get the wrong idea." She prayed Jean-Marc would never find out. What about Brenda? Had she looked at the painting? Could that be the reason for her dra-matic exit?

"Does it matter what people think?" His eyes were half closed as he gazed at her lips. Her legs went weak. He pulled her close and held her gently, as if he wanted to console her. He cra-dled her and caressed her hair. She tensed at first, but then relaxed under his touch. Then he bent his head to kiss her. Natalie turned her face away and took a step back. Jerry seemed surprised. She saw blood rushing to his face, as if he had been slapped.

"I have a boyfriend, and I just saw an angry woman storm-ing out of here," she said.

"We broke up. I'm free," Jerry replied.

Natalie remembered Simone mentioning that Jerry and Brenda regularly broke up but then got back together.

"Well, I'm not," she said tersely.

He looked deep into her eyes, as if to read her feelings. "I'm very attracted to you. Are you attracted to me?"

She didn't know what to answer. It wasn't just his physique

she was attracted to. She felt a deep connection to him through his art. It really spoke to her. His painting revealed her to herself as if it summoning her passionate side. As if he knew her better than she knew herself. And that was fascinating.

He came closer. "I want you," he whispered, kissing the lobe of her ear, then the side of her neck. She shuddered, and in spite of herself pressed her body against him.

"Can't you feel what's happening?" he whispered. "You can't deny that."

Her body felt so good against his. He kissed her eyes, her cheeks, and then her mouth. His tongue parted her lips, and she couldn't help but return his kiss with the same intensity. She couldn't believe this was happening. His hand slid under her t-shirt and caressed her back, but when it made its way to her breast, she caught it and pushed it away, breaking their embrace. For a moment she had forgotten Jean-Marc. She would never cheat on him. She stepped back.

"No," she said firmly.

He let his hands drop to his side and tried to regain his composure.

"I'm sorry," he said, running both hands through his hair as if he didn't know what to do with them.

She walked toward the door. When she glanced back, he was looking away.

Still under the spell of her own dizzying emotions, she took off running toward the hotel in a dreamlike state.

Wind whistled in her ears as invisible wings carried her faster and faster. She followed the Venice beach boardwalk for a while, cutting through the light morning crowd, her heart pumping in her chest as if it belonged to a teenager who had just been kissed for the first time. She wanted to jump, skip, and do cartwheels. How ridiculous, how childish, how amazing was that?

She slowed down to a fast walk. Droplets of sunshine made the palm trees glisten as if decorated with Christmas garlands. The unexpected kiss and the desire she had read in his eyes had filled her with a glee she was embarrassed to acknowledge. The places on her body he had touched still tingled. She wanted to savor the moment, but like a dark cloud, the thought of Jean-Marc waiting for her in Paris pierced her, obscuring the brightness and filling her with dread and remorse.

She took a shortcut through the shadowy backstreets and reached the hotel out of breath. The clerk raised an eyebrow when he saw her run in. She waved at him and took the stairs. Sweat from her forehead had gathered on the tip of her chin by the time she reached her room. She peeled off her clothes to jump in the shower but stopped to study her reflection in the closet's mirror. The woman Jerry painted had lean copper legs, a small waist, and smooth curves. Was that how he saw her?

In the shower, she opened her mouth under the fresh water. Jerry's desire made her feel vibrantly alive. But even though she acknowledged she wanted him, too, she could never let herself go any further. She would never do that to Jean-Marc.

She got out of the shower, her body somewhat cooled down. Slowly drying off with the large white hotel towel, she lathered her skin with vanilla body butter. Was Jerry responsible for the extra glow of her skin and the sparkle in her eyes? Maybe it was just a side effect of her own craving. She had no choice but to resist her physical attraction for him. It wouldn't bring anything but trouble into her life.

Her hair was still wet and dripping on her neck as she slipped into a pair of jeans and a brand new white tank top, and then stretched out on the bed.

The phone's insistent ring startled her. Nobody knew she was there besides Jerry. Could it be him? She picked up the phone carefully.

"A Simone is downstairs to see you," the desk clerk said.

Natalie sighed. "I'm coming down." She really didn't want to see Simone, but she was curious to hear what she would have to say.

Natalie stepped into the lobby and Simone hurried to her.

"What's going on? Jerry called me to scold me because *you* checked out into this hotel, and then he hung up." Simone sounded upset and self-righteous, which fueled Natalie's indignation.

"You have some nerve! You know why I left."

"What are you talking about?" Simone face was scrunched up, as if she had a headache—more than likely a hangover.

"Oh please! Don't pretend that you can't remember. You weren't *that* drunk."

Simone remained speechless, as if she didn't expect this. She looked stunned.

"Last thing I remember I was mixing margaritas. I have no idea what I did or said."

Natalie didn't believe her. After all, Simone was an actress.

"Well, at least I know your true feelings about me. Apparently you only say it when you are drunk."

"What the hell did I say?" Simone asked with eyes wide open, as if she had no idea. "What happened? I really don't remember!"

Still, Natalie wasn't convinced of her sincerity. "Why don't you ask Amanda?" she said. "I'm sure she does."

"Amanda's been bitter since her divorce. Her husband left her for an English photographer, and then she had a short fling with Jerry that messed her up even more. Was she mean to you?"

Simone always had the words to find her way out of a delicate situation. Natalie had to give her that. She made a mental note that Jerry had dated Amanda. He hadn't mentioned that to her, of course.

"She smeared lipstick on my dress," Natalie said, omitting Amanda's comments.

"That's crazy. I'm sorry that happened," Simone shook her head in disbelief. "I have to stop drinking so much. But you could probably see I wasn't myself. How can you write me off so quickly?"

"Don't try to turn things around; you are the one who betrayed me. You laughed and encouraged her." Natalie sat down on one of the hotel's lobby chair, feeling deflated as she relived the scene. Her eyes stung, tears close to bursting out. She noticed the man at the desk looking at them. He'd likely been listening the whole time. Now he pretended to shuffle some papers. She massaged her temples. The whole thing was giving her a headache.

"I'm sorry that happened, Natalie," Simone said softly as she also sat. She looked remorseful and a little teary herself. "I don't remember what Amanda said or did, but if it makes you feel better I can go slap the bitch right now."

"That won't be necessary. I already crushed lipstick on her face. Too bad you don't remember. But drunk or not, you were supposed to have my back."

"Again, I apologize." Simone looked contrite.

Natalie was still hurt, but there wasn't much more to say. "Anyway, what are you doing in this part of town? You should be in bed with a hangover."

"Oh, I had to go to a brunch at the Ivy. I was supposed to meet some industry people. But I don't think I made a good impression. I don't look my best today. Then Jerry called me." There was a silence between them. "You can move back to the guesthouse, Nat. Really."

Natalie looked at her. Simone seemed like a different person now. Somebody she couldn't trust anymore.

"Thank you, but I like it here. I'm going to stay in Venice Beach." Natalie hid the insidious feeling of loneliness with a sad smile. Now she was on her own.

CHAPTER SEVEN

Natalie sharpened her pencils and opened her new sketch-book to a blank page. Her intention was to draw Jerry's face. She hadn't seen him since their kiss two days before, but he occupied all her thoughts. There was nothing she could do about it even though she kept telling herself that, according to his own cousin, he was a womanizer and just wanted to sleep with her. She had tried to conjure up the image of Jean-Marc and what she liked about him, but even the guilt she felt couldn't keep her from burning hot each time she relived her kiss with Jerry.

It is probably what they call infatuation, she thought. Like the flu, it just had to run its course and there was nothing to do but wait until it passed.

She drew his eyes first, with their almond shape and straight eyelashes. She left the pupils empty like those of Greek sculptures. Then she outlined his eyebrows, slightly raised in the middle, remembering how tempted she had been to touch them and smooth them with her fingers. Then came the hard part: The expression of his eyes, deep with sometimes a touch of cynicism. She almost got it, but not quite.

Outlining his strong jaw line and wild hair, she erased frequently until his face finally emerged from the paper. At the end it did look like Jerry, but her drawing lacked detail and depth.

Natalie had never thought of drawing Jean-Marc's face. Thinking about him, she touched her locket and opened the little door again to read the inscription inside. Did Jean-Marc really love her? He knew the strong Natalie, whose fingers plunged inside people's bodies, and who kept her life and feelings under control. Did he even know of the lost woman with doubts, fears, and crazy dreams, who yearned to feel the rapture of life and be freed from the mundane? Jerry just wanted her; that she was sure of, but he had a sense of the self she had been hiding. With that painting, she was sensing another dimension to life, a mysterious, maybe even sacred realm that could be accessed through art. She had gotten to see herself through his eyes, and he had opened a door for her to get a peek at her own depth, her own yearning for a life full of passion. It was scary. What would happen if she forgot what was reasonable and let herself dive into her true desires? What did she truly want?

Then the thought of their passionate kiss made her chest swell for the thousandth time.

A knock at the door made her jump. She glanced at the clock near the bed. It was 9:30 p.m. It couldn't be housekeeping. She was almost ready to go to bed and wore only a long oversized t-shirt.

She closed her sketchbook and got up to cautiously open the door. Jerry stood in the doorway unshaven, his shirt fastened with only one button, as if he had put it on in a hurry. She couldn't articulate a single word. One moment she was drawing his face and the next he had materialized in front of her.

They stared at each other. He looked deep into her eyes, his eyelids heavy as if he were sick.

"What's going on?" she asked.

"I wanted to see you."

"How did you get the room number?"

"I tricked the lady at the reception desk."

She gave a nervous smile. "I was just thinking about you and you appeared."

"I can't think of anything but you," he said, his head down.

"Probably because you're not used to women resisting you."

He looked at her for a moment and she saw a spark light up in his eyes. "Why are you so scared?"

Because you come with a big price tag, she thought. "I'm not scared of anything," she said instead. "You have a longtime girl-friend that you break up with every now and then and I have a boyfriend I trust and who loves me." They were still standing in the doorway. She didn't want him in her bedroom. He reached out and grabbed her hand, pulling her to him.

"I don't like games. Tell me that you don't feel anything for me and I'll leave you alone. Be honest." She looked at him and saw the effort he'd made to come and speak from his heart. If she pushed him away now, she'd probably never see him again. The thought made her feel lightheaded. She had to accept the effect he had on her.

"I don't know you," she said, her voice almost inaudible.

He smiled as if it was all he wanted to hear and kissed the palm of her hand. Her heart skipped a few beats. He pulled her closer still. She turned her head and his kiss landed on her cheek. But they stood in a tight embrace.

"Can I come in?"

"No," she said.

"Then let's go out!" he said. "I want to show you something."

"Now? But I'm not dressed."

His eyes lingered on her body as if he could see through her t-shirt.

"I have to change too," he said. "I'll be right back." And he left.

Natalie wondered what had just happened. Only a few minutes ago, she was determined to resist him and just ride out her attraction for him, and now they were going on a date. A stab in her chest told her that she was on a dangerous path, but it was too late now. Jerry would be back soon.

Feeling out of breath, she changed into designer jeans, a silky silver top that bared her shoulders and crossed nicely across her breasts, and high heels. After she put the last touch to her makeup, Jerry knocked at her door. This time, he was closely shaved, his hair was brushed back into a ponytail, and he was dressed all in black. He chuckled when she whistled with admiration.

"You may want to take a jacket," he said. "We're taking my motorcycle."

Parked in front of the hotel was a midnight blue Harley-Davidson, with sparkling chrome gleaming under the street lights.

Natalie looked at Jerry. "You don't look like a Harley-Davidson type of guy."

"Really? What do they look like?"

"White guys with long hair, mustaches, and beards, like in *Easy Rider*."

Jerry laughed. "I guess I don't fit that description, but you may want to expand your assessment of Harley owners. I inherited this bike from my friend Harry and he was a black guy in his sixties, an artist like me. When he moved to London, he left it to me." He gave her a helmet to wear and climbed on.

Pressed against Jerry's back, her arms wrapped around his waist, Natalie felt at ease. She couldn't keep from smiling. People stared at them when the motorcycle stopped at red lights. She imagined that somehow they emanated a chemistry that others could detect.

Jerry turned his head toward her and winked as if he knew what was on her mind. They drove all the way to busy Sunset Boulevard, weaving through the traffic. A young crowd walked down the street in packs, gathering outside nightclubs and restaurants.

"Imagine how it is on the weekend," Jerry said.

They left Sunset to take Laurel Canyon, and then entered a gated area named Mount Olympus. The Harley climbed up winding streets named Achilles Drive, Venus Drive, Hercules Drive, all after the Greek gods. Huge mansions stood on each side of the street, some beautiful, others too ostentatious in their effort to imitate Greek architecture. The motorcycle finally turned onto Jupiter Drive, and by the number of cars parked on both sides of the street, Natalie realized that they were going to a house party. A crowd gathered in front of an impressive two-story mansion, lushly landscaped and lit. Jerry stopped just in front and parked between two luxury cars. Beautiful, stylish young people waited for two suited men to check their names off the guest list.

"You could have told me you were taking me to a party. I would have dressed up."

"You look great!" Jerry removed his helmet. He looked at

ease.

"Did you know that there was a dress-in-white theme?" Natalie said as she noticed that everyone except security was wearing white.

"I forgot but who cares, we're not really going to the party."

Jerry smiled at Natalie's puzzled face. He took her hand and led her through the crowd. He passed the security men, who nodded and let them through the gate. They went up large marble steps, but avoided the imposing front doorway to take a path on the side. He unlatched a little gate and they found themselves in a fragrant side garden.

A few couples were sitting on romantic benches beside a beautiful black-bottomed pool adorned with a cascading fountain. In the back of the spectacular villa, the crowd spread out onto a large terrace that overlooked the city lights sparkling in the distance like jewels. People were pressed up against each other, wandering around with their drinks.

Women stared at Jerry. Amused, Natalie let him lead her. They stepped down to the second level and went inside.

The huge room had twenty-foot high glass windows with amazing views. Giant abstract paintings decorated the other walls. In each corner, blond waif-like girls, dressed in white brassieres, tight white shorts and ten-inch heeled white boots, danced on top of tables covered with white cloths. They shook their shapely little butts with jerky moves.

Natalie observed everything as if it were happening to another person. She had never been to a party like this. Jerry shook a few hands, exchanged words here and there and took Natalie another flight down an iron staircase that led to a large hallway with several bedrooms. He lifted a heavy curtain and knocked at a hidden door. A booming male voice invited them in.

The room beyond was decorated in a Japanese minimalist style. A man in his fifties with a handsome, familiar face sat on a sofa with three young beauties surrounding him. They all smoked and drank.

The man stood up when he saw Jerry. "Hey man, I'm glad you could make it." They hugged and patted each other's back. "Oh! And who is this beautiful lady here with you?"

"This is Natalie, Natalie this is Bill."

Bill took Natalie's hand and kissed it seductively. "Natalie, what a beautiful face! But I know you from somewhere. Right?"

"I have the same feeling about you," Natalie said.

Bill laughed, and Jerry said, "Don't worry, it's not in another life. I'm sure that Bill's TV series made it to France."

Natalie still couldn't place him but lied, "Oh yeah! I know now. It's so nice to meet you."

"Bill is a successful producer now and he's also my godfather."

Bill smiled with satisfaction. He seemed pleased with himself.

"Welcome to my house. Now go have fun." He went back to the three young girls, who smiled seductively and made room for him.

Natalie and Jerry left, pulling the curtains behind them.

"I think that was a casting session in progress," Natalie whispered in Jerry's ear.

Jerry laughed. "How long have you been in Hollywood? You're a quick learner. Come this way. I want to show you something."

They went back up one flight and found themselves in a media room with several rows of seats facing a big screen.

"There it is," Jerry said. He leaned back against the wall near the doorway.

"What?" Natalie said, puzzled. "A home theater?"

She turned around and saw a gigantic nine-foot high painting on the wall opposite the screen. A painting of her! Almost the same as the one she had seen at Jerry's the other morning, only bigger. It showed her, half reclined on a red couch with the jungle landscape as a backdrop. She was painted in profile wearing a black evening dress.

She gasped and turned to Jerry.

"I don't understand. When did you have the time to do this one?"

Jerry looked deep into her eyes. "Three years ago."

"What? It doesn't make any sense."

"I woke up one morning with the vision of that face. I sketched it from memory, and I used it for this painting. Bill loved it and bought it." Jerry looked a little embarrassed.

Natalie went closer to the painting, her eyes glued on the face that looked so much like hers.

"It's unbelievable. It's me." How was this possible?

"When I first saw you, I didn't know what to think," Jerry said.

Natalie didn't know what to think either. Would she wake up and realize that she had dreamed all this? She couldn't quite believe that he had seen her in some kind of vision. It was surreal. A little dizzy, she returned to Jerry and, raising her hand to his face, smoothed his right eyebrow with her thumb.

"I've wanted to do that all day," she said.

He kissed her hair. "Let's go somewhere else," he said. "I don't like parties..."

They ended up in a French restaurant on Sunset Boulevard.

After they ordered iced teas and desserts, Natalie asked, "How did you become an artist?"

"I started to draw when I was twelve, after my father died. Bill offered me an easel and some professional art supplies. I entered some competitions, and started to win prizes. As soon as I was done with high school, I left home. I spent a few months in Haiti and in Amsterdam. In Paris I attended *Les Beaux Arts* for a while, and it was hard. I wanted to make it on my own, with no help. Eventually, I met some people who took interest in my art. They gave me a grant to come back to New York, and it all took off from there."

Jerry was obviously leaving out big chunks of his past, but Natalie wasn't ready for anything too heavy right now. She wanted to enjoy the evening with this gorgeous man, who might have gone through some hard times, but looked like he had overcome most of it.

"What about you?" he asked.

"There isn't much to say," she told him. "I had a protected childhood despite the fact that my father left when I was five. Both my mom and my dad are remarried. Mom was devastated after the divorce, but she devoted herself to us, and we didn't suffer too much except from a general distrust of men on my part."

"Distrust noted," Jerry said, holding his spoon in the air.

She looked at him, amused. "I still don't trust you. I'm sure there's a logical explanation for the woman in your painting looking like me. It could just be one of your many tricks to seduce women."

Jerry stopped eating his tiramisu, a shocked expression on his face.

"Damn it, woman! You're doing it again. Where does this come from? Your parents' divorce got to you more than you think. It's more than distrust; you probably think that most men are evil and perverted." He pushed his cake away as if he had lost his appetite.

Natalie laughed and kept eating, unfazed. "Most men *are* evil and perverted. That's a proven fact."

"Well, at least you got one thing right. I do want to seduce you." He placed his hand on her thigh and looked at her through his long lashes.

Natalie felt electricity traveling up her thighs, but she pushed his hands away.

"I'm not that easy to seduce."

"You certainly aren't, but you have no idea what you're missing," he said with a suggestive wink.

"Well, why don't you tell me then?"

"It's something that you have to experience for yourself. But you're playing so hard to get, I'm not sure I want to show you anymore."

"Oh, I'm sorry; I made you lose your appetite." She put a playful hand on his thigh.

"Ooh, I think my appetite is coming back." He placed his hand on top of hers and, squeezing it, hiked it a little higher. He looked deep into her eyes, his lips slightly opened; his eyes half-closed. She held his gaze. A current ran from his body into hers, the emotion between them building up until her body seemed to liquefy.

"Your place or my place?" he asked in a voice husky.

Natalie realized that she was at a point of no return. What was she doing? Her body was overriding her intellect. Her heart skipped a few beats. She had to stop what was happening but she couldn't, nor did she want to. It was as if she'd been caught by an underwater current and knew that all resistance was futile. "Your place," she said.

"Let's go then." He put a $50 bill on the table and got up. Natalie finished her last bite of chocolate cake, and a spoonful of Jerry's tiramisu, and then took a last sip of her iced tea while Jerry waited for her, feigning exasperation. He grabbed her hand and dragged her out. They left the restaurant laughing. Once outside they exchanged a long and torrid kiss. She felt his erection and her own body heat rising. She could have made love with him right then and there.

As the motorcycle hurried down the street, she kept her arms wrapped around him. Her mind presented her with images of Jean-Marc, but the sense of guilt was dulled by the powerful thought that Jerry was what she had always wanted. Her loyalty was slowly shifting to him. Maybe he really was the one. The desire in her body spread and her head spun. At red lights he placed his hands on her legs or pressed his hands on hers. He drove a little faster this time. They finally reached Speedway Street, and then turned into the alley leading to Jerry's house.

Jerry was driving slowly now, and the Harley emitted a soft hum. Natalie felt his body tense.

"What the hell?"

Natalie looked ahead and saw Brenda's Mercedes parked in front of Jerry's garage door. She shook her head in disbelief. The stereo playing sweet tunes in her head became silent and the world around her took an ugly tint.

"Looks like you have company. That's your girlfriend's car, right?" Natalie's voice was now cold. For a moment she had lowered her guard and let her body dictate her actions. But now it was as if someone had thrown a bucket of ice in her face to wake her up. She snickered, more upset with herself than anything else. All the way, she had fantasized that Jerry was some kind of soul mate. What a joke! How could she be so gullible?

"Brenda isn't my girlfriend anymore," Jerry said, with a tone that could pass for sincere. "She hasn't been for months. I have no idea what she's doing here; maybe she needs something. Let's go to your hotel."

"You can drop me at my hotel, or you can leave me here and go see what she wants. I'll walk." He had some nerve to think that she would sleep with him anyway.

"Come on, I'm not letting you walk. It's really not what you think."

"Whatever. Take me back to the hotel, please."

Jerry cursed, then made a U-turn. When he stopped the motorcycle in front of the hotel, Natalie got off as quickly as possible. But when she saw his face, she felt her anger dissolving a bit. He looked crestfallen. Still, the opportunity had passed. She had awakened from her moment of insanity.

"It wasn't meant to be," she said, almost gently.

"Let me come upstairs with you," he pleaded. "You can't

leave me like this."

She smiled sadly. "It was wrong anyway. Good night!" She turned away from him and walked inside.

CHAPTER EIGHT

Natalie spent the night reliving the evening. Like someone who had walked away from a terrible car wreck without a scratch, she was still shaking.

Without Brenda's impromptu visit, she would have made a huge mistake and woken up in Jerry's bed this morning riddled with remorse. The fact that he had painted her three years ago had messed with her head. But maybe there was no mystery. It could just be some kind of coincidence. He could have painted a model that looked a lot like her; as simple as that. She tugged the necklace around her neck and sighed in shame.

Was Jerry upset with Brenda for showing up at his house unexpectedly? Did she try to seduce him? Did they make up? Had they even broken up in the first place? Natalie would probably never know for sure.

She opened the curtains. The sun flooded inside, revealing the sky, cobalt blue, clear and crisp, and the lovely view of the beach with its miles of sand. Natalie forced herself to eject the thought of Jerry. Life was beautiful after all. And thank God, nothing irreversible had occurred.

She took a leisurely shower. But as she rinsed off, and touched the skin on her chest, she suddenly realized that her necklace was gone. Her heart jumped. No! She shut off the water and checked the bottom of the bathtub. Then she saw it. The broken chain was caught in the drain, with the locket still miraculously attached.

Troubled, Natalie dried herself off. The fracture of the chain was a disturbing coincidence. She imagined that her moment of craziness last night had somehow broken the bond between Jean-Marc and her. She found a little pocket in her toiletry bag where she placed the locket and its chain.

Her cell phone chimed, indicating that she had a voice message. Natalie's heart accelerated when she heard Jean-Marc's voice. He sounded disturbed, speaking slowly, as if he couldn't contain his irritation. "I'm in Paris. I'll be here for two days. I've tried to reach you many times since Sunday, but your phone wouldn't pick up. Yesterday I called Simone and found out you moved and went to a hotel. Why didn't you call me?"

Natalie's heart dropped to the bottom of her stomach. She had gone to Jerry's house, and nothing had been the same since. There was no plausible excuse for not having called Jean-Marc.

She dialed his number and he picked up right away.

"*Jean-Marc, c'est Natalie*, I was in the shower when you called."

"Natalie, what's going on?"

"Well, I didn't feel comfortable staying at Simone's parents' anymore so I moved in a hotel two days ago."

"Okay, why didn't you call me?"

"I *was* about to call you." She waited for him to say something but he stayed silent. "Come on, Jean-Marc, you're a pilot, I can't always reach you. You don't have to know where I am every second."

"Yes, I would like to know where you are and what you're

doing because I care about you. Obviously more than you care about me."

The now familiar wave of guilt engulfed Natalie. She managed to laugh, but her voice was a little unsteady. "Jean-Marc, don't be like that."

"Natalie, I want you to be honest with me. Did you meet somebody?"

Natalie stayed quiet for a few seconds. What would be the point of telling him about Jerry? She had been tempted, yes, but now it was different. "There's nobody to worry about," she said, and it felt like the truth.

"I'm not a fool, Natalie. There's something wrong. I can hear it in your voice. If you're not comfortable with Simone anymore why don't you come back home?"

"Because this is the first time in my life that I am free to do what I please without any demands on me. I finally have time to think. I need this time." She heard him sigh again.

"Nat, listen. You're in Los Angeles in a hotel room, by yourself. You're not on great terms with Simone. I'm worrying about you. I want you to let me know that you are okay on a regular basis. Do you need money?" Jean-Marc was so protective; it would be easy to let him take care of her. But it was also smothering.

"I'm fine, don't worry. I've been living alone in Paris for years, you know. *Je ne suis pas née de la dernière pluie.*"

"I know you weren't born yesterday. Still, be careful..."

"I will."

"Okay, I'll call you tomorrow then."

"I'll be there."

"*Je t'aime.*"

"Moi aussi, Je t'aime." Natalie couldn't blame Jean-Marc for worrying about her. She hadn't been particularly trustworthy and she wasn't proud of it. She silently vowed to make it up to him.

She hung up, stretched out on the bed and gazed at the California sky. Such a perfect day: no fog, no haze, no clouds. A tall palm tree swayed gently while seagulls crossed the azure sky.

She'd always loved places with palm trees. One rainy winter in Paris, when she was craving blue skies and sunshine, she spent an unreasonable amount of money on a coffee set she didn't need, only because it had delicate little palm trees painted on each cup. And there she was, staring at a great sky from a hotel room in Venice, California. She had no desire to go back to Paris.

Her cell phone rang again. To Natalie's surprise it was Simone.

"Hey Nat, I'll be in the neighborhood shopping for clothes. Do you want to join me?" Simone's voice was cautious. Natalie wasn't sure that she was ready to resume their friendship. The hurt was still there but at least Simone was trying. She agreed to meet her.

Their first stop on Main Street was Abigail, one of Simone's favorite stores that carried vintage clothes and designer rip-offs. Simone's intention was to find a dress with a floating skirt and spaghetti straps in the style of the fifties, for an audition the next day.

While Simone drove the sales lady over the edge by trying on dozens of dresses, Natalie wondered if their friendship could ever be restored. She tried not to think about Amanda, but it was almost impossible. She couldn't help but remember Simone's high-pitched laugh and Amanda's malevolent smirk. Natalie hadn't mentioned the party, but her interaction with Simone was more careful and guarded than it had ever been. Nothing was forgotten.

"Check this out!" Simone exploded, triumphant. She came out of the dressing room with a peach chiffon dress that hugged her breasts and small waist. It looked great on her and she spent at least another fifteen minutes admiring it, twirling in front of the mirror, pretending that she was not sure it fitted her. Simone seemed to enjoy making salespeople sweat before buying. Natalie was used to that trick, and it amused her to see that her old girl-friend hadn't changed in that way. She was sure that Simone would buy the dress, so she absorbed herself in the contemplation of a skirt from the rack; trying to speed the process would only delay it another fifteen minutes.

When they finally sat on the terrace of Starbucks for cappuccinos and muffins, Natalie was happy to rest her feet. She hadn't bought any clothes while shopping with Simone, but she promised herself to come back to the area at a later time.

"So I heard that you and Jerry were at Bill's party last night?" Simone asked around a mouthful of food. That caught Natalie off guard.

"How did you hear that?"

"Girl, this is my town. I have spies everywhere." Simone seemed to be studying the content of her plate, but Natalie knew that she was dying to get the details. That was probably the reason why she had called this morning.

Natalie smiled. "Your spies were correct."

"Come on, don't make me beg! I want to know what's going on between you guys. You know how nosy I am." She smiled expectantly.

Natalie took a bite of her pastry, chewing as slowly as possible. Simone made a gesture as if she was about to strangle her that made them both giggle.

"Okay, he just dropped me off at my hotel after the party and that's it. We didn't sleep together if it's what you want to know."

Simone wasn't convinced. "Really? I was told that he looked pretty into you."

"Who told you that?"

"A friend of mine who saw you at Ted's party last Saturday," Simone said, looking mysterious.

"Jerry just wanted to show me that big painting in Bill's media room. The woman he painted looks a lot like me. Do you know what painting I'm talking about?"

Simone frowned. "A big painting? I don't think I ever spent time in Bill's media room. But Jerry knows a lot of women. One of them could look like you." She picked up a cigarette from her designer bag, her lips slightly pinched. "He used it as an angle to get you? Guys! They're all the same."

"You're surely making him look bad." Simone obviously didn't want to see her with Jerry. Did she really think the painting was a coincidence, or did she just want to keep Natalie away from her cousin? Natalie was inclined to believe the latter.

"Jerry's my cousin and I love him. But if you want my advice, stay away unless you just want some good sex."

"Good sex? How would you know? Did you sleep with him?"

"Please! Don't be ridiculous. I'm just trying to warn you." Simone looked vexed.

"I think that I'm a good judge of character. I've been doing pretty good so far without your warnings, thank you."

"We used to be able to speak about guys without you getting on your high horse." Simone looked hurt.

"That's when you weren't trying to patronize me," Natalie replied.

They both stayed silent for a while.

Natalie felt cold; she had forgotten to bring a jacket. The weather changed so quickly in Los Angeles. She looked up at the sky and for a moment wished to be back in Martinique on her mother's verandah, loved and safe.

Simone finally broke the silence. "I'm sorry, Nat. I just don't want to see you make a mistake. You have Jean-Marc. By the way you described him, he seems like a great guy. And Jerry–I love him, he's a wonderful person, but he's as unstable and disturbed as an artist like him can be. It goes with the life. For us artists, nothing is ever set in stone. Not even success. The only thing we are ever loyal to is our art. People around us get hurt. You're a doctor; it's a totally different game." Simone looked sincere in her effort to explain herself, but Natalie didn't like what she was hearing.

"Implying that doctors and artists are incompatible because of their different lifestyles is preposterous. I personally know a few doctors happily married to artists."

"What I mean is that Jerry has only been consistent with his art. Everything else in his life is a mess. I don't know if you're up for all that."

"I have no intention of getting involved with Jerry, if that can reassure you. But for your information, messy lives are not the prerogative of artists." Natalie resented the cliché of doctors as people with rigid mindsets and strict codes. That was not the way she saw herself. What she wanted most right now was a life full of creativity and freedom.

Simone didn't answer but the look in her eyes indicated that she wasn't convinced.

"Now is there something specific about Jerry that I should know? Is he a psychopath?" Natalie asked.

Simone chuckled. "Not to my knowledge. But since you don't intend to get involved with him, there's nothing to worry about."

Before Natalie could say another word, a tall figure stopped at their table.

"Michael, what's up?" Simone rose to give him a hug. Natalie recognized the handsome black actor from Simone's party.

"Come sit with us." Simone looked happy with the diversion.

"Natalie, this is Michael, Michael, this is Natalie. She's visiting from Paris."

"Hi Natalie." Michael extended his hand and flashed a perfect smile.

Natalie smiled back and shook his hand. "We already met at your party Saturday," she said. Of course Simone couldn't remember.

Michael dragged a chair to their table and put down his latte. He sat back, confident and relaxed, opening his long legs wide.

"Hey!" Simone punched his shoulder. "Did you get that *Kamikaze* movie? Stan told me that he saw you at the audition."

"I got a call back for tomorrow. We'll see." He rubbed his arm as if Simone's punch had hurt him. *He's charming*, Natalie thought. She would've given him the part, whatever it was.

"I read the script. Poor Stan was really hoping he would get it." Simone had perked up. Her eyes shone with excitement. She seemed to love the world she lived in.

"I don't think we read for the same role, but did you go in for the part of Mitch's girlfriend? You would be perfect for it," Michael answered.

"My agent is trying to get me in, with no luck so far. I need a better agent." She went on about how incompetent her agent was, but how she couldn't afford to fire him yet.

Natalie stayed quiet, not wanting to get involved in their conversation. She didn't know the world they were talking about. It was probably a good time to bail and start looking for a furnished room to rent for her remaining twenty days in town.

"What about you? What have you been doing?" Michael said as if he had read her mind.

"Enjoying the beach mostly," Natalie answered.

"Venice is my favorite place in L.A.," Michael said. "I feel lucky to live here."

Natalie really liked the sound of his voice, deep but warm.

"Where are you staying?" he asked.

"At the Pacific Blue Hotel in Venice. I'll be there until the end of the week, but I would like to find something else for the next couple of weeks after that. Maybe a furnished studio?"

Simone frowned and opened her mouth to say something, but nothing came out. She shifted in her chair, looking uncomfortable.

Michael looked pensive, one hand on his chin. "I may be able to help," he said. "My neighbor Peggy, who's also an actress, got cast in an off-Broadway play. She has to leave in two days and she's still looking for somebody to sublet her apartment. I'll talk to her if you are interested."

Natalie was very interested. They exchanged phone numbers while Simone bit her lip. Michael and Simone resumed their conversation, but Michael's eyes often strayed to Natalie's face. It occurred to her that she was getting a lot of attention from guys lately; much more than in Paris. She wondered why. It was true that she often felt uprooted in Paris. Like everyone, she admired the old stones, the museums, and the architecture, but she didn't thrive there. The cold rainy weather and the general grumpiness often got to her. She felt out of place. Maybe that's why one of her first year med teachers nicknamed her the "Island Bird."

She touched her shell bracelet and closed her eyes. Leaning back on her chair, she pledged to enjoy every single moment of freedom she could steal during this vacation.

When she came back from her thoughts, Michael was watching her from the corner of his eye while listening to Simone. He acknowledged her with a faint nod and Natalie smiled. She liked him.

CHAPTER NINE

Natalie spent most of her afternoon roaming the aisles of an art store. The smell of fresh paper awakened memories of her childhood, when her favorite place was a book and art supply store in Fort-de-France. As a child, her hands caressed the soft bristles of sable brushes of all sizes and her eyes took delight in registering the paints, papers, and canvasses. She got absorbed in browsing art manuals, and finally stumbled on what she thought was the perfect book to learn the basics of drawing. On the first page was a list of recommended pencils. She bought them all and left the store with a bounce in her step.

What would Jean-Marc think about her newfound interest for art? He was pragmatic. His interest resided in politics, sports, and technology. He was goal oriented, and when he wanted something, he immediately strategized to get it. The problem was that he often wanted what Natalie couldn't give him. More love, more attention, more dependency on him. It smothered her. Then she remembered that she had been that close to having sex with another man, and that Jean-Marc's concerns were justified.

She drove back to the hotel, eager to use her new art supplies. Once in her room, she sat at the pine table in front of the large bay windows, neatly spread the art supplies she'd purchased in front of her, and dove into the drawing exercises in her book.

The sun had started to set when her cell phone interrupted her concentration. Before she picked up she knew it was Jerry.

"Hey Nat, what about dinner with me in an hour?" Natalie had been expecting his phone call, but she hadn't sorted out her thoughts yet. Jerry probably wanted to start back where they had left off, but with Brenda's interruption and Jean-Marc's call in the morning, things had changed. She didn't want to lie to Jean-Marc nor do anything that made her feel even guiltier.

Jerry sensed her hesitation. "Are you busy? Is this a bad time?"

"No. But tonight doesn't work for me." She didn't want to make it sound like she was upset with him, because she wasn't, not really. But she had to stop flirting with him.

"I have an art show in New York this weekend. I'll be gone for a few days," he said. "We can have dinner at my house. Come on, we need to talk."

Natalie paused. "I've changed my mind, Jerry. We can only be friends."

"Just a friendly dinner then," he insisted. "You have my word."

Natalie hesitated. She felt strong enough to resist him. Knowing that he was leaving soon for a few days would make it easier.

"Okay," she finally answered, hoping it wasn't another mistake.

"Great! I'll pick you up in an hour."

Less than a few seconds later her phone rang again. To Natalie's surprise it was Michael.

"Natalie, I spoke to my friend Peggy, the one who's looking

for someone to sublet her apartment," he said in his warm, charming voice. "I gave her your number."

"I appreciate your help, Michael. Thank you."

"Oh, it's my pleasure. I live in the same building, so hopefully I'll get to see you soon."

"That would be great," Natalie answered. Michael hung up and Natalie wondered if the universe was teasing her, or trying to test her. It was only now that she was seriously involved with a good guy that she met two other extremely attractive men. Where were they a few years ago? She remembered the time when she met either handsome dummies or smart and unappealing men. Couldn't she have met Jean-Marc, Jerry, and Michael one at a time and be allowed a little fun? The idea made her chuckle. She was getting far from the serious resident surgeon she had been only a week or so ago.

Jerry was shaved with a fresh black t-shirt and clean jeans when he appeared at her door.

They walked the few minutes to his house. She couldn't help but take pleasure in being so close to him, but when they arrived, she remembered Brenda. She made an effort not to ask him what had happened the night before with her.

Jerry fumbled in his pockets for his keys. "New locks, nobody can drop in this time," he said with a wink.

Eyebrows arched in question, Natalie looked at him without saying a word, waiting for him to go on.

"She just wanted to pick up some of her stuff. As I told you before, we aren't together anymore. She's moving to New York soon." He took her hand to lead her inside then faced her, looking straight in her eyes. "She left right away. She didn't sleep here."

Natalie shrugged. "It doesn't change anything, it still isn't–"

Jerry interrupted her, "Let's not talk about that now. I ordered some food. Are you hungry?" He brushed her hair away from her face.

"Not yet."

"Let's go upstairs then," he said. With a gesture of his hand, he invited her up the metal spiral staircase and followed her to his lofty living room, a marked contrast with the studio downstairs where the stained concrete was bare and the furnishings sparse.

Upstairs, colorful Oriental rugs were spread on dark hardwood floors. A beautiful black and plum colored sofa, an art piece in itself, stood out like a giant wave. The sofa and armchairs occupied most of the large room overlooking the first floor. A bronze sculpture of a man playing a saxophone rested on a heavy glass and metal coffee table. On the white walls there were no paintings but sculptures, all African art and shelves housing what looked like art and poetry books. A bar with granite counters stood by the wall facing the staircase. Every object looked tasteful and sophisticated.

Jerry wasn't a starving artist anymore. Natalie thought about her own apartment in Paris, which was warm and inviting. She remembered roaming the city's flea markets to find antique pieces that would look chic and still be affordable. Her place was small and cozy, with earthy colors like brown, terra cotta, and ochre for her pillows and curtains.

Natalie leaned on the railing to glance down at the first floor. Jerry watched her from behind the bar as if he was trying to read her. Was he waiting for her comment? The room was beautiful, if a little cold. Exactly what she had thought of Jerry the first time they'd met.

"Interesting room," she finally said. "Somehow it looks like you."

"I'm not sure how to take that."

"It's beautiful... Did you make those sculptures?"

"Only this one." He pointed to the statue on the coffee table. She was surprised. The statue looked like an antique.

"I did it a long time ago when I was experimenting with different styles." Jerry pulled a bottle of red wine from under the bar and showed it to Natalie, who nodded her approval. She sat on the floor near the coffee table to contemplate the statue and followed its contours with her fingers. Jerry, carrying two glasses of red wine, came to sit on the couch behind her. He offered her one of the glasses. Natalie leaned back and exhaled when she heard the first notes of Miles Davis' *"Kind of Blue"* soaring and filling the room.

"I love Miles," she said almost to herself. They listened silently for a while. The room seemed to spin slowly around her. Jerry kissed her hair. She turned her head toward him, looking closely at his face. She traced the contour of his lips with her finger then smoothed his unruly eyebrows. He kissed her fingers. She sighed.

"I have known Jean-Marc since we were kids."

Jerry sat up. "I don't want to talk about him. I don't want to hear that he had you all that time."

"I said I've known him for a long time, but we were just friends. We started dating a year ago."

Jerry frowned. "I'm sorry. I wish I could walk away from you and let him have you. He met you first and I'm sure he doesn't want to lose you. But I can't help it. I keep telling myself thank God you're not married."

Natalie lifted herself up from the floor onto the sofa, realizing that sitting there with Jerry, she felt complete–something she never felt with Jean-Marc. And it scared her because it was probably an illusion. Natalie didn't trust life much. She remembered feeling so triumphant after she had passed the difficult contest to be accepted into medical school, only to realize after a few months that she had committed herself to a life that was far from easy. Now, she could sniff out a cosmic trap ready to open up and swallow her as soon as she let her guard down.

Then Bob Marley's "*I Shot the Sheriff*" replaced Miles Davis and Natalie nodded her appreciation. "I love reggae," she said. "Especially the old stuff. Bob Marley and Peter Tosh. I grew up with this music." She took another sip of her glass and giggled for no particular reason. Wine usually went to her head very quickly.

"We're very similar," Jerry said. "*Yes,* we are," he repeated when he saw Natalie's incredulous expression. "Like me, you're very passionate. I hear it in your laugh and I can see it in your eyes. But you try to hide it. Why? Give yourself permission to live how you want."

Maybe Jerry understood her better than she thought. "What I want isn't always practical," she said, chuckling. "I've often fantasized about jumping on a table in the hospital's cafeteria and doing a wild African dance. But if I give myself permission to live that, they'll put me in the psychiatric ward."

Jerry laughed. There was a pause. "I'm falling for you," he said, suddenly serious, his head down as if in defeat. "There's not much I can do about it."

Did he just say he was falling for me? All of a sudden, she questioned her understanding of the English language. "What do you mean by falling?"

He looked at her with a twinkle in his eyes. "You heard it right." He leaned over to kiss her, but she shifted her head to avoid it.

"I'm leaving in less than three weeks. Let's just be friends."

Jerry seriously considered what she just had said. "You could stay in L.A. longer... If you wanted to," he suggested carefully.

"I can't just stay in L.A. I have a whole life in Paris." She felt a little indignant.

"Would you like to stay?" Jerry's expression was hard to read.

"I don't know!" She leaned back, looking straight ahead.

"Tell me about your life in Paris."

"My life in Paris..." Natalie got lost in thoughts. "I spend most of my time at the hospital dealing with life and death situations. It can be difficult. I remember my first day as an intern. I had to deal with two suicide attempts, a construction worker who fell off the fourth floor of a building, and a domestic dispute that turned to butchery. One of the suicide attempts survived; everybody else died. I was devastated." Natalie's eyes widened. She stayed silent for a while then waved her hand in front of her eyes as if she could shoo away her thoughts. Jerry waited for her to speak again.

"I have a pager that rules my life and I don't get paged for fun," she finally said. "When I save a life or help alleviate someone's suffering it seems to be worth it. But sometimes it gets overwhelming and I wish there was something else I could do." Natalie would have liked to draw a more attractive picture of her life, but at the present moment she couldn't.

"What about this Jean-Marc? Doesn't he make you happy?" There was jealousy in his voice.

"Yes, he does," Natalie said quickly. "But he is an airline pilot and he's gone a lot."

"You haven't been with him that long; why don't you give us a chance?" Jerry asked, his voice hopeful.

"We have a long history together," Natalie replied. "We flirted when we were teens …"

"Yeah, yeah! I see the picture." Jerry faked a yawn and Natalie stopped talking, surprised. "You're the one who asked about him."

"Yeah! But I didn't expect a childhood sweetheart's story. Actually, I don't want to know about any other men in your life."

"Too late, I'm on a roll now. Before Jean-Marc, there was Yves. We stayed together four years, and the last one was horrible. We had a very painful breakup." Natalie stopped smiling, remembering Yves yelling obscenities as if he had lost his mind.

Jerry was interested now. "What happened with him?"

"We were going different ways. He settled into a routine after he became a dentist. We liked different people, different foods, developed different hobbies. He was a true Parisian and I am an island girl… I guess life just happened."

"I like Paris," Jerry said. "For an artist there is so much to see and learn over there. Even the gray and rainy weather can be depressing and uplifting at the same time. It's really your state of mind that makes you transform an experience into a good one or a painful one."

"I suppose you're right. I do appreciate Paris' architectural beauty, but sometimes I feel displaced. I can enjoy myself, but I never feel complete. Sun and sea are essential to my being. Actually, I feel better here than in Paris." Jerry placed his head on her lap, stretching his legs on the sofa. She ran her hand through his hair. Maybe because her thoughts were still in Paris she didn't feel physically affected yet by his proximity.

"Why did you choose to become a physician?" Jerry asked.

Natalie thought for a moment. "I wanted to do something meaningful, to be able to help people and alleviate suffering. But when I think about it, I was also trying to make my mother happy. She always wanted to be a physician, but her family couldn't afford to send her to Paris to study, so she became a nurse. She made sure her children wouldn't have the same problem. My older brother is a surgeon and I followed his steps, as was expected of me. I was too young to really understand what I was getting into. In France, you can start pre-med right after high school. So I started med school when I was seventeen years old." She stopped a moment to sip her wine. "It's funny the surprise on some people's faces when I tell them what I do. Especially when I know that they have misjudged me as being stupid."

"I know what you're talking about. Painters aren't usually considered stupid, but models or actors are often underestimated when many of them are extremely smart."

Was Brenda one of the smart models? Natalie wondered. She stopped playing with his hair.

"I would love to have enough talent to be a painter." She hadn't meant to let her secret desire out. The words had escaped from her mouth without her consent.

Jerry smiled. "It's not too late."

Natalie remembered how hard it had been for her to adapt to her life in Paris. She had secretly cried her whole first year. She had felt scared looking at older medical students who seemed so serious, and so lacking in joy. Her mother encouraged her to take it one day at a time. Ginette had been so proud and happy when her daughter had passed the contest and got into med school; the last thing Natalie wanted was to disappoint her. Like a girl forced into an arranged marriage, she had never felt free to change her mind. Little by little she had gotten absorbed by her studies and was determined to be the best physician she could be. Only now was she able to see clearly that she hadn't really thought out her path.

"If you have the desire to paint, you should definitely explore it,'" Jerry was saying.

Natalie gave a nervous smile. She was so far from ever becoming an artist of Jerry's caliber. Telling him about it made her feel even more inadequate. "What about dinner? I think I'm hungry now."

They sat at the kitchen counter downstairs to eat seafood pasta and sip a very good French Merlot.

If Jerry was disappointed when she asked him to take her back to the hotel after they had coffee, then he didn't show it.

He insisted on walking her all the way to her room, but he stopped at the door.

"I had a wonderful time. Thank you," she said.

"My pleasure," he said. "I'll call you before I leave on Saturday." He kissed her on her cheek, ran his hand over her hair, kissed her once more and left. Natalie watched him retreat down the hallway, grateful that their dinner had stayed friendly as he'd promised. But she also realized that life seemed much brighter and more colorful when he was around. Now that he had left, part of her craved for him to come back and stay.

Natalie was going crazy from the rush of thoughts and impulses running through her mind. One second she wanted to be loyal and true to Jean-Marc, the next she wanted to race to Jerry's house and jump in his arms. She wished she could confide in someone. Maybe it would help her see clearly inside her own mind. She couldn't talk to her mom, who loved Jean-Marc and wouldn't understand. Confessing her dilemma to Simone was not an option. Simone's mind was already made up. Natalie thought about her brother Roger. He usually saw things from a higher perspective. She could try to call him now, but it was past midnight in Los Angeles. That made it 9 a.m. in Paris. Roger was already at work. She decided to email him.

Hé Roger,

I'm enjoying my vacation. Los Angeles is much more interesting that I expected. Last time we talked, I was telling you how happy I was to have Jean-Marc in my life, but now I'm confused. I've met someone I'm really attracted to. He's a really amazing artist and I don't know what to do about it. Is this just a test from life to see if I can resist temptation? Or does it mean that Jean-Marc may not be the one for me? I need your big brotherly advice. Bisous.

CHAPTER TEN

Natalie had thought that emailing Roger would give her some relief, but she was restless. She stayed awake most of the night, finally drifting into a half-dream state. Then images from her childhood slowly emerged.

Four children, from five to seven years old, played in front of her childhood home.

"Cowboys are the best. They have guns," the cute little boy with beautiful honey-colored eyes shouted, a triumphant smile on his face as he waved his toy gun at Natalie and her cousin Suzy.

"That's right! And they always win!" exclaimed Jean-Marc's brother, Claude, a pudgy six- year-old.

Natalie and Suzy had their hands on their ears. "I like Indians," five-year-old Natalie yelled back. "Cowboys are mean. They are thieves and liars." Then the discussion turned into war. The cowboys emptied their guns and the Indians fought back with salvoes of arrows. None of them admitted to being wounded.

Natalie smiled at the memories of the kids who more than once parted as enemies for real.

Then she remembered her 15-year-old self during summer camp in Barbados, behind her, the lovely sight of white sand, coconut trees, and emerald waters. She was hurrying to meet the other kids on the beach when Jean-Marc, now a lanky 16-year-old with strikingly clear eyes lighting up his brown face, planted himself in front of her. She hadn't seen him for a while, as her parents had moved to another town years ago. And she hadn't paid him any special attention when she realized that they attended the same summer camp, but there he was, towering over her, blocking her every way she went, brushing his bare skin against hers.

"You're not going anywhere until you kiss me," he said. Natalie just laughed but she couldn't get past him. She finally looked up.

There was a little bit of hair above his crooked smile. He looked vibrant, confident, and very cute. His audacity won her over and she became curious. His lips were hot and salty. It was a good kiss.

They kissed again, many times, whenever no one was looking. But after two weeks, when it was time to fly back to Martinique, Natalie told him they could only be friends. He didn't protest.

Then Natalie's mind floated to two years later, to the awful day of Jean-Marc's older brother's funeral. Claude had died in a motorcycle accident. Tears filled her eyes at the memory of his family standing outside the church after the service, receiving condolences from friends and relatives. The sun was merciless and the sky so clear everything around appeared crisp and luminous. Claude's father almost had a heart attack when he learned the news. His mother had reportedly lost her mind and yet, here they were, standing with dignity, accepting words of sympathy.

Dressed in a black suit, Jean-Marc stood straight next to his father, his face haggard and his eyes red. He looked taller and less boyish than she remembered. When he saw Natalie, his face lit up and he managed a smile. There was nothing she could say, but her tears just kept rolling down her face. She saw concern in his eyes before he gave a very warm and compassionate look. He patted her back when they hugged. She was the one being comforted, and that gesture profoundly touched her. From then, she saw him with different eyes. He had gained her respect.

She didn't see him again for many years. Last June, she was returning from a medical conference and hurrying to exit Charles-de-Gaulle terminal when she saw him, a handsome man wearing an airline pilot's uniform, coming toward her. Their eyes met and they appraised each other before she recognized the golden eyes. It was as if destiny had finally reunited her with Jean-Marc. They were both fully grown and free. No games were played this time. Dinner had followed, then bed, and they had been together ever since.

Warm under the comforter, Natalie kept her eyes closed. It was as if she was getting to fall in love again with all the different versions of Jean-Marc. Her heart softened at the thought of the cute and spirited little boy, the impetuous teenager he had been, and the attractive man he had become. She hadn't realized how much he meant to her or how entangled he was in her childhood memories. It wasn't something she would ever be able to discard. She trusted him because she'd known him forever. No harm would ever come from him. He was worth fighting temptation.

Buried deep under the covers, she listened to the soothing sound of rain against her hotel room's window. She curled up under the comforter and lingered in her memories of Jean-Marc, reviving their moments of intimacy. She remembered the feeling of his weight on her body and the way his hands shook the first time they made love. He told her that he'd loved her since they were kids, and that now that he finally had her he would never let her go. She replayed those moments over and over again. For the first time since she'd left Paris, she longed for him.

The window let in a meek light that reminded her of Paris and its wet sidewalks. The beach was deserted. Most of the stores still looked closed, as if nobody was expected to shop on such a day. Natalie's first rainy day in Los Angeles seemed to signal the end of her vacation. It was time to go back home to Jean-Marc. She realized that she could have loved him better if she hadn't been so self-absorbed. Now she was ready to shorten her vacation and pour all of her love on him, without holding back.

CHAPTER ELEVEN

Jean-Marc didn't answer his cell phone. Nor was he at home. Natalie spent the next two hours trying to book an earlier flight, but most were sold out. Her only option was two stops before Paris, and it would cost a fortune. Of course, she could always ask Jean-Marc to use his connections to get one of those stand-by tickets, but she was reluctant to do so.

She sat down on her bed and tried to organize her thoughts. Dominique, Roger's wife, had once told her that she believed angels were always around us, guiding us with signs. Things always happened for a reason. At the time, Natalie thought that Dominique was a little weird, but it stuck in her mind and since then she paid attention to signs. For example, if she had to make an important phone call and the line was busy, she would pause and wonder if there was something else to consider before making the call. So now that she had attempted in vain to book a flight, she wondered if she was right to leave earlier. Now, a subtle pang in her chest made her suddenly feel as if she was quitting in the middle of a task.

She was still trying to untangle her thoughts when her cell phone rang. An unknown female voice identified herself as Peggy, Michael's neighbor.

"Michael told me that you were looking for a place to rent for two or three weeks, is that right?" Peggy was very articulate.

Her voice reminded Natalie of the standard American voices in TV commercials. "I'm leaving tomorrow," Peggy continued. "Can we meet this morning?"

An hour ago Natalie was looking for an airplane ticket out of Los Angeles; now it looked like fate had decided otherwise.

Peggy's apartment was only a ten-minute walk away. Natalie just had to follow the boardwalk where the shops, open but empty, blasted reggae music. Avoiding the large puddles, she kept a fast pace while making mental notes of the clothing stores to come back to at a later time. The fresh air cleared her head from the tension of the morning. Now that she had made the choice to stay in Los Angeles, her energy seemed to come back. The idea of making new friends put a smile on her face.

"Hey miss, would you be interested in working on a pilot for Fox television?" A tall man with thinning blond hair stood in front of Natalie. His tanned face was wrinkled, probably by too much sun exposure, and he offered a large smile full of yellow teeth.

"Huh? Well, I'm not an actress," Natalie said.

"I can get you a meeting with the producers," the guy said. There was something phony in the smile pasted on his face.

Natalie declined his offer with a polite smile and kept walking. But all the way she fantasized about what it must feel like to be an actress and get a big break on a movie.

Peggy lived in an unassuming white building facing the beach. Natalie went up a few stairs to locked double glass doors and rang Peggy's apartment. She was quickly buzzed into a bare but clean lobby. She then walked two flights up a carpeted hallway and she found her destination two doors down on her right. She knocked and the bark of a small dog greeted her.

A dog! She hoped that taking care of him wasn't part of the deal. She wouldn't want that responsibility. The door opened a few seconds later revealing a lean Asian girl with light brown hair cut in a short bob, and porcelain white skin delicately painted with touches of color. She held a small white Yorkshire terrier in her arms.

"Hi Natalie, come on in," she said, opening the door wider. She almost sang the words. "I'm still packing so it's a little messy."

The foyer opened to a bright living room. The first thing Natalie noticed was the splendid unobstructed view of the ocean. Right then, she knew that she had found the perfect place to finish her vacation. Standing in the little foyer she looked around, unable to detect any sign of the announced mess. She took in the lime green sofa with colorful pillows, the brown chenille armchair, the Indian rugs on the wood floors, the small coffee table covered with magazines, and the old wooden table with four antique chairs.

Black and white photographs of Peggy, some of them very artistically shot, hung on the walls. Healthy looking plants spread their luscious shiny leaves every corner of the room and on each side of the window. They worried Natalie a little. She had never been too good with plants. She hoped she wouldn't have time to kill them all in two weeks.

"Nice place," Natalie said. The apartment reminded her of her own place in Paris. No expensive or bulky furniture, but the colorful pillows, curtains, and throws made it agreeable to the eye.

"Thank you," Peggy said, and she blushed a little.

Natalie looked at the little dog.

"He's so cute, what's his name?"

"This is Annabel, she's a girl." Peggy put Annabel down and the little dog danced around Natalie. "She likes you, and she is a good judge of character."

Natalie was charmed by Annabel's perkiness and good nature. She kneeled down to pet her and the little dog licked her hand thoroughly. "Is she staying in L.A?" she asked, warming to the idea.

"Oh no! She's going with me; she's used to traveling."

Natalie was almost disappointed. Annabel had managed to win over her in only a few minutes.

"Let me show you around," Peggy said. She led Natalie to the bedroom, which was painted sky blue with white moldings on the ceiling. It also had a wonderful view of the beach. On the wall by the window, a medium-size painting depicted a boat sailing on the ocean. A large bed stood in the middle of the room, decorated with sheer curtains and a white lace bedspread. It overflowed with pillows of all sizes and shapes, all of them white. It looked like a bed prepared for a wedding night or the fantasy of a little girl. The room looked like a sanctuary flooded with light.

A few open boxes and luggage on the floor represented the only sign of the mess Peggy had referred to earlier. Actually, it looked as if she was finished with her packing and had found the time to straighten up the apartment before Natalie came by. The small bathroom outside of the bedroom was entirely tiled in white and featured the tiniest tub Natalie had ever seen. A real Ficus tree leaned toward the window.

"I have to leave some clothes, but you should have enough room to put your things away," Peggy explained, showing a small closet still half full of clothes.

"That's fine," Natalie said. She would have to leave some of her clothes in her luggage, but it was only a small inconvenience. She loved the place. "It's a beautiful room. It feels so peaceful. And I love that bed," she added. Peggy seemed pleased with the compliment.

"You can watch the most beautiful sunsets from this window," she said. "I would have preferred not to rent my apartment at all, but theater in New York doesn't pay much, so I have to. Michael said that you were a physician?" It seemed to be enough of a reference for Peggy.

"Yes. I just finished my residency." Natalie didn't remember telling Michael her profession, so she assumed that he got the information from Simone.

Peggy showed her the kitchen, tiny but bright, equipped with a washer and dryer for laundry.

"How much would you rent it for two weeks?" Natalie finally asked.

They worked out the details of the rent. It wasn't cheap, but two weeks at the hotel would cost more than double.

"I'm leaving tomorrow morning and you can move right in. Michael lives one flight up. But you probably knew that already. Let me show you where you can park your car. I'll leave mine at my sister's house so that you'll have a parking space." As she kept talking about how hard it was to park on the beach, Natalie wondered how it would affect her to have Michael as a neighbor. It made her pause. She hoped that it wouldn't complicate her already complicated life.

She agreed to come back later that day with Peggy's rent, and walked back to her hotel.

Natalie wondered if she should have talked to Jean-Marc before renting Peggy's apartment. He would have found a way to get her to Paris or to Martinique for sure, but Peggy's call seemed like a kind of divine intervention–a sign that she should stay.

She thought about calling Simone. She missed talking to her daily. Would things have played out differently if she had made more effort with Simone's friends? No! Blaming herself was a bad habit she'd gotten from her childhood; she wouldn't do that anymore.

To put a stop to her internal dialogue, Natalie called Simone anyway and left a message on her voice mail.

Natalie sat at the table on the little balcony outside her hotel room with her sketching pad and drawing pencils and practiced the exercises in her drawing book until her eyes ached. When she finally emerged from her drawing session it was almost 5 p.m., and she had skipped lunch. It was time to go back to Peggy's.

By 5:30 p.m. Natalie was knocking at Peggy's door. The sky was getting clearer, but it was still chilly and windy.

A smiling Peggy opened the door. Annabel started dancing joyfully on her two rear paws when she saw Natalie.

"Hey Natalie, come on in. I'm done with my packing, if you can believe it."

Natalie gasped at the view from the open window. The sun was hiding behind pink and orange clouds, and the living room, warm and inviting, was bathed in a gold light as if lit by a fireplace. This view was magical.

"I think I'm going to sit by the window all day for two weeks," Natalie said, a wide smile on her face.

"That's what I did the first month I got this place," Peggy

laughed.

"Here is your money. Thank you so much for letting me rent your apartment." Natalie felt a little awkward as she retrieved an envelope filled with twenty-dollar bills.

"Great! Thank you. If you can fill this paper with your info..." Peggy handed Natalie a typed letter asking basic background information. There was no lease, no contract, and no deposit. Peggy was basing her trust solely on Michael's recommendation and her own assessment.

"Do you want to drink something?" Peggy asked. "I have carrot ginger juice, herbal teas, wine…"

"A glass of wine would be great."

"Sure, I'll have a glass with you." She got glasses from the kitchen cupboard and poured wine from an opened bottle.

"Actually, we should call Michael and invite him over for a drink. I think he's home." She picked up the phone and fifteen minutes later the party was on.

Michael had brought his friend Jimmy, a short and stocky light-skinned black guy with a big head shaped like a potato. Natalie had seen him before in a well-received independent movie released last year in Paris. Jimmy's laugh could probably be heard all the way from the open window to the boardwalk. Michael and he cracked jokes that Natalie didn't get, but Peggy seemed right there with them. Jimmy spoke fast, and sometimes with a heavy accent that Natalie guessed was Southern, and he seemed to do it on purpose just to confuse her. One glass of wine was enough to make her feel drunk and doubt her language skills.

"Smile!" Jimmy barked after a speech that seemed addressed to her. Tired of being the butt of Jimmy's jokes, Natalie answered in French and gave him her most seductive smile.

She just told Jimmy that she could embarrass him also if she chose too, but she finished her sentence with a sexy wink that made him choke on his beer. He coughed out the peanuts he was eating, and the motion knocked over Michael's beer and the bowl of nuts. While trying to clean up, he made an even bigger mess, which sent Michael into fits of laughter.

"Damn! She really got you!" Michael said while Peggy rolled her eyes at Jimmy, not too happy with the mess he had created. Natalie had neutralized Jimmy and knew that he would leave her alone for the rest of the night. Her phone rang from her bag. It was Simone.

"Hey girl, where are you?" Simone said. "I can hear some action in the background."

"Hey, Simone. I'm at Peggy's, Michael's friend. I'll be renting her apartment for the next two weeks. We are about to go out for dinner," Natalie said.

"Ask her to join us," Michael shouted before Simone had time to answer.

"Do you want to come with us?"

"I'm on my way to see a movie with Ted, but I can meet you for drinks," Simone said after a short hesitation. "I'll call you when it's over. Maybe we can all go to a club afterwards."

Michael proposed dinner at an all-you-can-eat sushi bar in Santa Monica. They all agreed.

Propped on her pillow in the kitchen with several little stuffed animals waiting to be chewed on, Annabel looked at them all with a blasé attitude. She delicately accepted the little bone-shaped treat offered by Peggy, but gave a disapproving stare when they all left the apartment.

Natalie warmed up quickly to her new friends. Michael had a magnetic presence, like an athlete after a good performance, relaxed and confident. Peggy was easygoing, and even Jimmy was fun to be with now that he had stopped teasing her.

An hour and a half later, they were stuffed with sushi and warmed up by sake. As they loaded into Michael's Jeep to head back to the beach, Simone called again.

"Joel, Ted's cousin, is having a birthday party at Club Hollywood. Why don't you guys join us there? Joel's crazy and he knows everybody. It's going to be fun." Peggy's mind was set on going home, but Michael and Jimmy were game.

"I left my number and address in New York on the fridge," Peggy told Nat as she exited Michael's car. "Here is a set of keys for the front door; everything else will be on the kitchen counter. I'll call you this weekend." They hugged. "Too bad we didn't meet earlier, we could have hung out. But let's stay in touch."

Natalie was ready to call it a night, too, but she didn't want to reject Simone's invitation. Anyway, Jimmy wouldn't let her go home.

"Come on, girl. Don't tell me you don't need to get your groove on. When you're back in Paris, you're going to say 'Damn, I wish I was at Club Hollywood right now.' You got to have fun while you can, girl! Life's short."

"Okay, but I'm not dressed to go to a night club," Natalie said, suddenly concerned with her jeans and black shirt.

Jimmy rolled his eyes and Michael inspected her.

"You look great like that. This is L.A; everything goes. You could go topless and nobody would complain." He obviously had absorbed too much sake.

"Yeah, that's how we flow," Jimmy added seriously.

"Well, I'll think about your suggestion," Natalie said, "but I think I should drive."

"Don't worry, you're with me. Nothing will happen to you." Michael's expression turned sober.

Natalie shrugged as if she had been overpowered, but she was glad to spend more time with them. Michael and Jimmy were a lot of fun. Staying in L.A. was the right decision.

CHAPTER TWELVE

"If all the girls in Martinique look like you, I'm getting an airline ticket tomorrow," Jimmy said. "Are you sure your boyfriend is sane letting you roam L.A. on your own?"

Natalie laughed at Jimmy's nonstop rambling while Michael stayed quiet and concentrated on driving safely. He tried to keep Jimmy in check every once in a while, but Natalie was getting used to Jimmy's way. Riding with them reminded her of her younger years in Martinique when she had countless friends to hang out with.

Club Hollywood was located in an enormous complex with multiple shops and a state-of-the-art new theater. The underground parking below the complex was the biggest that Natalie had ever seen. The traffic inside was dense, but so well organized that to Natalie's surprise, they parked and took the four escalators up to lobby level in less than ten minutes.

They had to take a fifth escalator to the upper level to get to the Club. Young men and women waited outside to be chosen by egotistical bouncers checking names on the guest list.

Fortunately, as soon as they approached, Natalie spotted Simone and Ted waiting for them. A maitre d' who looked like Brad Pitt's better-looking younger brother hustled them inside. Simone looked like her regular gorgeous self in black snakeskin pants and halter-top. She greeted Natalie warmly and seemed sincerely happy to see her.

Club Hollywood was a monument: multiple levels hosted different parties, each with their own DJ's. People ate and drank on terraces with amazing views of the city. Michael and Jimmy seemed tempted to crash a party where everyone wore Afro wigs and seventies outfits. Natalie wouldn't have minded either, but they weren't wearing the right clothes so they kept following Brad Pitt's brother to Joel's party. There, beautiful young Hollywood specimens stood near the bar and sat drinking on Italian leather sofas. All looked a little bored.

Simone introduced Joel, a skinny boy with long dark hair. He looked like an English rock musician. Then she sat on Ted's lap and they happily stared at each other, kissing every thirty seconds. Jimmy decided to explore the other rooms.

Michael invited Natalie to dance. "Okay, but I have to follow your advice to go topless first," she said, winking at him. As she unbuttoned her shirt, Michael's eyes opened wide. "Tada…" She triumphantly stood up in a black camisole. Michael exhaled, wiping imaginary sweat from his forehead.

"You shouldn't play with my heart like that," he said, shaking his head and acting wounded.

They went looking for Jimmy and ended up in a gigantic room where the DJ played old disco hits that made the crowd wild. As at Bill's party, blond girls undulated on a platform above the pack. Jimmy was dancing next to two pretty girls in miniskirts.

Simone and Ted came to join them. To Natalie's relief, it seemed that the tension between her and Simone was gone. The music was pumping, and Natalie lost herself on the dance floor. She didn't remember having so much fun in years. Michael was a pleasure to dance with, and he looked hot. Hours passed unnoticed with Natalie reveling in the lively Hollywood scene.

On the way back to the beach, Jimmy didn't make a sound. Instead, he passed out on the back seat, even snoring on occasion. Michael, the designated driver, looked perfectly sober.

"Jimmy is a handful," Natalie said after he let out a particularly loud snore.

"Yeah! But he's a good guy," Michael said. "A very loyal friend."

Natalie nodded but didn't add anything. She had thought she had a trustworthy friend in Simone. Now she couldn't vouch for her loyalty.

"You look serious. Are you okay?" Michael asked.

"I'm fine. Just reflecting on friendship."

Michael nodded and stayed silent for a little while. "Tell me about you," he said, keeping his eyes on the road. "What makes you get up in the morning?"

The question surprised Natalie. She wasn't sure how to answer it. The expected response to a question like his had something to do with saving lives or fulfilling one's mission on earth. But the only thing that came to her mind was coffee and guava jelly on her croissant.

"To be truthful," she said, "if it wasn't for coffee and sugar, some days I would stay in bed. What about you? What makes *you* get up?"

"I see each day as an opportunity to enjoy and share whatever talent I have," Michael said after a second of reflection.

"Same for me," Jimmy quipped from the backseat. Then he went back to snoring.

Natalie chuckled then got serious again as she tried to collect her thoughts. "I can't quite say the same thing. Even though I like what I do and it gives me great satisfaction, there are days when it takes too much from me. You know, we are taught to stay detached, but I can't. Sometimes I have nightmares about the people I couldn't save."

"What do you do to unwind?" Michael asked.

"That's the problem. Those past years I didn't get a lot of occasions to unwind. When I'm free, I sleep or spend time with my boyfriend. I don't have a lot of time to blow."

"You must," Michael said, his voice soothing but firm. "Making time to meditate and feeling connected to a higher power than yourself is the only way to harmonize your life. If not, you're going to end up sick or addicted to something."

Natalie thought about her anti-anxiety pills. At least she hadn't taken any since her arrival in L.A. "You're right. I can feel the difference now that I have some time alone. The simplest things give me pleasure."

"What things, for example?"

Natalie noticed how easy it was to confide in Michael. He looked genuinely interested in what she had to say. "Well, don't laugh, but I took up drawing. I bought art supplies and a book to teach me some basics and I spend hours drawing every day."

"I would never laugh at something like that. Artistic expression is what I live for," Michael said. They drove in silence for a while.

"What does your boyfriend do?" Michael finally asked.

"He's an airline pilot."

"Are you happy with him?"

Why did he ask that question? Did she look unhappy? "He's a great guy. Yes! I'm happy with him," Natalie answered after a pause.

Michael nodded and didn't add anything for another few minutes. They were getting close to their destination. Natalie recognized the now familiar streets of Venice.

"What would happen if you slowed down and made time to draw when you went back to Paris?" he asked.

"When you work in a hospital, it's impossible to slow down, especially at the beginning of your career," Natalie said.

"Nothing's impossible. It's all about making choices and setting priorities," Michael said, stopping in front of Natalie's hotel.

Natalie smiled. "I'll try to remember that."

Jimmy opened an eye. "Man, can I crash at your pad?" he asked Michael.

"You can sleep on the couch," Michael said, getting out of the car to open the door for Natalie.

"Would you marry me?" Jimmy asked Natalie as she got out of the car.

"I'll think about it," she answered, smiling.

"Don't give him any hope," Michael said, "or you won't be able to get rid of him. Do you need some help moving tomorrow?"

"I'm sure I'll be fine. Thank you, Michael." They hugged like old friends.

Michael waited for Natalie to step inside the lobby to drive away. Natalie waved, and then turned around to meet the raised eyebrows of the reception clerk, who had seen her the previous night with Jerry. No doubt, she was living the party girl's dream.

The smile on Natalie's face vanished when she pulled out her cell phone and realized that she had missed Jean-Marc's call. Her heart jumped in her chest as if she had been caught cheating.

The low energy in Jean-Marc's voice did nothing to reassure her. "Hey Natalie, I missed you again. I had a long day and some issues at work. Call me..."

Something was wrong with him. His message was short and his voice somewhat somber, as if he was trying to control his anger. Another jab of anxiety cut through her chest. It was 2 a.m. in Los Angeles, and if she called now she would have to admit that she had been out partying. It would be wiser to wait until morning when she was sober. She fell on her bed and just couldn't get up to remove her makeup. A voice in her head told her that if she had to hide having a good time from Jean-Marc, then something in their relationship needed work, but she was too tired to think. The floor and the ceiling seemed to move toward each other, crushing her in between as she dove into sleep.

When she opened her eyes the room was still plunged in darkness. The alarm clock said 6:30 a.m. She had a dull headache. Her first thought was of Jean-Marc. She painfully sat up on her bed and caught her reflection in the mirror across the room. With her makeup smudged on her face and her tousled hair, she looked like someone who'd had a wild night. Wishing in vain for coffee and a croissant, she dialed Jean-Marc's number. He answered immediately.

"*Jean-Marc, c'est Natalie.*" She made an effort to sound as cheerful as possible in spite of her voice still hoarse with sleep. "I tried to call you all morning yesterday; I really wanted to talk to you. I miss you." She reminded herself of a guilty spouse eager to please.

"Really?" He sounded guarded.

"Yes, I can't wait to see you. You sound tired. How was your flight?"

"It was okay, but we were delayed two hours because of technical problems, and then I had to fly above the airport for an hour because of other planes with technical problems. It was a long day."

"I'm sorry about that. I wish I was there with you."

He seemed to perk up. "I can find you a seat on an Air France flight. It would be great if you came back now. You know, I really need you with me."

Natalie felt her chest tightening up. "Oh. I met a woman who was subletting her apartment on the beach and I rented it for the next two weeks... But don't worry; two weeks will go fast... Jean-Marc, are you there?"

"What do you want me to tell you, Natalie?" Jean-Marc finally answered. "I don't understand. You're saying that you want to be with me, but you rented a place for two weeks? It doesn't make any sense." Natalie had never heard him talk to her with that irritated tone of voice.

"It's not like two weeks will make a big difference."

"A day can make a big difference, Natalie. I've been thinking about our relationship, and I don't think that we are on the same wavelength. I can feel in your voice that something's not right."

Natalie knew that she had been walking a fine line with Jean-Marc, but she had not seen this coming. "Not at all. On the contrary, everything's great," she said, thinking of her new insight of how important he was to her.

But he seemed to misunderstand her and sounded even more

upset. "If you're not sure that you want me in your life, then forget about us. I don't want to worry about what you're doing or who you're seeing."

Natalie was shocked by the anger in his voice. "I don't know what you're talking about. Is it forbidden to have a vacation unless we're together?"

"Please, Natalie. Be honest with yourself and with me. You went over there because you are looking for something that you are not finding here with me." Natalie had never heard Jean-Marc be so blunt.

"I work hard, Jean-Marc, I needed to breathe and to feel free of any constraints for a change. It doesn't mean that—"

"If you really loved me, you wouldn't need to breathe and feel free, Natalie."

"That's not true, Jerry…" *No!* She didn't just say that. She covered her mouth with her hand, horrified she'd made such a slip at the worst possible moment. The silence between them weighed two tons.

"Who's Jerry?" Jean-Marc's voice was low and menacing.

"Jerry is Simone's cousin…"

"So that's what's going on. I knew it…"

"Jean-Marc, there's nothing going on. Don't be silly. You know I love you..." Her tone was indignant, but then she remembered that a lot had been going on.

"I'm not a fool, Natalie; don't underestimate me. I… I think that we need time to rethink our relationship." Jean-Marc's icy tone could hardly contain his anger. "You need to feel free? You are free. You don't need to ever call me again," he spat. "And don't think that you're the only one with options here. You're not that much fun to be around with all your hospital drama, and you're not irreplaceable." He hung up.

Natalie sat on the bed in total shock, her heart pounding fast and loud. What had just happened? Just when she had discovered how important he was to her, Jean-Marc was dumping her? His final words hammered themselves into her head. He sounded like he hated her. And he had implied that he would be replacing her easily. Was it somebody she knew? Why did she have to slip and call him Jerry just then? What was wrong with her? It had to be her punishment for what she had done.

Tears finally came, relieving the pressure in her head. She had never considered that he would break up with her, not like that, not that quickly. She had taken him for granted. Now he was gone and she could only blame herself.

CHAPTER THIRTEEN

Natalie lay motionless on her bed, silently shedding tears, until the reception desk called to ask if she was checking out. It took more than an hour to gather her things into her two pieces of luggage.

The reception clerk, probably noticing her red eyes, didn't charge her for late check out. Instead, he helped her load her luggage in her car. She thanked him with a ten-dollar bill and drove off.

A few minutes later, she was parked under the white building on Thornton in the parking space Peggy had left empty. She dragged her luggage up the stairs.

When she opened the door to Peggy's apartment, the living room was bathed in sunlight coming through the open curtains. The pleasant scent of vanilla floated in the air. The sight of the ocean in the distance made her exhale. Instead of unpacking, she removed her sketchpad and pencils from her carry-on, pulled a stool from the kitchen to the living room window, and sketched her new view of Venice Beach.

Her cell phone rang more than once, but she ignored it and kept working until she felt too hungry to concentrate anymore. Then she got up to scramble two eggs from the fridge and gobbled them hastily before going back to her window. This time she drew a picture of herself, watching her reflection in the mirror created by the window's glass. The woman in the picture looked older with sad, sunken eyes.

She was about her to tear up her drawing when the phone in the living room rang. Peggy's answering machine picked it up and Natalie heard Michael's warm voice.

"Natalie, are you there? I saw your car on in the garage; let me know if you need anything…"

She picked it up without thinking then regretted her impulsive gesture when she heard the sound of her own voice.

"Hey, Michael. How are you? Yes, I'm okay. No, I don't need anything. I'm a little tired, that's all. Okay, talk to you later." Michael sounded a little puzzled by her lack of energy, but he didn't try to pry and wished her a good evening. She meant to tell him that she had had a good time and enjoyed their conversation on the way back from the club, but she was too tired and drowsy for that. She put her attention back on her drawing and decided to keep it.

Her neck and her back ached when she got up. Stretching out on Peggy's white bed, she stayed there, her eyes fixed on the white ceiling until sleep fell over her.

The next morning, when the rousing beat of her cell phone woke her up, she didn't recognize her surroundings. An alarm clock on the nightstand indicated 8:30 a.m. Then it all came back. Peggy 's apartment… Jean-Marc… She answered her phone almost as a way to chase away the dark thoughts already crowding in and was relieved to hear her mother's cheerful voice.

"*C'est toi, ma chérie*? I was worrying. I haven't talked to you in a while. Where are you?" Natalie had to wait for the flow of questions to finish before she could answer. Out of her head came lies that wouldn't alarm Ginette, who sounded enthusiastic today.

Since the death of her grandfather, Papa Eugene, those days had become rare. Natalie missed her mother, and she missed the sweet flavors of her childhood home. She wished she could go back to waking up in her childhood bed, to the aroma of freshly brewed coffee and *pain doux,* the cake her mother liked to bake.

"Last night I saw a great South African dance group at the Grand Carbet," Ginette was saying enthusiastically. "They came for the festival of Fort-de-France. *C'était super!* Guess who I met who asked about you? You remember Jocelyne Victor?"

Talking to her mother soothed her. Ginette busied herself with trivial things, but at times, it was comforting. Natalie thought for a moment of confiding in her mom but she didn't want to upset her. Her mother's chatter brought back the carefree comfort of her childhood, when life didn't require a meaning but was just to be lived. What happened to the delicious time when there was nothing better than dressing her new litter of puppies with doll clothes or reading adventure books on the verandah surrounded by hibiscus flowers?

After so many days spent in Paris, studying at her desk or attending to someone in distress, she had forgotten what it felt like to be carefree. But during this vacation, she had found a new enthusiasm for life. If Jean-Marc couldn't understand that, then he was not the one for her. She replayed the conversation with Jean-Marc in her head, this time with the right words, until she realized that it was a futile exercise. It wouldn't change what happened.

Remembering that her cell phone had rung the day before, she checked it and found a message from Jerry asking her to come to New York with him for the weekend. She thought he had already left, but apparently his flight was to take off in the evening. If she had answered the phone the day before she would have declined his invitation, but today was a new day and she was single. Just the mention of New York City made her heart leap with excitement. Manhattan, in her mind, was one of the most thrilling places on earth. Before she realized what she was doing, she dialed Jerry's number. He picked up just when she changed her mind and was about to hang up. Her cautious side had started to consider the possible implications of the trip.

"Hey, Nat. Are you coming with me to New York?"

"I don't think so, Jerry. It's a little short notice."

"Come on, Nat. An art lover like you has to visit New York. Plus, I have a first-class ticket for you. You can't possibly miss that. It's going to be fun, I promise."

"It's tempting, but you should have asked me before buying me a ticket."

"I didn't buy it. I'm redeeming my frequent traveler's mileage. It's completely free. It would be a shame to waste it."

The thought of Jean-Marc crept back in the corner of her mind.

"I moved out of the hotel yesterday into a sublet on Thornton Avenue. I can't leave it already."

"Why can't you? There's no law that says so. And why did you rent? You could have stayed with me."

"Well, thank you, but you only have one bed in your house," Natalie said. "Speaking of which, do you have only one hotel room in New York?"

"I actually have a one bedroom apartment with a sofa bed. It's going to be hard, but I promise I'll be good," Jerry said, chuckling.

"Yeah, right! You promised that before."

"Well, you're still in one piece."

Natalie sighed. It was tempting. And it wasn't as if her agenda was full for this weekend. "What time is the flight?" she said.

"All right! We leave at 10:45 tonight. Give me your address; I'll come pick you up around 9 o'clock."

After she hung up Natalie wondered what had gotten into her, accepting Jerry's invitation. The sensation in her stomach told her that it might not be the wisest decision. Now she was feeling some guilt toward Jean-Marc. Wasn't she moving a little too quickly? Was there a proper amount of time for mourning a relationship?

Yves, her ex before Jean-Marc, would have told her that her obsession to be proper was typical of her island background. He always thought he knew so much about her, but in reality, he had never understood her. But had she just agreed to have sex with Jerry? Couldn't they just share a great friendship? *Yeah, right!* She pushed away her own skeptical thoughts, refusing to think ahead.

She hadn't unpacked yet, so it would be quite easy to put on some clothes and her toiletry in her carry-on bag. There was plenty of time before the flight. After showering, and getting dressed, she picked up the phone and called Simone.

Simone answered in a voice so low it scared Natalie.

"Simone, what's going on? Are you okay?" She imagined the worst.

"I'm sorry, Nat, I'm... It's... I don't want to talk about it, not on the phone." Her voice seemed desperate.

"Where are you?"

"I'm in Culver City."

"That's not too far from Venice, right? Let's meet somewhere."

Simone gave Natalie directions to a coffee shop on Culver Boulevard. Natalie grabbed her handbag and left right away. When she parked in front of the coffee shop, Simone was waiting for her at a table outside. Her eyes were red and puffy.

"What happened?" Natalie asked, hugging her friend.

"It's that bastard," Simone answered, her eyes watering again.

"Who? What bastard?"

"Ted, who else? The asshole got a directing job for a TV movie, with a lead role that would have been perfect for me. But guess what? He said that he was only a gun for hire and had nothing to do with the casting. Victoria Tweed was chosen for the part." Simone sounded so angry she could hardly talk. "He told me that she had already been attached to the project before the producers hired him. I wasn't too happy but I thought that if the movie advanced his career he would have more power later. What the son of the bitch didn't know was that I would meet Vicky this morning at the Beverly Center." Simone pointed an angry finger toward Natalie, who felt lucky she wasn't in Ted's shoes.

"You see, I know Vicky," Simone continued. "We took some acting classes together before she got a part in some silly soap opera. So I ask her what's up and she tells me that she got that TV movie. So I say, 'Oh yes! I know Ted O'Neal, the director.' And you know what she tells me? 'Oh, he was great at the audition; he gave me some good notes.' I thought that I would die on the spot. I was so mad I had to make up a fake phone call and an emergency so I could disappear before I made a fool of myself." She pulled out a tissue out of her bag to dab her eyes.

"Did you ask Ted for some explanations?" Natalie asked indignantly.

"You bet I did! I just went to his office. The bastard couldn't deny anymore that he was involved in the casting. He said that he'd tried to bring me in, but the producers wouldn't see me. They wanted an actress with a name. As if Vicky has a name! That's really typical of those bastards to betray you and try to make you feel insecure on top of it." She started to sob.

Her pain touched Natalie. Betrayal was an awful experience. Natalie had gone through it not that long ago when she had felt betrayed by Simone.

"I was so upset," Simone continued. "I slapped him and told him to go to hell. I never wanted to see his stupid face ever again."

"Oh! I'm so sorry, Sims." She hugged Simone again, staying in a tight embrace for a moment. Natalie noticed a few curious stares from other customers.

Simone dried her eyes and took a deep breath. She looked calmer.

"I'm so humiliated, Nat. I... I wish you'd let him choke on that olive." She fetched another tissue paper from her handbag and blew her nose. "Anyway, I've got another shitty audition to go to on Monday, but I won't be denied. I'm going to use that anger; you'll see. It's a waitress part, but it's going to be the angriest waitress on the face of earth. I'm considering spitting in the casting lady's face if necessary."

Natalie smiled. "I don't think that's a good idea."

"You can come with me if you like. Maybe you can keep me out of trouble."

"Well, I accepted Jerry's offer to fly to New York with him until Tuesday." Natalie braced herself.

"You what? Natalie!"

"What? Is Jerry a serial killer or something? It's time you tell me what I have to be so careful about."

"It's nothing like that, Nat. Jerry's just dangerous because he's... Jerry. One day he's all a woman can hope for, the next day he'll want nothing to do with you. Brenda's the only one who managed to hang with him that long. I'll feel responsible if you get hurt."

"Don't worry about me. Anyway, Jean-Marc dumped me and I need to think about something else."

"What? Are you kidding me? That's impossible! Jean-Marc would never do something like that." The news seemed to distract Simone from her personal drama.

"You don't know him."

"From what you told me, it sounds like he adores you. What happened?"

"He got upset because he wanted me to leave L.A. earlier and come back to him. I did try to shorten my trip but I couldn't. On top of that, I called him Jerry by accident."

"Nat, no! You didn't!" Simone looked scandalized.

"I couldn't believe I made that slip," Natalie moaned. "It really pissed him off, and he said that he was 'setting me free.'"

"Nat, that's not really dumping. In the States we call that having a fight."

"You didn't hear his tone," Natalie argued. "I think that he hates me now."

"If you need a pretext to have sex with Jerry, go ahead. But I don't think it's necessarily over with Jean-Marc."

"Believe me, it's over. And don't worry, I can handle Jerry."

"Wow! I can't believe we broke up with our guys almost at the same time. Well, I hope I'll get over Ted quickly. He had a small penis, but he was such a good lover. The bastard." Her eyes watered again but Natalie couldn't help but smile.

"I have to go, Nat. I promised one of my friends that I would help her prepare for her audition, but I'm late. Thank you for coming to talk to me. I do feel better." They hugged again. "Call me when you come back, and if you have any problems, call me from New York."

"I'll be fine. Take care of yourself, and break a leg for your audition."

"All right. I love you…"

"I love you, too."

As she drove back to the beach, Natalie rejoiced that her friendship with Simone had survived, but she felt sorry for Simone and Ted. They were the cutest couple, both blond and pretty. Apparently, Ted's ambition was stronger than his feelings for Simone. Would Simone have done the same under the same circumstances? According to Jerry, Hollywood changed people. The initial freshness and enthusiasm often faded and was replaced by calculation and deceit.

Back in her apartment, Natalie packed three outfits for three days, but she added her favorite chic black dress, curve-hugging and strapless, which bared her back nicely. She'd bought it on Rue de Rennes in Paris for a small fortune, but it was worth it. When she wore it with four-inch-high black pumps, she got nothing but compliments.

She decided to call Michael to let him know that she was leaving and a few minutes later he was ringing the doorbell, dressed casually in jeans and a long sleeve t-shirt that clung to his fit body. Natalie wondered how he looked without his clothes and had to mentally slap her hand for her inappropriate thoughts.

"Care for something to eat?" Michael said.

They exited the building and emerged into the sunny day.

"It looks like everything's going well today. Yesterday I was a little worried about you. You sounded depressed."

"I was," Natalie answered with a faint smile. "I feel better today."

"I'm glad to hear that. Let me know if I can help in any way." His tone was warm and compassionate.

"Thank you." They walked side by side toward the Boardwalk Café a few blocks from the building.

"Oh! By the way, I got the part in that *Kamikaze* movie," Michael said quietly.

"How wonderful!" Natalie exclaimed. "When is it starting?"

"In two weeks. We're shooting in Thailand. I'll be gone for five weeks." There was a look of quiet contentment on his face.

"How exciting! Do you have a good part?"

Michael smiled broadly this time. "One of the leads. It could be my big break." He gave her a side look, watching the effect of his words.

"I'm so proud of you. You have what it takes to be a big star. I could see that right away." Michael placed his right hand on his heart and bowed slightly to thank her.

"I guess I'll see the movie in Paris," she continued. "I'm leaving in two weeks myself."

"Too bad you're leaving so soon," he said.

"You're leaving also, so what do you care?" Natalie joked. "Oh! By the way, I'm going to New York for the weekend. So when you don't see me around, don't think that I've been kidnapped."

"You're going to New York? Really?" Michael looked surprised.

"A friend who's going there for business invited me to come with him." Natalie smiled as she saw Michael frowning.

They reached the restaurant. It was packed, but there was no waiting list.

"You said *him*. Who's this *him*? Do your parents know about it? Is your boyfriend okay with it? How long have you known *him*?" Michael made fake freaked-out faces and Natalie chuckled.

"Are you worrying about me?"

"Of course I am…" The waiter took them to a tiny table on the outside patio facing the boardwalk. The tables were really close to each other and Michael had to lower his voice.

"Okay. Now tell me everything. You're not going there with your boyfriend, right?"

"Right," Natalie said.

"May I ask who's the happy man you're cheating with is?"

"First of all, I'm not cheating. I don't have a boyfriend."

"What? You were talking about your boyfriend the other day." His tone had changed from joking to serious.

"Well, I was in a serious relationship until two days ago. That's why I was so depressed yesterday."

"And today you're already leaving with another man. Damn! That was a quick recovery," Michael said, frowning.

Natalie frowned, feeling a little insulted. "Why do you care, anyway?" she asked.

"I do care. Let's say that I think good things about you. I mean, I thought good things about you; now I'm not so sure." Michael had recovered his joking tone, but there was something in his eyes that didn't smile.

"I can assure you, Jerry's just a friend. There is nothing between us…"

Michael interrupted her. "Jerry? Don't tell me that you're leaving with Simone's cousin Jerry!"

"Yes. Why?" The waiter came back to take their order, a hamburger with fries for Michael and a chicken salad for Natalie. Michael waited for the waiter to leave.

"Are you sure about this?"

"Sure about what? Of course I'm not sure about anything. Right now I'm just trying to take things moment by moment. Now if there is a serious reason why I shouldn't go, like you know that Jerry's a psychopath or has a contagious disease, you should tell me frankly."

Michael smiled. "I don't know anything like that. I think he's a cool dude. Jimmy's going to be disappointed, though."

"Jimmy? What are you talking about?"

"Yes, my man Jimmy. I told him that you were engaged so he wouldn't call you every day to ask you out." They both laughed.

"I'm not really sure why I agreed to go to New York with Jerry. I don't even know why he asked me…"

Michael raised an eyebrow. "Come on now. We're adults

here. You know perfectly well why he asked you."

"No, I mean, we already went through that. There was that initial attraction between us, but nothing happened because I wasn't free and he finally understood that. He doesn't even know that Jean-Marc and I broke up…"

Michael sighed and shook his head in disbelief. "Ah, stop it! I know that you're not a dumb pretty girl. Just don't try to fool yourself. There's no one here to judge you."

Natalie opened her mouth to answer, but nothing making sense would come out. She wondered if Michael was a little bit jealous that she was going away with Jerry. She watched him as he added ketchup on his huge hamburger and took a giant bite. He could be blunt and speak his mind, but she couldn't really hold it against him. She liked that he was authentic. If she had met him six months ago, she might have had a crush on him. After Yves, she had wondered if she would ever meet the right man. And now it was raining men.

She had met three handsome, smart, and talented men, all of them in the same short period of time. The universe was playing jokes with her. You want a man? Here you go! Have three!

Michael raised his head from his food. He seemed to have ejected the subject of her trip from his mind. "Is your salad okay?" he asked as if it was really important.

"It's perfect. Thank you."

The huge Saturday crowd moved slowly up and down the boardwalk. Girls displayed their tans in shorts and bikini tops while rubbing shoulders with Rastas with blond dreadlocks, pale rockers in black leather jackets, and German-looking tourists in Bermuda shorts. Musicians and performers did their thing, and homeless men sat on benches wearing all the clothes they owned despite the warm weather.

On the way back to their apartment building, Natalie and Michael stopped to watch a Michael Jackson impersonator and a nearly naked man with a sculpted, oiled body holding fake snakes. They managed to avoid the guitar player on roller skates.

"I love Venice beach," Michael said. "I can't see myself living anywhere else in L.A."

"Same here. I'm an island girl. I need the proximity to the ocean."

As Michael escorted her to her door, Natalie offered him her cheek to kiss, but he also gave her a big bear hug. She enjoyed the feeling of his broad shoulders embracing her and the smell of his cologne.

"Let me know if you need anything, okay? And don't give my man Jerry too much hell." She made a face as he ran away, climbing the stairs up to his place in two jumps, his laugh resounding in the hallway.

Natalie was more than ready when Jerry knocked on the door just after 9 p.m.

Her heart leaped when she saw him. She had almost forgotten how good he looked. He wore jeans and a white linen shirt, his unruly, frizzy curls framing his beautiful face.

"Nice spot," he said, looking around. He saw her carry-on bag waiting by the door. "Are you ready?" The enthusiasm in his voice was contagious.

"Let's go." She grabbed her handbag and tan leather jacket. As she turned off the lights she looked back, making a silent wish to have a great trip and get back in one piece from this adventure.

CHAPTER FOURTEEN

The yellow cab double-parked in front of a rundown building on 4th Street between avenues A and B. The street looked like a playground run by the dozens of kids skateboarding and sitting on curbs. Trash bags lined the sidewalk, and salsa music blasted from an open garage, a far cry from the quiet sleepiness of Santa Monica's streets. A distinct pulse could be felt here.

"Welcome to New York," Jerry said with a chuckle. He unlocked the building's front door, which opened on a narrow hallway leading to a steep wooden staircase. Even though he carried their bags, Natalie's thighs burned by the time they reached the fourth floor.

"There are probably no fat people in this building," she said, huffing and puffing.

"One more flight," Jerry encouraged, smiling at her protests. He dropped their bags in front of a door on the fifth floor, and fumbled in his jacket's pocket for the key. He had already opened the door and gotten the bags inside when Natalie reached the floor, her tongue sticking out, feigning total exhaustion. He playfully bent down and lifted her despite her protests, carrying her over his shoulder. As he reached toward the switch to turn on the lights, he tripped over one of the bags and they almost crashed to the floor. Jerry managed to unload her before reaching the floor, almost in slow motion. They laughed hard as he lay on his back with Natalie sitting on the floor beside him.

They had laughed the whole trip. Natalie felt quite comfortable with him now. She'd studied his face while he dozed on the plane and felt a stir just looking at him. She'd watched him, unobserved, with the foolish thought of engraving the shape of his eyes in her mind. He must've been an incredibly beautiful child. What price did he have to pay for being such a beautiful and talented man? Because Natalie knew there was always a price.

They got up. The hallway opened to a large room with high ceilings. Near the large window, a drafting table supported all kinds of painting supplies but she didn't see an easel. The red brick walls were covered with paintings of different formats and styles, but only one or two seemed to be Jerry's work. Books were stacked everywhere on overcrowded bookshelves, piled on the coffee table, or on the floor. An open door revealed a small bedroom, hardly big enough for the large bed. Natalie could see a large abstract painting hanging above it. This place had a warm and lived-in vibe, and it made a surprising contrast to Jerry's house on Venice Beach.

"So this is where you come when you are tired of L.A?" Natalie said. The apartment was more revealing than she expected.

"Yep! I actually spend more time here than in L.A." Jerry kept his eyes on her as if he was trying to read her thoughts.

"But you don't paint here very much, right?" she said as she walked around the room and studied the paintings on the wall.

"I used to, but now I have a studio in SoHo, where I can paint my large pieces," Jerry answered patiently.

"I like this place; it has an intimate feel," Natalie said as she plopped on a sofa covered with a colorful Indian blanket. Then she grinned and gave Jerry a sideways look. "But where am I supposed to sleep?"

"This is your bed. You can stay here, and I'll sleep in my studio. Unless you feel lonely and want me to stay... In which case I'll sleep on this sofa here," he said with a smile as he pointed to the sofa she was sitting on.

"I was just kidding." She repressed a yawn. She hadn't gotten any sleep on the plane.

"Do you want some coffee?" Jerry disappeared in the kitchen, but came back out with an empty can of coffee. "I have to get some groceries but make yourself comfortable. There are clean towels in the closet near the bathroom if you want to take a shower."

Natalie felt grateful for the time by herself in the bathroom. It was so tiny that you could practically take a shower while sitting on the toilet, but it was very clean.

She showered with delight, brushed her teeth, and would have been tempted to put on pajamas and jump in bed if it wasn't 11 a.m. She carefully stepped out of the bathroom with a towel wrapped around her body, but Jerry was still gone. Relieved, she retrieved fresh underwear from her bags and slipped on soft off-white pants and a fitted tunic. Jerry was still gone after she was fully dressed, so she lay down on the bed for a nap.

When she opened her eyes again a quick glance at her watch told her that she had slept more than two hours. She got up quickly and walked to the living room. Jerry was lying down on the couch and reading his mail. He looked at her with a smile.

"Feeling rested?" he asked.

"I guess so. I didn't want to sleep, it just happened while I was waiting for you."

"You did good; when I came back I also took a nap. Do you

want to go out for lunch?"

"I do," Natalie said enthusiastically. "I don't want to waste another minute. I want to see New York."

They had lunch in a little Italian restaurant where everyone seemed to know Jerry. Danny, the owner, a very charming Italian-American man in his sixties, sat at their table and made them laugh with stories of his youth when he was the lead singer of a band called The Ones. After lunch Jerry took her to his studio, a huge loft with concrete floors and cathedral windows, and showed her his unfinished nine-foot high painting commissioned by the city of Orange in New Jersey. The scale and mastery of the urban scene impressed her deeply. Something important had always been missing in her life, she realized. And that something was the ability to speak in the language of art. If she could rewind time and start her life over, art would be an essential part of her existence.

After they left the studio, they walked through SoHo and the Village, where the air was thick with the smell of asphalt, incense, spicy food, and sometimes marijuana. Not a second passed without loud honks from swarms of yellow cabs. Natalie could feel her body charging as if it could suck up the energy of the city.

It was almost 6 p.m. when they returned to the apartment. Jerry disappeared in the bathroom and Natalie heard the sound of running water. She sat down on the sofa and noticed the pile of mail on the coffee table. The first piece bore an exotic stamp. The return address printed on the front of the envelope showed that it came from Ingrid in Sweden.

Who was Ingrid? Was she a lover, a fellow artist, or a friend? She knew so little about Jerry. The truth was that she didn't know enough about him to be with him in this apartment. She wondered what had made her accept. It was bold and crazy, and very unlike her. But she had done it, and it was too late to second-guess her decision.

Jerry came out of the bathroom bare-chested, wearing only his jeans. His wet hair, coiled in tight curls, dripped on his shoulders. Natalie admired the V-shape of his body, lean and firm, with tight abs and small hips. His copper skin had a warm, reddish-brown glow. He had been reserved so far; he hadn't tried to kiss her or touch her. But there he was, half-naked.

"Are you trying to seduce me?" Natalie asked.

"Of course. How am I doing?" Jerry said with a smirk.

"Pretty well. Put on some clothes before something bad happens to you."

"Yeah, promises, promises." He came to sit near Natalie on the sofa. "You're wondering why I asked you to come with me, aren't you?" He looked straight into her eyes. "I wanted you to see this side of my life. I like the light in my house in Venice and the view on the ocean, but I have almost no social life in L.A. I get most of my inspiration here."

"Why do you want me to see this other part of you?" she asked.

Jerry sighed, looking exasperated. "I want you to really know me."

"Who are you, Jerry?"

"I'm a guy who wants to be with you. I want to let myself fall in love with you. I've made dozens of drawings of you. I've drawn you naked from every angle I could think of. I've made love to you many times in my mind. Not many women affect me the way you do." His fingers caressed her face and followed the contour of her neck, down to her shoulder and her arm. He played with the shell bracelet around her wrist. "What else do you want to know?"

He picked up her hand and kissed her palm. A burning sensation spread all over her body. "I'm crazy about you, can't you see that?" he said, his eyelids heavy.

She saw a short struggle in his eyes and then he suddenly rose and scooped her up in his arms. The voice in her head that said "no" was too tiny and weak for her to resist. Right now she didn't care if what she felt was only physical; she wanted him, probably as much as he wanted her. When they kissed, she knew that there was no going back. Her own desire swelled from the middle of her chest and submerged her like a big wave, but she was not afraid of drowning anymore.

He carried her to the bed and undressed her slowly, as he would unwrap a present. Then he got up as if to get a full look at her, stepped out of his jeans and stood before her, naked and unashamed. His face was tense as his eyes followed the contours of her body with intensity. She didn't feel embarrassed to lie naked in front of him. "You're so beautiful!" he whispered, saying out loud what she thought about him.

She pulled him toward her. The contact of his body almost hurt, his mouth leaving a burning trail all over her body. He took his time tasting every part of her. When his lips reached the skin inside her thighs she became totally present, her body receptive to his touch, pleasure building up until it was almost too much to take. When they couldn't wait anymore, their bodies collided as if they couldn't get close enough to each other, the pleasure so intense she could cry. She also took charge, learning his body with all her senses, caressing and teasing, making him moan, then riding him in a wild sensual dance. His hands keeping her tight against him, his mouth hot on her breast, he took her far beyond what she'd experienced before.

She was surprised that they could give each other so much pleasure. Their bodies seemed made to fit together. They made love again, the sensations in her body even more acute and as she looked into his eyes, the fire that she had lit inside of them made her shudder.

She woke up to the whistling of an espresso machine and the smell of coffee from the kitchen, daylight piercing through the light curtains and Jerry's scent still on her skin. He had gotten up without waking her. Some of their clothes were spread on the floor along with torn condom packets. No contest, that was the hottest, wildest night of her life. Making love to Jerry had been like an act of liberation. She realized only now that before him she'd always held back in an unconscious attempt to keep control. But last night had been different. Natalie had no regrets about what had happened.

Where was he? She slipped off the bed into the bathroom, splashed her face with cold water, brushed her teeth and smiled at her reflection in the mirror. Picking up his shirt from a chair, she put it on and made her way to the kitchen to surprise him.

The kitchen was empty. A steaming pot of coffee waited on the counter, but Jerry was gone. He'd left without leaving a word. Natalie felt a pit in her stomach. Had he lost interest already? The sound of keys unlocking the front door interrupted her downward spiraling thoughts. Jerry appeared with a box of something smelling delicious. His face lit up with a smile when he saw her.

"Hey gorgeous, I thought I'd be back before you got up. I went to get breakfast." He put down the box. "My shirt looks good on you," he said, pulling her toward him and kissing her lips with ardor.

"I thought that you went straight to your studio to paint and left me on my own," she said kissing him back reluctantly.

"What are you talking about? I would never do that. I wanted to cook breakfast but I forgot to buy eggs yesterday." The Styrofoam boxes contained croissants filled with eggs, bacon and jelly. Natalie sat down to eat. Sweet and salty melted on her tongue in the most delicious way. She stretched her toes with pleasure. Jerry laughed at her appetite. They finished eating then went straight back to bed.

"All I want to do is make love to you," Jerry whispered as they came out of a post-coital nap. "I don't know if I can manage anything else."

"I do want to see more of New York, though," Natalie said, sitting up. "I can't leave without seeing the Empire State Building and Central Park, or else I'm going to think that I fell into a trap."

Jerry laughed and she poked his dimples with her index finger. He kissed her hand. "Okay, get dressed then. We are going for a tour, and tonight we'll do that reception thing."

"What reception?" Natalie asked.

"Just a party for the opening of my art exhibition. There is a gallery representing my work in SoHo."

Jerry couldn't completely mask his satisfaction in saying those words, and Natalie picked up his pride under the blasé tone of voice.

It was only 11:30 a.m. and there was plenty of time to see

some of New York before the party. Natalie jumped in the shower, refusing Jerry's offer to take it together, and got dressed in no time, making sure to put on some flat shoes in case they did a lot of walking.

Half an hour later, they were inside a beaten-down yellow cab on their way to the Empire State Building. Natalie insisted on going all the way to the top. It was something Jerry hadn't done since his ninth birthday. Admiring the dizzying concentration of skyscrapers, Natalie thought of the romantic movies featuring the famous rooftop. Jerry seemed amused by her enthusiasm, observing her with an indulgent smile. When Natalie was finally satisfied, he insisted they go buy some donuts in Harlem. They found a Haitian driver who seemed to know the exact spot.

"This place has the best donuts in town and Harlem is no more dangerous than anywhere else in New York," Jerry told Natalie when she asked about his choice to go all the way there. "I used to live on 139th Street. The Bronx may be another story, but Harlem is safe enough nowadays."

The cab driver was rewarded with a donut and a generous tip when he dropped them off in Central Park. The shadowy trees offered a welcome respite from the scorching heat everywhere else.

Jerry seemed at ease everywhere, whether he was buying donuts in Harlem or strolling in wealthier surroundings in Central Park. "How does it affect you to have a white mother and a black father?" Natalie asked as she buried her mouth in the cotton candy they'd purchased from a street vendor. She'd already eaten two donuts, but the cotton candy looked like the pink cloud she'd walked on all morning. She couldn't remember ingesting this much sugar in such a short period of time since her childhood.

Jerry lifted an eyebrow. "I was sent to all white schools, and the kids never let me forget that I was different from them. I didn't really care; I always felt black. I was very close to my father and proud of him, but I always wondered how my parents ever ended up with each other." Jerry's face became serious. He paused for a while and looked into the distance as if he were reliving some memories. Natalie said nothing but hooked her arm around his.

"To this day, it's a mystery to me," he continued finally, shaking his head as if he was still in disbelief. "They were so radically different. My father was so cool and my mother, well, she has always been such a pain in the ass. I hope you never have to meet her." He looked straight ahead and his body seemed to tense up.

"Really?" Natalie was disturbed. What had Jerry's mother done to him? Or did the problem come from him? She suddenly had had enough of her cotton candy. Her lips puckered, she dropped the rest of it in an overflowing garbage can. Jerry placed his arm on her shoulder.

"If you had the misfortune to meet my mother, you'd understand what I am talking about. But I don't want to take that risk. I don't even want to get started on the subject."

"You must have had a rough childhood."

They sat on a bench. Jerry didn't answer right away; he seemed absorbed for a moment with the sight of a pretty little girl in a red dress sitting on the grass in front of them. Her long black hair floated around her while she blew a storm of bubbles. Jerry took out a small sketchbook and pencil from his back pocket and quickly sketched the scene in front of him, adding notes about colors on his drawing. Natalie assumed that the woman reading a book on the nearby bench was the little girl's mother. She wondered what that scene would become in his painting.

He put back his little notepad in his jean pocket. "My child-hood sucked, but that's the past. I survived it." Jerry took a deep breath and looked at Natalie. "And here I am sitting next to a smart and beautiful woman to whom I made love all night and all morning. Life is wonderful!" His charming smile was back.

He pulled Natalie toward him and kissed her with passion. The thought that they were lovers gave her a jolt of pleasure.

"What if we skip the visit to the MOMA and go back home," Jerry whispered in her ear.

"Hmm! I don't think I'll get another occasion to visit that museum anytime soon... Let's do the MOMA." She kissed his right eye, the one with the rebellious eyebrow. It would be so easy to lose control with him, but she had to stay vigilant; being his lover didn't mean that she should let her guard down. She was still waiting for the Jerry she had been warned against to show his face.

Natalie loved their visit to the MOMA. Jerry guided her through the current exhibition on the themes of Seasons and Moments, landscapes as a Retreat and Escape from Urban Life. She admired works by Monet, Miro, Cézanne, Edward Munch, and Emil Nolde, and woodcuts by Paul Gauguin. Surrounded with all this art, a great peace descended on her. Her breathing deepened, the lightness in her chest felt like joy. She had found her passion. But trying to live it was such a foolish dream.

Jerry, who had already seen this exhibition, stayed silent most of the time. Sometimes he would pull out his little sketch-book and jot down a few words or comments. He sketched her standing in front of Matisse's *The Piano Lesson*, awestruck.

As she watched the street scene through the dirty window of

their yellow cab, Natalie understood why Jerry liked New York so much. The city had a palpable energy that made it exciting and alive. Was it because of the concentration of people? Living piled up in those high buildings probably necessitated a pouring of energy into the streets and an escape through art. She loved it. But could she live here for a long period of time? She doubted it. Something inside of her yearned for peaceful horizons.

They got back to the apartment around 6:30 p.m. and had to hurry to change clothes. Natalie was glad she brought along her strapless black dress.

"You look amazing!" Jerry said as she came out of the bathroom dressed and made up, her eyes accented with charcoal for a glamorous look.

"You have to pose for me in that dress." Jerry wanted to sketch her right away, but Natalie convinced him that it could wait until they came back. They left the apartment at 7:30 and she wondered if he was dragging his feet. Was he nervous? He wore a black suit with an open white shirt and looked like a male model even with those unruly curls framing his face.

All of a sudden she was not so sure that she wanted to go anywhere. Most of his business relations or friends who didn't flee New York for the summer would probably be there. They would compare her to his previous conquests. Natalie decided she would give him plenty of space.

The yellow cab stopped in front of a chic-looking brick building. As Jerry helped Natalie get out, a red-haired woman in her late forties ran up to them and grabbed Jerry's arm.

"Where have you been? Mart Wiseman is here. He has somewhere else to go, but he wants to meet you…"

"Samantha, this is Natalie. Nat, this is my agent, Samantha."
Jerry seemed completely unaffected by Samantha's hype.

"Nice to meet you, Natalie," Samantha said with a large fake
smile. She then turned her attention back to Jerry, and led him
through the front door. A dense crowd already filled the bright aer-
ial space. Jerry grabbed Natalie's hand, but she didn't want to be
dragged along.

"Go meet that man, I'll be right here," Natalie said to reassure Jerry. She really didn't feel like following Samantha.

"You'll be okay?" Jerry asked, eyebrows lifted.

"Absolutely," she answered. He gave her a peck on the lips
and disappeared into the crowd, preceded by Samantha. Natalie
looked around. The artwork was displayed on tall walls arranged in
a labyrinth. She was fascinated. Jerry's surrealistic style combined
imagination with an impressive accuracy of details.

She got particularly caught in the painting of a black saxophonist playing by a pool filled with golden water the color of
whiskey. In the water, you could see the ghostly reflection of a
woman's face, beautiful but cold, with flowing blond hair blending
into the pool's water. The setting around the pool was a jungle,
which was recurrent in some of his other paintings. Jerry's father
was a saxophonist, and Simone had said that he had been found
dead in a pool. The thought gave Natalie chills.

Could the reflection in the pool be his mother's? Was he
blaming her for his father's death? Was it why he seemed to dislike
her so much? That would explain whatever difficult behavior he
had in the past.

The truth was that he looked and acted like a perfectly sane
human being. So far she had seen no trace of mental disorders, or

even the unpredictability she had been warned against. *Let's go see what other secrets I can find in his paintings,* she thought to herself. She went from painting to painting, forgetting the scene around her, impressed by all of them, even those she liked less. But as she didn't find any more references to his parents, she attributed her insight to her own imagination.

At some point, she spotted Jerry across the room, talking with a heavyset man with gray hair whom she assumed was Mart Wiseman. The man had the confident posture of someone who had everything he could want from life. Jerry sported the guarded expression he had the first time she'd seen him.

"How long have you known Jerry McDane?" a voice said in her ear.

Startled, Natalie turned around to see an attractive middle-aged woman with long dark hair dressed in a black designer pantsuit.

"Hi, how are you?" Natalie answered, smiling but ignoring the question.

"I'm Lucia, but everybody calls me Lou. Samantha and I represent Jerry." Lou's voice had switched from intimate to professional. Natalie was immediately on her guard. Unlike Samantha, who had dismissed her immediately, Lou was evaluating Natalie from every angle.

"Oh! Very nice meeting you, I'm Natalie Dorel."

"I can hear an accent there. Are you French?"

"Yes, I am." Natalie promised herself she'd work on her accent.

"It's such a nice accent," Lou purred. "I saw you come in with Jerry," she continued. "He's so talented and so handsome, isn't he?"

"Yes, he is." Natalie braced herself for the next inquiry.

"So how long have you known him?" Lou's lips were bright red and contrasted dramatically with her very dark eyes and hair. She emanated the sensuality of a flamenco dancer. Natalie wondered if there had been something between Jerry and his agent.

"I've known him a month or so," Natalie answered making her tone as pleasant as possible. "How long have you been his agent?" Natalie instinctively knew that Lou didn't wish her well.

"We have been representing him for almost a year." She paused for a moment. "So Natalie, are you a model?"

"I'm a physician." Natalie registered the surprise on Lou's face with a certain pleasure.

"Oh! How interesting! Jerry's girlfriends are usually models," Lou replied with a wicked sideways smile.

There we go! Natalie thought. Lou was informing her that she was only one of Jerry's many conquests. Two days ago they were only friends, now they were lovers. She looked at Jerry, who was still speaking with the fat guy, and felt proud of him. She should make an announcement: *Ladies and Gentlemen, your attention please! That man over there, yes the man who painted all this great stuff that you came to admire, is my lover.*

She eyed Lou with a new fire in her eyes. "It's a wonderful evening, congratulations! I'm going to get something to drink. Nice talking to you." With her most innocent smile, she moved toward the cocktail area across the room, knowing that she hadn't made a friend. Lou was probably raking her brain right now to find a way to spoil her relationship with Jerry.

CHAPTER FIFTEEN

Natalie raised the bubbling glass of pink champagne to her lips. She saw Jerry, free from his interlocutor, looking around, but as he turned in her direction, new admirers surrounded him.

In a flash of insight, she understood that she was attracted to Jerry because he lived the life of his choice. He led the kind of life she wanted to live. She found satisfaction and a sense of purpose in taking care of people, but she had never taken the time to ask herself if it made her happy. If she could do it all over again she would have chosen to heal people through art.

Was it too late to start painting? Was it a gift from God, something that you were born with, like having a beautiful voice? Or could you acquire it later in life with hard work and passion? Jerry started when he was twelve years old. How crazy would it be for her to enroll in art school and put aside her career as a physician? How would Ginette take it? Roger would be disappointed and her father would be upset. Everyone had been so enthusiastic about her "choice" to go into medicine.

What if she dared to stay in New York and go to art school? That could be so much fun! She let the thought sink in. Yes, but it would be selfish. There would be no sympathy for a surgeon who decided not to operate anymore so that she could paint. Plus, she couldn't see herself telling Jerry that she wanted to leave medicine to be an artist just like him. That would sound ridiculous. Jerry looked impressed with her occupation as a physician. He had enough artist friends, successful or not.

For some reason she thought about Michael telling her that she had to make time for herself if she wanted to stay healthy. He would be supportive of her. She liked him and his open-mindedness. Her thoughts drifted to Jean-Marc. He had always wanted to be an airline pilot and that's just what he did. And he had always loved her. Or he used to. She had been careless with him. The thought enveloped her like a heavy cloak.

"You should go get him now."

Natalie, landing back on earth, almost spilled her drink at the sound of a male voice behind her. A distinguished-looking man with impeccable gray hair looked at her with an enigmatic smile. He wore a dark suit with a lavender shirt and a matching silk scarf around his neck. The man looked like an older James Bond.

"He's practically getting mugged," he said, looking briefly toward Jerry, and Natalie felt relieved. For a moment she thought that she had been thinking aloud.

How many people had noticed her coming in with Jerry? She glanced toward him and saw a stunning woman in a miniskirt and colorful short jacket hanging on his arm. Thousands of short golden curls were framing her exquisite face, and she wore color-ful jewels around her neck. She seemed to come straight out of a fashion magazine. Natalie didn't feel jealous; she knew that there would always be someone prettier or younger, and that was just life. She deliberately turned her back on Jerry and faced James Bond.

"Hello, my name is Natalie. Are you a friend of Jerry?"

"Nice meeting you, Natalie. I'm George, the gallery owner," the man said with a kind smile. "How do you like the expo?"

"I love it. I also saw a showing of Jerry's work in Los Angeles last month. These are different paintings. He's really prolific."

"Yes. And his paintings are selling well on both coasts. Jerry McDane has become quite a name in the art world." Natalie had nothing to add to that. She simply smiled, finishing the last sip on her glass of champagne.

"How long have you known him?" George asked. Natalie almost sighed out loud. Why did they all want to know that? So they could place their relationship into a box? Or maybe they wondered what happened to Brenda?

Before she could answer, she felt a familiar arm around her shoulder. Good! Jerry had managed to free himself from the crowd and the pretty blond.

"There you are. I was looking for you everywhere," Jerry said. He looked so good Natalie felt her heart swell with pride. "Hey George, how is it going?"

"We're doing great. Lots of interest and already some sales, and I met beautiful Natalie. You're a lucky man."

"I know," Jerry said, caressing Natalie's cheek with his finger. "Listen, I'll call you tomorrow. We have to go."

"No problem. Call me at the office tomorrow before noon." They shook hands, and Jerry led Natalie to the exit. They found a cab immediately.

"Take us to the Blue Light," Jerry told the driver. He turned toward Natalie. "There's a great jazz quartet playing tonight, but I'm not even sure if we can get in. Do you feel like listening to jazz?" he asked Natalie.

"I would love to," Natalie said. Jerry put his arm around her shoulders and they rode silently for a while. Jerry seemed a little absent.

"It was very impressive," Natalie said, breaking the silence. "It looked like you were being mobbed."

"Whatever, let's not talk about it." Jerry dismissed her with a gesture of his hand.

Surprised, Natalie tensed up a bit. "What else do you want to talk about?" She wasn't just a groupie trying to make conversation. She sat up, letting his arm slide on her back.

"I'm sorry, it's just that I don't really like being in the spotlight," Jerry said, looking contrite. "Actually, I hate being in the spotlight. I come to those events because I have to. It helps sell my paintings. But I remember a few years back when all those people looked at me as if I were a bum. If it weren't for my friend Harry introducing me to his agent, I would still be out in the streets. I don't like all the fuss. I don't believe it's sincere. I'm happy to get out of there."

"I see." Natalie was still on the defensive. "I met your agents. They look very possessive."

"Forget about them, they're always like that. The only way they like to see me is alone in my studio, painting. They think they own me." He caressed Natalie's back as if to reassure her but his caress irritated her.

"Come on, don't get mad at me. I'm sorry I snapped at you." He made an exaggerated apologetic face, looking sorrier by the second. Natalie finally softened, but she didn't add anything.

The cab stopped in front of the Blue Light. A cosmopolitan crowd waited in line to get into what seemed to be a tiny hole in the wall.

One of the men guarding the entrance signaled him to come to the front and hustled him in as if he was a movie star.

"Thanks, man," Jerry said, shaking his hand. "How is it going?"

"Everything's all right. Good to see you." The man escorted them past the cashier so they didn't have to pay, and Jerry slipped him a few bills while shaking his hand.

A woman with long braided hair approached them. "Do you have a reservation?"

Jerry shook his head no. The woman made them wait a moment in the hallway, where they could hear the clapping and loud approval of the crowd. The hostess finally came back and directed them to a small table close to the stage, which seemed to have been added for them.

Natalie was surprised to see how small and intimate the room was. Many of the jazz lovers sat or stood at the bar. The audience erupted in applause and howls when the quartet began their rendition of "Take Five." The sweet notes of saxophone and piano made Natalie euphoric.

After a few numbers, the band stopped for break, and Natalie and Jerry ordered a bottle of red wine and appetizers. Jerry seemed relaxed, but absent. Natalie could feel a subtle change in his attitude. What had happened?

A new flow of listeners was allowed in the bar. Natalie scanned the room and stopped on a familiar face. Standing at the bar laughing with abandon was the fashion plate from the art show, the one that Natalie had spotted swooning over Jerry. The girl looked at them for a second. Had Jerry seen her? He looked in the other direction. He excused himself to go to the restroom, and Natalie followed him with her eyes. She noticed that she wasn't the only one. Jerry was turning heads, men's and women's.

Natalie turned her gaze back toward the bar to look for the girl, but she was also gone. They were both gone! Natalie felt her cheeks becoming hot with suspicion. It could just be a coincidence but Simone had warned that Jerry was a playboy, and Michael had too, in his own way. Pride kept her in her seat. Under no circumstances did she want to behave like a jealous woman.

She could worry about Jerry's loyalty and fight for him each time a pretty woman came into the picture, or she could give up getting involved with him now. The choice was hers. She remembered how her mother Ginette had fought for Natalie's dad, and managed to forgive him even after finding a woman in their bed. And still, she'd ended up with a broken heart and a divorce. Natalie had always promised herself that it wouldn't happen to her.

When Jerry reappeared alone Natalie relaxed a bit, but when the girl came out from the same hallway, she thought that she might not have been that crazy after all.

In a split second, her decision was made. She wouldn't agonize or fight over Jerry. That was not for her; she wasn't even sure that she liked his world or would fit into it. She had wanted him, and it had been a physical attraction as much for her as for him, but their story had no future.

Jerry sat down and smiled, apparently unaware of all the drama that had been playing in Natalie's head. She observed the girl going back to her friends with a bounce in her steps, the thousands of curls on her head dancing like little snakes.

"Can we leave now?" Natalie asked. "I'm getting a headache."

Jerry looked surprised and a little concerned. "Sure, let's go." He reached in his pocket for his wallet, paid the bill, and left a generous tip as usual. Natalie watched Jerry closely as they made their way to the exit, but he didn't look toward the bar or make eye contact with the snake-haired girl.

Once outside Jerry put his arm around her shoulders.

"Are you okay?"

"I'm fine, just a headache."

"I have some aspirin at home." He hailed a taxi.

They rode back to the apartment in silence. Natalie could see Jerry looking at her with some concern. At least she had his full attention. Her headache, which had been very faint when she first complained about it, was now full-blown. When they got back to the apartment, Jerry went immediately in the kitchen and came back with two white pills and a glass of water. Natalie would have normally asked to check a label or investigate to know what exactly she was taking, but this time she didn't care. She sat at the kitchen table and slowly drank her glass of water.

Jerry sat, too, and looked at her until she glanced at him. They stared at each other for a moment.

"Tell me what's wrong," Jerry finally said, a concerned look on his face.

"Nothing's wrong, I just have a headache." Natalie couldn't really understand why she felt so deflated.

"Are you still upset because I didn't want to talk about the art show?" Jerry asked.

"I guess not," Natalie said, even though she was frowning.

"You have to know," Jerry said, "I don't like talking about

my work and what it means and all that. Once it's out there I'm not interested in analyzing it."

Natalie judged his comment as somehow condescending. "You don't have to explain anything. I wasn't asking you to discuss your paintings; I was just making a comment on the number of people there. Besides, I wasn't even thinking about your artwork." Now she knew that Jerry wouldn't explain the strange painting of the saxophonist by the pool.

"So what's the problem?"

Natalie finished her glass of water. "You tell me. You are the one looking weird."

"Actually, there is something bothering me…" Jerry said after a pause. Natalie looked at him, inviting him to keep going. "I may have to stay in New York to finish the piece New Jersey commissioned. They moved the inauguration to an earlier date and they are asking me if I can have it finished by then. I'll need to work on it for the next two weeks."

"I see." *Could this be the work of Samantha and Lou?* Natalie wondered.

"When did you learn about this?" Natalie asked.

"Lou told me before we left the gallery and it kind of pissed me off."

Was this why he had seemed preoccupied? "That's okay. I'll go back to L.A. alone," she said with a forced smile.

"Why don't you just stay with me? Relax and visit New York. I would have to work a lot but we could be back in L.A. by next Friday," Jerry said in an engaging way.

"I don't think so," Natalie answered. "Anyway, now or in two weeks our relationship has to end. When my vacation is over

I'll have to go back to Paris." She spoke softly, realizing that she didn't really want to leave.

"It doesn't have to end. I can paint anywhere in the world. I can go to Paris as often as I want."

"Yeah! I guess so," Natalie said unconvinced. "But for the next two weeks you need to focus on your work. I'd be a distraction. So I'm leaving tomorrow."

"Nat, what's going on? Why don't you tell me what's bothering you?" Jerry pulled her to him, making her sit on his lap. Natalie's body was responding to his touch, but she didn't want to give in. She got up.

"I should be the one asking you that. Oh! Forget it, I'm tired," she announced, rising to leave the kitchen. Jerry caught her by her wrist.

"Hold on! We're going to discuss this. What are you're talking about?"

"Please! You are the one who started it."

"Started what? What I said in the cab? I already apologized. And you just said that you weren't thinking about it. So what is it? Are you already tired of me? If so, just say it." He looked upset now. No doubt, they were having an argument.

"Maybe you are the one ready to move on because you met somebody else."

Jerry looked surprised. "What are you talking about? Met who? Where? At the art show? Is that what this is? You're jealous?"

"Oh! Please. I'm not jealous. I saw all the girls swooning around you. I'm not naïve."

Jerry's face relaxed and he almost smiled. "I thought that

you'd be a little more secure. There's nobody to be jealous of."

"I'm secure, Jerry," Natalie said. "But everybody who knows you warned me. You have a reputation for being the worst kind of playboy."

"I'm glad to know that my own cousin Simone has been stabbing me in the back," Jerry replied, a sarcastic smile on his face. "Listen, yes, I'm not perfect. I did some things that I probably wouldn't do now. But I'm not who I was a few years ago, and you're a very special woman. Don't you think?" He made a step toward her but she stepped back and left the kitchen. She sat on the sofa in the living room, her arms crossed. She wished she knew what she was so upset about. *You're afraid to get hurt,* the voice in her head answered. It was fear that made her react this way. She had to calm down.

"Anyway, I prefer to go back to L.A. while you work here," she said softly. "Knowing you, you're probably going to work night and day. I don't feel like visiting New York by myself. Besides, I promised to take care of Peggy's plants."

Jerry, as if he had perceived the shift in her mood, sat closer to her, and pulling her toward him, kissed the side of her neck. Natalie sighed and rubbed her forehead with both hands. Part of her just wanted to enjoy whatever time they had together. Jerry took one of her hands and kissed the palm.

"I'm going back with you. I can always come back to New York right away."

"No, that would be ridiculous. I can travel alone. How do you think I made it to L.A. in the first place?"

"I don't want you to leave," Jerry said.

"I know," she whispered.

It was probably their last night together. Natalie knew that she had feelings for Jerry. The moments spent with him had been wonderful, but could their story last? She didn't think so.

When they made love that night it had the tenderness and the eagerness of a last time. In her attempt to register every sensation and retain every second of pleasure as if it would never be experienced again, Natalie also felt a certain detachment as if she was watching all of it from above.

Jerry fell asleep, one arm across her waist. Lying on her back, her eyes toward the window, Natalie's thoughts drifted back to Jean-Marc. Jerry had never asked about him. Had he figured out that they had broken up, or did he just think that she had chosen him? She felt ashamed when she thought of Jean-Marc. Simone had suggested that their split was just a fight. Had Natalie used it to give herself permission to have sex with Jerry? The little pit in her stomach seemed to indicate that it could be the truth. What was going on with her? Why was she so confused?

In spite of the humming of the air conditioning unit on the windowsill, Natalie could hear the sensual beat of a slow Cuban song coming from the street. The Caribbean music took her back to the hot sweaty nights in Martinique, when she partied all night with her friends and found herself at dawn drinking coconut water and eating spicy sausages bought from a street vendor. That was before she had gone to study in Paris. Life was quite simple then.

How could she not love Jerry? He was amazing. But staying with him would be a sort of annihilation. She didn't want to lose her identity by depending too much on him, his moods, or worrying about the women he met. He would absorb her and occupy all her thoughts. She would probably become like her mother, who used to start all her sentences with: "Raymond thinks that..." No way!

Maybe she was just afraid to fall too hard for Jerry. Jerry was a great lover, but he wasn't fit for a long-term relationship. And she wasn't over Jean-Marc. In spite of the harsh words exchanged, she missed him. The truth came to her slowly but clearly. Now lying down in another man's arms, she felt guilty toward them both.

CHAPTER SIXTEEN

Natalie rolled down the taxicab's window to let the cool ocean breeze clear her mind. The weather in Los Angeles contrasted sharply with New York's, where the temperature had reached 105 degrees in the morning. Jerry looked sorry to see her leave. They kissed and acted as if they would see each other soon, but she had the feeling that their time together was up.

She tried to convince herself that it was better this way. She had wanted Jerry, they had a short passionate summer fling, but now it was over, and in a week and a half all of this would be a memory. It had felt so good to slow down to observe the world around her and attempt to reproduce it on her sketchpad. Soon enough, she would have to go back to Paris, look for a position in a Parisian hospital, then for the rest of her professional life she'd have to be strong, confident, and all-knowing. Still, the thought of going back to work in a hospital filled her with dread. Squirming in her seat, she tried to think of something else, but this time it didn't work.

A battle was taking place in her mind between a mature voice that told her that it was selfish, childish, and irresponsible to consider not going back to the hospital and a younger but defiant voice that insisted that she had every right to change her path even this late in the game. The L.A. taxicab stopped in front of the familiar white building on Thornton. The cab driver, a chubby man who hadn't said more than three sentences along the way, carried her small luggage to the front of the building and smiled only when she tipped him. Would she call Jerry to let him know that she had landed safely? She decided not. She had to get used to life without a man to check in with.

Natalie found the apartment bathed by the last rays of the sun. The window offered the vision of a grandiose sky with shades of orange, pink and purple tinting the clouds. She dropped her bags to get her cell phone and took three pictures of the sunset, including herself in the last one by extending her right arm in front of her. Then, sitting by the windowsill, she watched the sun go down into the silvery ocean until she saw the last green ray.

That night, she slept twelve hours and dreamed that she was zooming above the ocean on a wooden swing attached to the sky. She still had a smile on her lips when her phone woke her up. She jumped out of the bed to answer it, hoping it was Jerry.

"*C'est toi, ma chérie?*" Ginette's voice was surprisingly close. She seemed relieved to have finally gotten hold of her daughter. She asked so many questions that Natalie felt dizzy. Ginette wanted to know every little detail of her life. Natalie's newfound feeling of freedom was starting to fade until she realized that she didn't have to answer all the questions, so she didn't mention Jerry and the trip to New York. Ginette was still coping with Papa Eugene's recent death. Months after his passing, his children were dumbfounded when they discovered that he had saved 200,000 euros.

"How did he save so much money?" Natalie asked. Her grandfather had worked all his life as a mechanic in a sugar cane manufactory.

"You know how your grandfather loved cockfights. He was

betting a lot and Maman Amelie and he didn't spend much." Papa Eugene had always been secretive about how much money he made betting.

Natalie and Ginette shared a laugh, remembering how nothing was too good for Papa Eugene's roosters, which were shipped in from Spain. He would feed them a special secret diet including corn, oil, and soggy bread, mixed with some mysterious other ingredients, and would train them on his bed in spite of Maman Amelie's protests. Natalie missed her island. It would be good to spend a few months there to reconnect with her roots and enjoy the slower-paced life.

"I'm having a good time here, *maman*," Natalie said, changing the subject. "I don't know if I'm ready to go back to the hospital yet."

"*Ah bon?* You need more vacation? Be careful not to leave Jean-Marc alone too long. He's a good guy, but men will always be men."

Natalie sighed. She didn't want to talk about Jean-Marc. "We broke up," she said.

"What? What happened? He found somebody else? I knew it."

"It's not that. He got upset because he thought I had too much fun without him. He's much too possessive." Natalie wasn't sure she was being fair to Jean-Marc.

"I always thought that you shouldn't leave on a vacation like that by yourself. Too bad you lost him, because good guys like him aren't easy to find. Only last week, I met his mother at Dr. Marcelin's funeral. We talked about you. And she told me that every time he calls her, he mentions you." Ginette seemed quite upset and lamented the loss of Jean-Marc for a while. Natalie didn't even dare imagine how her mother would feel if she also announced that she wanted to take a break from her medical career.

After Ginette hung up, Natalie sat for a while, reflecting on the chaotic turn her life had taken. A knock at the door made her jump. She looked through the peephole, and recognizing Michael's silhouette, cracked the door open.

"Hey girl, you're back!" Michael had a big smile for her.

"Yep! I'm back in one piece, but I'm not dressed. I just spent almost an hour on the phone with my mother."

"Oh! I just wanted to say hi. I'm on my way to the gym." He wore long shorts and a sleeveless t-shirt.

"Okay, I'll see you later then." She gave herself another mental slap when she caught herself admiring Michael's physique. *Enough chaos!*

"I'm going to a seminar tonight, you want to come?" Michael asked, as if it was a sudden inspiration.

"What type of seminar?"

"It's a motivational seminar about taking your destiny in your own hands."

"Sounds like just what I need, but I thought that you already had a tight hold on your destiny."

Michael laughed. "The seminars keep me focused. It's quite easy to fall back into negative thought patterns."

"You are absolutely right. I'd love to go. What time tonight?"

"Seven. I'll pick you up at six!" Michael was already running down the stairs.

Natalie felt more cheerful. She really liked Michael's positive energy. She took a quick shower, put on a white t-shirt and exercise pants, and pushed the table in front of the window.

She got her pencils, pad, and drawing book from the bedroom closet and sat at the table, but after a few minutes she found herself restless.

What was Jerry doing now? Was he in his studio, working? She pictured him vividly, painting the pretty girl from his art show as she sat on some type of red sofa. There was always a red sofa wherever Jerry was painting. She sighed. The phone rang just at that moment, and even though she hoped that it was Jerry, she was happy to recognize her brother's voice. He sounded as clear as if he were in the room.

"*Hey Nat, comment ça va?*" He sounded full of energy.

"*Roger! Je suis contente*, how is everything?"

"Everything is good around here, but what about you? I got your email."

"Oh! You took so long to answer, I forgot about my email." Natalie wondered if she wanted to confide in her brother anymore. "Well, everything is different now," she said with some hesitation. "Jean-Marc dumped me. I hooked up with this artist I told you about, Jerry, but it won't work with him, either..."

"What? Jean-Marc dumped you? That's hard to believe." Roger sounded dumbfounded.

"He didn't want me to come here in the first place. And as I was not staying by the phone to wait for his calls, he got upset. Anyway, it's over."

"Just like that? And then you went out with this Jerry guy? I hope that you're being careful?" Roger was always telling her to be careful, but this time his remark bothered her.

"What are you talking about?" she said guardedly.

"I'm not judging you, Nat. I just want to make sure that you are safe."

"I always play it safe," Natalie replied, trying not to sound angry. It had been a mistake to think that Roger could help in any way.

"I trust you. It's just the big brother thing; don't get mad. Listen, I like Jean-Marc and I'm pretty sure that he loves you. I'm sure that he's waiting for you to call him back."

"He broke up with me. I'm not calling him back. Besides, if he can't accept that I need to be my own person, he's not the one for me. I needed this vacation to figure out what I want to do with my life."

"With your life? I don't understand."

"Roger, I'm not sure that I want to keep working in a hospital. It's too stressful. I need beauty, light, and peace in my life right now. If I had the talent, I'd much rather become an artist." Natalie felt like she was pleading for his understanding.

"Come on, Nat, most artists stress like hell to make ends meet. It's fun at twenty, but when they reach forty or fifty years old and they didn't manage to be Picasso…"

"So you think that I have zero chances to ever become Picasso?" Natalie felt anger from her chest rising to her face. "What if I could have been Picasso but never even tried? You know what they say: in every child there is a Mozart that is murdered."

"You're not a child anymore, and you never expressed the desire to be an artist before. Come on, Natalie, don't you remember how many people wanted to be in your shoes when you got your residency in a prestigious hospital like *Val-Dieu*? You got in because you were a motivated top student." Roger's voice was now indignant. "You are saving lives every day. Isn't that more important that making art? Plus, I had to work my connections to get you a position at *Charité* hospital. I wanted to keep the surprise for when you come back."

As Natalie stayed silent, Roger's voice softened. "Nothing keeps you from taking art classes if you want it, but don't throw away a promising career like yours."

"They want me at *Charité*?" Natalie finally said.

"Yes! They want to see you when you come back."

Natalie sighed and rubbed her temples. "What if... that career doesn't make me happy? I always did what was reasonable. I never had enough time to think about what I really wanted." Natalie felt like she was standing up for herself for the first time. "I'm pretty sure that I don't want to spend my life working in a hospital. I may have to branch out into something else like, acupuncture... I don't know." She imagined Roger listening to her, his mouth wide open in disbelief. "I'm not you, Roger," she continued. "The world needs surgeons like you, but I'd rather help people stay healthy by putting beauty and love in their heart. It's another way to heal."

Roger paused for a while. Natalie could sense his disapproval even in his silence.

"You're old enough to make your own decisions," he finally said. "I'm sorry if you feel like that because you put a lot of time and effort into your studies. Personally, I'm happy with my career choice. There's nothing else that I'd rather do."

"I know, but I'm not you. I have to follow my own path. Can you understand that?" Natalie pleaded.

"Kind of," Roger sighed. "Maybe you just need a longer

break." With that, he hung up.

Natalie paused for a while. It was the first time that she had been so clear, even to herself, about the way she felt. Roger must have been quite surprised. He was probably worrying about her right now, but she felt empowered.

She wished she could talk to someone who could understand her. She tried Simone's home and cell without any success, but she knew that Simone would call back immediately to get the details of the trip with Jerry. He still hadn't called. Natalie didn't want to think anymore; she needed to feel the sun on her skin. She grabbed her purse and ran outside.

CHAPTER SEVENTEEN

Natalie spent almost an hour at the Native American art shop on the boardwalk, wandering from jewels shaped like feathers or totem animals to intriguing objects like the one called a dream catcher. The sound of flutes and drums made her think of wild open spaces, mountains, canyons, deserts, and new possibilities.

When her cell phone rang in her bag she knew it was Simone. She put down the dream catcher and answered the call.

"Hello, girlie, it's me. How was New York?"

"Hey, it's good to hear your voice. New York was great! Where are you?"

"Not very far from you. I had an audition in Santa Monica, so let's have lunch. I want you to tell me everything–I repeat, *everything* about your trip."

Natalie laughed. "Okay for lunch, let's meet at the Boardwalk Café. How long will it take for you to get there?"

"I'll be there in 20 minutes. See you then." Simone's voice was full of anticipation.

Natalie paid for the dream catcher, but stayed in the shop a few more minutes to enjoy the music and the smell of burnt sage, which quieted her mind.

At the restaurant, she chose a seat where she could survey the boardwalk, then removed the dream catcher from its clear plastic bag. The round wooden frame was crisscrossed with strings arranged in a spider web design. Trapped in the web, a small solitary turquoise bead seemed to have lost its way. A tag explained that when you hung the whole thing by your window or your bed, the web caught bad dreams and the bead absorbed them, while good dreams found their way through a hole in the center. Would it be able to catch all of her recurrent surgery nightmares? She remembered her dream last night, which spoke of freedom.

"Oh! You bought a dream catcher!" Simone was standing beside her. She had changed her hair color from blond to copper, and the cascading locks bounced around her face. She wore an elegant gray business suit with high heels and the silk Hermes scarf that Natalie had brought her from Paris. Natalie, in a t-shirt and yoga pants, became conscious that she had run outside without paying any attention to her appearance.

They hugged. Simone sat, making so much noise with her chair that she attracted glances from the other tables.

"You look great!" Natalie exclaimed.

"I had to look professional for my audition," Simone answered.

"How did it go?"

"What can I say? I think I rocked it. The director and producers were there, but I got no feedback from them. Sometimes, I feel like smacking them when they tell me 'thank you for coming, we'll let you know.'" Natalie laughed as Simone pointed to the dream catcher. "I used to have one of those but I lost it."

"Did it work?" Natalie asked.

"Kind of, but dreaming isn't enough for me anymore. Now I'm only interested in action and concrete results."

"Someone famous said 'nothing happens unless first a

dream,'" Natalie said.

"True, but you get tired of dreaming and not seeing it come true. It's time for me to stop dreaming and wake up. Screw dream catchers, give me success catchers!" Simone had raised her voice and a few of the restaurant's patrons looked in her direction.

"I'm sorry, Nat," she said, in a lower tone. "I've become bitchy lately." Natalie remembered Simone's recent breakup with Ted and didn't say anything.

The waiter came to take their orders, but neither of them had looked at the menu. He promised to come back later.

"So how was your trip? Start from the first moment to when Jerry came to pick you up."

"Let's order first," Natalie answered. "We don't want to send that waiter away a second time; the place is starting to fill up." Natalie didn't feel like talking about Jerry right then.

"I hope they have something healthy," Simone said.

The waiter was back before they had time to fully scan the menu. Natalie decided to go for it. "I'll get the breakfast combo with a banana and walnut topping for my waffle, and orange juice."

Simone looked at her in shock.

"Girl, you are so lucky. I can't have anything spicy or greasy right now." She turned to the waiter. "What can you recommend not spicy or greasy?"

"Not much, I'm afraid." The waiter was ruggedly handsome with red hair and freckles. The smirk on his face showed that he wasn't taking his job too seriously. *Probably an actor*, Natalie thought.

Simone frowned. The waiter noticed and became more affable. "The Spinach Omelet is pretty bland. We can make it easy cheese, if you want."

"Okay, let's make it no cheese, and just water with that." Simone closed the menu, looking relieved.

"Why can't you eat spicy or greasy? That doesn't sound like you," Natalie asked when the waiter was gone.

Simone sighed. "I've had heartburn for the past few days. The doctor says it's stress. I guess I was already stressed out, but breaking up with Ted must have triggered it."

"Did you talk to him?" Natalie asked.

"Hell no! And he better avoid me for the rest of his days," Simone said, a threatening look on her face.

"But you said that you were stressed out before the problem with Ted. I know that being an actor isn't easy, but at least you are doing what you chose to do, right? Doesn't that make you feel good about yourself?" Natalie said.

Simone shrugged and didn't answer.

"Right now, I'm thinking of taking a break from hospital life and enrolling into art school. Don't tell me that following your dreams doesn't make you happy either," Natalie continued, almost pleading for an answer.

Simone looked surprised. She shook her head as if Natalie were speaking nonsense.

"Girl, yes, I'm doing what I want to do, but that doesn't mean that everything is rosy. I have to deal with rejection on a daily basis and still stay cheerful and enthusiastic if I want a chance to succeed in this business. I don't know what happy means to you, a permanent state of bliss? Wake up! It doesn't exist. I'm an actress because there's nothing else I want to do. And yes, it's my choice, but that doesn't mean that I don't question it or that I will never get tired of it." Her voice cracked a bit.

"Sometimes I feel so discouraged." She looked like she was about to cry and Natalie felt her own eyes prickling.

"I go to all those auditions feeling like I nailed them," Simone continued. "And I still don't get the job. And then, every once in a while, I don't know why, something breaks and I get hired. The worst part is when I have to ask my parents for help. When that happens I'm mortified." She used the paper napkin on the table to dab under her eyes. "That's when I start to consider my backup plans like marrying an old rich fart, or worst of all, working at the restaurant with my parents. It's really pathetic."

"But you feel good most of the time, right?" Natalie insisted.

Simone struggled a moment with what she was about to say.

"You don't know what I have to go through to live my *dream*." She drew quotes in the air. "There are times where I have to flatter egomaniacs, let them touch my ass and smile, laugh at their stupid jokes, let them think that I'm nothing but an empty head with boobs, go to their freaky parties and come back home nauseated. And what do I have to show for that? You think that it's clichéd, stereotypical actress bullshit, right? This wasn't my dream. Sometimes it looks like a nightmare!"

Natalie had never seen such a stern expression on her friend's face. She stayed silent as the waiter appeared with their food. He placed the plates in front of them and disappeared quickly. Detaching her eyes from Simone's, Natalie looked at the boardwalk. Bicyclists and roller skaters glided gracefully on the bicycle path; almost everyone wore sunglasses and a happy grin. But what hid beyond the masks? How many broken dreams? Lost illusions?

Natalie's eyes went back to Simone who looked absently at her nails. "I know that doing what you love isn't enough to solve all your problems, Sims; I'm not that naïve," Natalie said as she felt a surge of love and compassion for her friend. "But you should still give yourself credit for being on the road toward achieving what *you* have envisioned for yourself," she continued. "You have to be able to enjoy the process, the small victories, and to remember what the original intention is about. At least that's what I think." Natalie's own words gave her a little bit of peace, as if somebody else had said them.

Simone lifted an eyebrow. "Yeah! I guess so," she answered simply, picking up her fork. They ate in silence but the tension was gone.

"You don't have to tell me anything. I know what happened with Jerry," Simone said.

"What do you think happened?"

"I think that you had sex with Jerry, and realized later that it was a mistake."

"I don't regret anything," Natalie answered. "And I don't think that it was a mistake. We had a wonderful time and everything was perfect. It was actually too good." She sighed. "Then we went to his art show, and he seemed to me like a different person to me. There were all these people gravitating around him. And there was one girl in particular. I don't know, but I could feel the chemistry between them. I realized that I didn't want to be in love with him. I didn't want to think about him day and night and worry about other women. So I think that I'll leave it at that; a short-term relationship that'll end as soon as I go back to Paris. On top of it, he had to stay in New York to finish a painting, so I won't get to see him much more. So that's about it."

Simone seemed to listen intently. "Jerry always had a ton of girls ready to give him anything he wanted," she said. "He's great looking, so he gets attention. It's something that anybody in a relationship with him has to get used to, but he has matured, thank God. You know, I don't think that he ever recovered from his father's death. The way he used to go through women could've been an attempt to forget all that, or some kind of way to cheat death. I don't know. His mother wasn't much of a mother to him, and he was a suicidal teenager. Until a few years ago, he was drinking too much and smoking too much pot. Then his mentor and good friend died, and he got sober, but I always wondered how long it would last."

"I see." Natalie now understood Simone's reserve about her going out with Jerry. But she also felt new compassion for him.

"Did you say that you were thinking about enrolling in art school?" Simone asked, observing her friend sharply.

"I did say that." Natalie sighed again. "The truth is that I realized that I don't want to perform gruesome surgeries all the days of my life. I was so caught up in the process I didn't see the price I was paying. It's so stressful, patients are scared, their families are scared, there's no room for mistakes. I'm walking around exhausted all the time, and when I finally go to bed, I have nightmares. You have no idea how much I needed this vacation. Until I came here, I didn't even think that I had a choice to live my life any other way. People like Jerry and you all go for what they want in spite of the obstacles. And I have to tell you, Simone, you have been an inspiration. I admire your strength. It takes guts to take the rejection and keep going at it the way you do. Even if you yell and curse all the way, you still go to that next audition and give it all you have. You'll always be my hero for that, and I'm sure that it'll all pay off one day."

Simone reached out and placed her hand on Natalie's. She looked touched.

"That's weird. I always thought that you enjoyed doing something so important. For me, the courage is doing what you do. You're a doctor. You're out there saving lives; people respect you. Who's the real hero here?" Simone said softly.

"The question is: Am I cut out for it? I'd love to introduce creativity and art into my life," Natalie answered.

"Can't you do both?" Simone asked.

Natalie felt misunderstood again. "Simone, you are turning into my brother. I can probably do both. But If I do that, I'll get sucked up in my old life again, it will just be like starting a new hobby."

"In that case, don't you want to stay in L.A?" Simone said.

"I don't think so. I'll probably go back to Paris for a while and present my thesis just because it's already done, and then enroll in art school there."

"Wow. When did you decide that?"

"It just came to me right now," Natalie chuckled.

"Okay, if you say so. What about Jerry?" Nicole shot back.

"What about him? You were the one telling me not to go out with him," Natalie said, a little defensively.

"I just said that if you go out with him, you'd have to be careful because he is who he is. Now there's no doubt that he's a great guy in many ways." Simone's face showed genuine concern. She looked like the old Simone Natalie loved, and Natalie relaxed a bit.

"I'm going out with Michael tonight," she announced and she laughed at Simone's facial expression: Her eyebrows lifted up to her hairline.

"We are just going to a motivational seminar. Do you want to come, too?"

"I don't think so. I've gone to a lot of those already, and I think I'm motivated enough. I'll save my money and crash early tonight."

Natalie felt grateful that her friendship with Simone had been restored. She insisted on paying the bill and walked Simone to her car.

The sound of Caribbean drums reached their ears. A crowd had gathered around a group of black musicians playing some rousing rhythms. Some of the musicians wore heavy army jackets and looked displaced. It was as if their souls were still wherever they'd come from. Natalie felt one with them. They were all strangers in a vast unknown land, strange and colorful birds that flew away from home.

The music stopped abruptly. The lead drum player, very dark with long dreadlocks, threw his arms up to the sun.

"Venice Beach," he cried out. "As far West as one can go."

Was this why we had left? Natalie wondered. *To go as far West as one could go?* What tribulations, deceptions, and heartbreaks had this man encountered before finding himself right here, unable to go farther, as if all roads ended in Hollywood? How many dreams had washed up on this shore?

Simone's car was parked in front of Jerry's garage just a few blocks from the restaurant.

"That's a good plan," Natalie laughed.

"I do it all the time, especially when I know Jerry's out of town. Okay, I'm out of here. Give a big hug to Michael and…" The sight of a big pearly-white Mercedes, pulling up next to her car interrupted her. At the wheel was a blond woman in her late fifties. Natalie saw a look of recognition on Simone's face.

"Aunt May!" Simone exclaimed.

Natalie studied the lady who must have been Jerry's mother. She remembered the painting with the jazz musician and the face in the pool. So this was Jerry's mother. She looked…rich. The woman smiled to Simone, showing teeth that were too white and too perfect. She stepped out of her car with elegance and stood royally in an off-white silk pantsuit, a long silk scarf floating lightly in the breeze. Natalie cursed herself for the choice of her own clothes. The day she'd left the house in a hurry without paying attention to what she wore had to be the day she would meet Jerry's mother. Even Simone was at her best. *Zut alors*! She cursed silently.

"Helloooo, darling!" Jerry's mother stood in front of her car as if she was being photographed by paparazzi. Simone walked over to her Aunt May and they air kissed twice as May removed her large Chanel sunglasses. Natalie could see where Jerry got his looks. He had inherited his mother's perfectly straight nose and the shape of her eyes, except hers were green. They also had the same square jaws.

"You look fabulous darling, how are you?" Jerry's mother said.

"I'm great, Aunt May, and you look amazing, as always." They complimented each other for a while and Natalie felt completely ignored. She was considering leaving quietly when Simone, finally able to change the conversation, turned toward her.

"Aunt May, this is my friend Natalie; I probably told you about her."

May turned her green eyes toward Natalie and gave her an inquisitive look up and down that made Natalie uncomfortable. May's lips turned downward, revealing that she wasn't impressed.

"Hello there!" Her tone was condescending as she waved the tip of her fingers.

"Nice to meet you," Natalie mumbled, feeling an instant dislike for Jerry's mother. May, probably noticing her accent, looked slightly more interested.

"Have I met you before, dear? You look vaguely familiar." Natalie shrugged but Simone intervened. "Natalie is my friend from Paris. You may have seen photos of her, Aunt May."

"Maybe." Then May's eyes opened a little as if she could finally place Natalie. "You are one of Jerry's models, aren't you?" There was disdain in her voice. The word "model" in May's mouth sounded like a dirty word, and Natalie felt as if she had been insulted. Was she talking about one of Jerry's girlfriend-models, or the models who posed for his paintings? Unless one function encompassed the other. May's eyes sharpened as if she knew that she had stumbled on something.

"You know my son Jerry, right?" she inquired.

"Yes, I know him," Natalie answered shortly. She was in a hurry to escape the scrutiny of her green eyes. May snickered and turned back to Simone. "Well! Is he home? He isn't answering his phone, as usual."

"He's still in New York, Aunt May. He was delayed there,

but he's coming back next week. I was just parked in front of the garage." Why was Simone sounding like a little girl?

"Okay, dear. I guess I'll catch up with him later. I must go now." May gave Simone another air kiss and got in her car, without another look at Natalie. As she disappeared Natalie and Simone stayed silent. Simone was the first one to speak.

"Aunt May is something else. I think that Jerry's remarkably sane, considering. Life was not easy with a mother like that." Simone seemed perplexed.

"How come my face looks familiar to her?" Natalie asked. She still felt the sting of May's words. "I look like one of Jerry's models? What is she talking about?" Natalie was feeling more and more piqued. Simone gave her an apologetic smile.

"I think I showed her pictures from Paris; she probably remembered your face."

"I doubt it; it must be something else."

"Well, you remember telling me about the painting at Bill's, the one that looked like you?" Simone said. "May is a good friend of Bill. She could have seen the painting. By the way, I remembered that I had shown Jerry some photos of you from when I lived in Paris. "

"So that's what happened? I knew there was a logical explanation. But he said that he woke up one day and painted my face out of the blue. What a liar!" Natalie felt more and more indignant by the minute.

Simone shrugged. "It's possible he forgot that he saw it, woke up one day and painted your face. That was during a time when he smoked a lot of pot." She rubbed Natalie's shoulder as if to soothe her.

"Are you defending him now? He implied that there was some type of cosmic meaning to him painting me before we met. It was just a trick to get me."

"I'm not sure that you understand how Jerry's brain works. He was probably sincere. Do you have regrets now?"

Natalie took a sharp breath. She felt confused. "I'm not sure."

"Well, it may be easy to say, but I often tell myself to have no regrets and consider everything like an experience."

"I guess you're right." Natalie tried to smile.

After Simone left, she stood for a moment in front of the building watching the car disappear. Natalie was pensive. Did she have regrets? Jean-Marc came to her mind. She had lost him because of Jerry. She'd made many mistakes, but she had to take responsibility for them and go forward.

She took a deep breath and looked up at the cloudless sky, taking strength in its immensity. All she wanted now was to sit at her table in front of the window and find solace with her pencils and sketchpad.

CHAPTER EIGHTEEN

Natalie sat in front of the open window with her colored pencils and sketchpad, and watched the way the sky and the ocean merged at the horizon in a soft blue line. She got up with regret when the phone rang.

Peggy's voice greeted her on the other end of the line. "Natalie, how have you been?"

"Hey Peggy, good to hear from you." Natalie was truly glad to hear Peggy's voice.

"Same here," Peggy said. "Listen, I was trying to reach Michael, but he's not home and he isn't answering his cell phone. Did you see him?"

"He passed by earlier; he was on his way to the gym. He must still be there."

"Oh!" Peggy sounded disappointed.

"How are things going for you in New York?" Natalie asked. It hadn't even crossed her mind that she could have visited Peggy in New York.

Peggy admitted that she was unhappy about the playwright who kept revising her role, the director who couldn't direct actors, and the other actors, all seasoned pros, concerned only about their own performances. Obviously, she needed an ear.

"At least you are working," Natalie said after Peggy finally spilled everything out. "Imagine all the actresses who would die to be in your shoes right now doing a play in New York City with those renowned actors."

"You're right. It's a very challenging part, and it does have the potential to be my big career break," Peggy said after a pause, her voice recovering a certain calm.

Natalie was always amazed to see how a little bit of encouragement could change someone's attitude toward life. She had seen patients' faces light up and their breathing deepen at the suggestion that they were doing better or that their ailment was curable. Doctors were encouraged not to give their patients false hopes. But what if there wasn't such a thing as a false hope? Circumstances could always get better with the proper mindset.

Natalie's thoughts went back to Jerry's mother. It was almost impossible to imagine her married to an artist with a fluctuating income. *Having lots of money seemed to be as essential to her as breathing*, Natalie thought. But maybe she was being harsh.

And what about Jerry leading her to believe that his painting of someone looking like her was some kind of act of clairvoyance? She wanted to talk to him about that. She got her cell phone from her handbag to call him, and found out that he had left her a voice message. He must have called just as she was meeting his mother. She returned the call without listening to the message.

"Hey love!" His voice was warm and intimate.

"Hey!" Natalie responded, a little guarded. But somehow it felt good to hear his voice.

"I've been trying to reach you; did you get my message?" Jerry asked.

"Yeah! I saw that. You know, I met your mother today."

"You did?" There was some alarm in his voice. A silence followed.

"How did you meet her?"

"I had lunch with Simone on the beach, and she had parked her car in front of your garage. Your mother pulled up as we were leaving."

"You sound pissed off," Jerry said. "Let me guess. She was disagreeable?"

"She seemed to remember me from the painting in Bill's den," Natalie replied. "And then Simone said that she had showed you photos of me a long time ago." Again, there was a short silence.

"What are you saying? I'm not following." Now, Jerry sounded guarded.

"Oh please Jerry, you told me you had a vision of me one morning and that's how you made that painting, but you just remembered a photograph. Of course I didn't believe you, but why did you say that? I thought that you didn't like to play games."

"I wasn't playing a game and I don't remember seeing a photo of you. Your face did come as an inspiration. Why does this matter anyway?"

"Nothing matters except that I didn't believe you then, and I just found out that I was right."

"Nat, what's going on? You're acting so strange. What happened? You left only yesterday morning, and now you sound like a totally different person. Is it because you met my mother? She's a pain, and everybody knows that, but I warned you. You can't take it personally."

"It has nothing to do with meeting your mother; not really.

It's just me. I'm leaving next week and you'll be in New York until next week. So I don't think that our relationship will go any further."

"I guess that you didn't listen to my message. I'll be in L.A. in two days. My agents made a mistake. The city didn't push the date of the center's inauguration. I still have a few people to meet here, but I don't have to stay."

"A mistake?" Natalie wasn't surprised. It was probably something his agent Lou came up with.

"Yeah! Who cares! Listen, we need to talk," Jerry said. "I want you in my life. I told you that. I'll try to find a flight for tomorrow. We'll make it work, babe, don't worry, okay?"

So she would get to see Jerry again. A tremor in her body made her realize that part of her rejoiced wildly. The other part was really confused. She would probably get even more attached to him, and then what?

"I'll be there soon," Jerry insisted, his voice low and tender.

Her body melted at the sound of his voice. It was hard to resist.

"Okay. See you soon," she said, her voice softer.

A fresh breeze lifted the veil curtains of the living room window. Natalie dragged the one comfortable armchair in front of the window and placed her feet on the sill.

Contradictory thoughts rushed through her mind until her head felt heavy. She didn't know what to do, and couldn't articulate what she wanted. The fact that Jerry was coming back to Los Angeles disturbed her relative peace with their short relationship. It would have been easier to go on with her life and use her freedom to find the right direction for herself.

It had gotten chilly, but Natalie had no desire or energy to move. Drifting into a state between sleep and daydream, her body was at rest but her mind couldn't really relax. What was Jean-Marc doing right now? Had he already met another girl?

When she finally got up from the chair, the sun was still high, but she felt cold. She closed the window and went to lie down on the bed.

The sound of the doorbell woke her up. Her head ached and her throat was sore. The bedroom was bathed in the afternoon golden red light. Natalie got up painfully and opened the door. Michael looked freshly showered and wore a dark blue shirt. His smile disappeared when he looked at her.

"Nat, what's going on? You look sick!"

"Sorry, I don't feel so good. You'll have to go without me," Natalie said, her voice weak. Michael pushed his way in.

"What happened?" he asked.

"I just got cold sitting by the window for too long."

"Did you take any medicine?"

"Not yet, I just woke up."

"Let me get you something."

Natalie hesitated. "I don't want you to miss your seminar."

"Don't worry about it," Michael said with authority. "I can always go another time. I'll be right back."

Natalie lay down on the sofa unaware of how much time had gone by before she heard the doorbell again.

"It's open!" she yelled as loud as she could, her headache intensifying from the effort. Michael let himself in and went to the kitchen, where he turned on the light above the stove. He filled a pan with water, lit up the stove and a few minutes later he brought her a cup of a hot yellow liquid smelling of citrus.

"Drink that, it's good for what you have." Natalie was touched by the gesture.

"What is it?" Natalie asked.

"Something for cold and flu. Trust me; it will make you feel better."

Natalie was too tired to investigate further. She sipped the bitter liquid obediently, making a face each time she swallowed. Michael sat down and looked at her with an amused smile. He took the cup as she was about to put it on the floor and placed it on the coffee table.

"What's going on?" he asked in a soothing voice.

"Just the onset of a cold," she answered. "Thank you for the medicine… Can you still make it on time to the seminar?"

Michael ignored her question. "People usually get sick when something isn't going their way. So what is it?" He placed his arm around her shoulders and pulled her closer. "Come on, tell me what's bothering you."

Natalie smiled and relaxed a little bit, her head resting on his shoulder. "I'm not quite sure. I may be depressed because I'm leaving soon, and I still don't have definite answers to my questions."

"What questions?" Michael asked.

"What am I going to do with my life? This vacation made it clear to me that I enjoy being away from my busy life at the hospital, but I have a position waiting for me in Paris. I know that it doesn't make sense, but I don't even know if I can bear going back to the hospital even for one day."

"Because you think that if you go back to it, you'll end up doing it forever?" Michael said.

"Exactly! How do you know that?"

"My parents begged me to get a profession before I started acting. You can always act any time you want, they said, but if it doesn't work you will have a profession to fall back on. That's precisely what I didn't want. If I had a secure job to fall back on, I'd probably never be an actor. It's quite hard to leave the path of security for the unknown."

"Yes, I agree," Natalie said. "But you didn't listen to your parents. I only knew that I wanted to be of service, to help people. But the way I chose to do it doesn't work for me. I've known that subconsciously for a while, but I refused to admit it. When Simone suggested that I should come visit her, I thought that I just wanted some mindless fun, but I realize now that it was more than that. I needed some time alone to think and redirect my life."

"Do you know what other direction you want to take?" he asked, stroking her hair. She could smell his cologne and feel the warmth emanating from his body, and she sensed that he was stirred by their physical closeness. If there were a little bit of physical attraction between them, it had no place in their lives. Natalie extracted herself from Michael's arms as if his question required that she sit up straighter to answer it correctly.

"I would love to go to art school, but is that realistic?" she asked shyly.

"I think that if you have a real desire to do it, you probably have what it takes. You're the only one responsible for your life, you know, and perseverance and hard work are the main ingredients to succeed in any field. In my opinion, the worst thing that can happen to people is to realize at the end of their lives that they didn't live fully, that they just played it safe doing what they thought they were supposed to do, and now it's over. If you want to explore art, by all means do it. I support that one hundred percent." He gave her a big, reassuring smile and she felt grateful.

He took a deep breath and asked, "Where are you at with Jerry?"

Natalie sighed. "I don't know. He was supposed to stay in New York and I thought that I wouldn't see him again. Now he's saying that he's coming back before I leave..." Natalie had meant to be more truthful, but it was hard to talk about Jerry with Michael. "It's not easy." She didn't know for sure what she was referring to.

"No, but nothing is. We all have to overcome our fears." His reflective tone made Natalie curious.

"What fears did you have to overcome?" she asked.

"I was painfully shy in high school. If I had to speak in public or talk to anybody I didn't know, my heart would be racing, I'd break into cold sweats, and I would feel physically ill. It made my life so difficult it became unbearable. I had to do something about it. So I forced myself to do the very things I was terrified of. I took public speaking classes. I enrolled in the church choir. I even went to spoken-word nights and recited poetry even though it made me sick. The more terrifying it was to me, the more I would force myself to do it. I couldn't think of anything less appealing to do than theatre. That's when I decided to take acting classes. I fell in love with acting, and I started to enjoy performing in spite of the fear. It wasn't easy, but it was definitely worth it."

"Wow! Seeing you now, I would never have thought that. You look so confident."

"I am now but there are still some fears I'm working on," he said after some hesitation.

"Like what?"

"Well…" he took a deep breath, "…I never told this girl what a wonderful person she is and how she makes me feel. I think about her all the time. She's the first thing on my mind when I wake up, and my last thought when I go to bed." He had an uneasy laugh. "She has a lot on her mind right now, and most of all I want her to be happy. So I am content with just being her friend." He laughed again nervously and ran his hands on his thighs.

Natalie felt a little pang of envy for whoever Michael was talking about. "She's a lucky girl. You should tell her. I'll be surprised if she rejects you."

Michael chuckled then looked at her with an undisguised yearning in his eyes.

"I'm telling her now."

Natalie opened her mouth, but no sound came out. Michael's confession was a surprise, but it also felt like a gift. His words had touched her even though he seemed embarrassed to have voiced them. She took his hand and looked straight at him. "Thank you for sharing that with me. I have no doubt that if this girl didn't have so much on her mind she would also feel the same for you."

He pulled her close to him again and she closed her eyes, allowing her body to receive his hug. He caressed her hair then kissed it. She pressed herself a little closer and rested in this loving embrace. Burying her face in his neck to avoid his kiss on her lips, she knew she had encouraged this by downplaying her relationship with Jerry, and she felt guilty about it. There was no way she could give into the sexual tension between them. It would be too much of a mess with the unfinished business with Jerry and the thought of

Jean-Marc still lingering in her mind. There was no room in her life for Michael.

They both sighed and kept hugging, and then they relaxed their embrace, Natalie's head still resting on Michael's shoulder. The living room was now plunged in darkness, the only light coming from the kitchen stove and the streetlight through the veil curtains.

"Are you feeling better?" Michael asked.

"Yes. I'm just tired now. I hope you won't get my cold."

"Don't worry about it, I never get anything. Let me take you to bed, sweetie." He got up and bent to scoop up Natalie in his arms, carrying her effortlessly to the bedroom and dropping her gently on the bed. He removed her flip-flops, helped her get under the sheets and tucked her in as if she were a little girl. She felt drowsy and warm.

"Rest now. Call me if you need anything," he said.

She grabbed his hand. "Thank you, Michael. Too bad we missed the empowerment seminar."

"That's okay. We'll go to the Meditation Gardens when you feel better." He kissed her cheek and left. The front door lock clicked behind him. *What a great guy*, she thought as she dozed off. Why did she have to meet him now?

CHAPTER NINETEEN

"Meditation is meant to stop our incessant compulsive thinking, and let us rest and open up to new and unlimited possibilities," Michael said to Natalie. They sat on a ceramic bench by a lake in the Self Realization Gardens in Pacific Palisades. Two swans gracefully glided on the green waters.

"Just the scenery is enough to make me feel renewed," Natalie said. "This place is so serene." Her eyes delighted in the idyllic landscape, waterfalls, luscious trees and fragrant flowerbeds courted by red and blue dragonflies. The gardens were alive with the rustling of running waters, the whispering of the wind in the foliage, and the chirp of birds. Side by side on the small bench, their shoulders touched as they watched the movements of brown ducks, turtles, and red fish in the lake.

Natalie broke the silence. "So how do you meditate?"

"You have to understand first that meditation is the act of going within to a place that exists beyond thoughts. From this silent place, you get insights and inspiration. All you have to do is to observe your breathing and stay present. When thoughts come, you just observe them and let them pass."

"How often do you meditate?" Natalie asked softly.

"Me? Every day, sometimes twice a day."

"That's probably what I need to do to figure out my next course of action," she said, almost to herself. Michael nodded.

Natalie thought of her life in Paris, waking up everyday at

6:30 a.m. and rushing from one activity to another until she finally got back to bed and fell asleep as soon as her head touched the pillow. An existence without time to breathe deeply and reflect wasn't a real one. She wanted much more out of her life. She owed it to herself. And Michael was helping her find the state of mind that would help her in her decision.

They sat by the lake for an hour before they got up and walked back slowly to the parking lot holding hands. An observer would have sworn that they were lovers. Natalie did feel some love for Michael; but it was a platonic feeling with a little bit of physical attraction. Most of all, she was happy to be his friend. He hadn't talked again about his feelings for her, probably because he didn't want to pressure her. And for that also she felt grateful.

She declined his invitation to come to the wardrobe fitting for his upcoming movie; the more she spent time with him, she reasoned, the more she would like him. That begged for trouble. So when he dropped her by the apartment on Thornton, she went straight to the ocean. She sat on her heels, only a few feet from where the waves retreated from the shore. She had brought her sketchbook but hadn't opened it. Instead, she inhaled deeply, filling her lungs with the morning breeze. Thoughts of Martinique and its small beaches of emerald waters bordered by coconut trees came back to her. Her eyes closed, she dove into the warm Caribbean Sea. *Swoosh*... The delicious freshness of the water enveloped her as she listened to the muted sounds from under the sea.

She opened her eyes again to the immense California beach. No coconut trees here. Only palm trees way behind the boardwalk and the dark green waters of Venice Beach. She wasn't even tempted to swim in this cold ocean, but its sight was still majestic.

She could see the Malibu Mountains far on the right and Marina del Rey on the left. Tire tracks were drawn on the sand almost all the way to the water, probably made the beach patrol. She had no choice but to sit on one of those tire tracks, and somehow it spoiled the pleasure. She stretched out her legs and buried her toes in the sand, thinking of the many dreams of love and glory that had been sent to the cosmos from this beach.

She thought of the man she'd just passed on her way to the water. He was sitting on the small pier, his head bowed down, long dreadlocks covering his face. It was not exactly an attitude of victory. A black man decently dressed with clean pants and almost new shoes, he had a duffel bag near him. Natalie wanted to ask him if he was okay but he didn't look sick, just down on his luck. She didn't want to know the demons he had met during the night. Hollywood seemed to be the capital of dreams and nightmares. One day you could be living the dream, there was money in your pocket and the world seemed to go your way; and the next day you could wake up with nothing and end up on the beach like debris washed on the shore. So she passed by, silently asking God to bless this stranger.

She sighed. Now, a week from leaving Los Angeles, she had more questions than when she came. The chill from the wind made her shiver and she zipped up her light jacket.

There were three men in her life, too many by most of the world's standards, and she cared for all three. She admired Jean-Marc's confidence, Jerry's talent, and Michael's strength. But Jean-Marc was also possessive, Jerry fickle, and Michael an actor whose life was shaped by his roles and where they took him. She was not ready for any of them, not before finding her own truth. She felt grateful for her life-changing voyage. It was if some of the city's creative vibe had imprinted itself on her, gifting her with a burning desire for artistic expression. Sitting there, contemplating the silvery ocean, she felt a special connection with this land of dreamers.

Her cell phone rang, interrupting her meditative state. Jerry's number flashed on the little screen.

"Hey gorgeous, what are you doing?"

She smiled at the sound of his voice. "Watching the waves crash on the shore, what about you?"

"I'm watching you watching the waves," he answered. She turned around and saw him sitting on the sand thirty feet behind her. He wore khaki shorts and a white t-shirt, looking relaxed and incredibly handsome. He got up and came toward her with a big smile.

She couldn't help but feel happy to see him. They embraced and exchanged a long kiss before she broke away.

"How did you find me?" she asked.

"I was coming to your place to surprise you and I saw you walking toward the shore."

"I thought you'd be back tomorrow."

"I couldn't wait. I took an earlier flight. Hey, can I see?" He pointed to her sketchbook.

She handed him the sketchbook after some hesitation. "Don't laugh at me." He opened it with a smile of anticipation and looked at the drawings carefully, nodding his approval.

"That's pretty good," he said as he turned the pages. "Hey, that's me! From memory, I like it." After closely examining all the drawings, he returned to a sketch of a little boy making sandcastles.

"This one is my favorite. You captured the concentration of the boy, as if he were doing something really important with a hidden meaning. I like that." He closed the sketchbook and gave it back to her.

"Really? Or are you just being nice?" Natalie asked.

"No, I mean it. You should go for it," he added.

"Go for what?"

"Give it your all; you obviously love it. Don't be afraid. Stick with it."

Natalie's eyes watered, she wasn't sure why. "Thank you, that's very nice of you." It wasn't what she meant to say. She was talking to him as if he were a stranger. Jerry pulled her toward him and looked into her eyes.

"It's not nice, baby. I don't say nice things. It's just the truth. For me, a painting or a drawing is successful if it can communicate an emotion. It's a language. You have to be honest and reveal yourself to arouse emotions through art. And when you do, it works."

They hugged, and in that moment Natalie was happy. But her thoughts somehow went to Michael, and for a moment she struggled with her conflicted emotions. She had wanted to put an end to her story with Jerry, but now that he was there, she felt wonderful in his arms.

Holding hands, they walked back to the boardwalk. As they passed the pier, Natalie noticed that the man with the duffel bag was gone. She mentally sent him more blessings and good will.

That could have been Jerry at some point of his life, sitting on that pier. He had spoken of hard and desperate times. It was difficult to believe now, but she could sense in him some of the passion and enthusiasm of those who have come back from real physical or mental suffering. Jerry's attention was anchored in the moment. He seemed to enjoy life day by day, reminding Natalie of those patients who had survived life-threatening surgeries, or had miraculously recovered their health. For a while they had a new understanding of life. Everything was brighter and they could appreciate the beauty of simple moments and the miracles of living.

At 11 on a Friday morning, it was still early by Venice Beach standards. Joggers and bikers replaced the usual crowd. The day promised to be beautiful: no clouds, no early fog, and a nice breeze. They left the boardwalk and reached the relatively calmer pace of Speedway. Jerry's arm rested on her shoulder, while she'd wrapped hers around his waist. His body felt warm and firm. They walked slowly back to his house. Natalie knew that she would always remember the perfection of the moment.

When Jerry unlocked his front door, the expression on his face as he let her go in first didn't leave much doubt about his immediate intention. He closed the door behind them, pulled her toward him and pinned her arms to the wall in the foyer.

"I missed you so much," he whispered in her ear. Then he kissed her face, her neck, waking up every part of her body until he kneeled in front of her and removed her jeans.

They made passionate love standing up in the hallway, then upstairs in his bedroom. Natalie lost track of time and even forgot her troubles, surrendering to the heat of their lovemaking in a room that seemed suspended in the air, and on a bed from which she could see the sky above.

But hours later, as she sat up in his bed, his head resting on her lap, her hands stroking his hair, she remembered that their time together was short.

"Next Saturday all this will be a souvenir," she sighed.

Jerry looked at her attentively. "You don't really have to go back now, do you?"

"I have to go back, my ticket is not open."

"Baby, you know that's not a problem. We could go back together as soon as I'm done with this painting."

For a moment the thought of Jerry coming to Paris with her made her heart jump with excitement. Then fear crept in. What if he got bored with her tedious life in Paris? Jerry was part of the dream. Paris was the harsh reality. Would their story survive her Parisian daily grind? She didn't want Jerry in Paris, not if she was going back to the hospital. And if she wasn't going back, could she get deeply involved before untangling her own life? Would loving him interfere with the hard choices she knew she had to make for her career? Why was she getting so agitated?

"I have bills to pay, a thesis to present. I cannot extend my stay any longer. Anyway, your life is in New York and L.A., and mine is in Paris and Martinique…" Why was she making all these excuses?

Jerry sat up to look at her straight in the eye. "My life is anywhere I want it to be. I'm a free man. I could meet you in Paris after I deliver my painting, and fly back and forth to New York. I can paint anywhere." Natalie stayed silent. "That's if you want me with you, of course," Jerry added hesitantly.

"Jerry, I don't know if this can work. I may not stay in Paris you know. I may just want to go back to Martinique, and it's much too small for you…"

"Hold on, Natalie! You got it all figured out? You know everything, huh? You even know what's good for me. Why do you have to think so much? What you need to do is to stop taking everything so damn seriously and take it one day at a time. Take it one moment at a time instead of trying to control everything in the future."

Jerry jumped out of bed and got dressed in ten seconds while Natalie looked around for her clothes. As she couldn't find them, she sank deeper into the bed, gathering the sheets around her. She had never seen him upset.

"The way I see it," he said, his forehead knotted with a frown, "nothing is ever written in stone. As far as I'm concerned, the only life worth living is right now. Hell! We don't know if we'll be alive tomorrow, so why spoil a perfectly great moment with bullshit thoughts of fear? No one knows the future. What you are afraid of may never happen anyway. And if it does, why not then enjoy yourself now? If you don't want me in your life, you can just say so. You don't have to invent some crazy story about me keeping you from being who you are…You are what you are now; nobody can make you do anything that you don't agree to do. And I'm certainly not the kind of man who would force anybody into a particular lifestyle. I'm not a basketball player asking his wife to sit through all his matches. All I said is that it doesn't have to end on Saturday. I didn't ask you to live your life my damn way…"

Natalie felt herself blush under his outburst. It was humiliating to be yelled at while naked in a bed. "I need to find my clothes," she said, feeling tears ready to burst out.

Jerry took his head in his hands and sat back on the bed.

"I'm sorry, Nat. I didn't mean to lose my temper."

"I just have to get out of here," Natalie said, her lips pinched so she wouldn't cry. She might deserve to be yelled at, but her only desire right now was to get dressed. She wrapped the sheet around her body and got up to look for her clothes.

"Damn!" Jerry got up, ran down the stairs, and left the house.

CHAPTER TWENTY

Natalie walked down the stairs to find her clothes. Jerry's words still stung because somehow he was right. She did worry too much about the future. But that wasn't something she felt she had total control of. And she didn't want him to yell at her.

She picked up her clothes scattered on the floor, and got dressed in haste, anxious to get out of the house before he came back. His cell phone, left on a small table in the foyer, rang just as she was picking up her beach tote to leave. The phone was propped on the top of a black folder that caught Natalie's interest, and it stopped ringing just as she got closer.

On the folder's cover, the word "Projects" was painted in white. Natalie didn't resist the temptation to open it. It was stuffed with pictures, sketches on paper napkins, envelopes, representing scenes of everyday life, drawings of people eating in restaurants, sitting on a bench, or children at play. Her heart softened when she recognized several drawings of her at the Museum of Modern Art. There were also black and white photos of buildings and street scenes, and a postcard of a very pretty girl with curly golden hair.

Natalie felt a pinch in her stomach as she recognized the snake-haired girl from the opening night in New York, the one who had mysteriously reappeared at the jazz concert. The name printed on the front of the postcard read: "Lizzie Wilson, Actress." On the back there was an address, phone number, and e-mail. The woman reminded Natalie of someone. Her head started to ache as some faint memories made their ways to her conscious thoughts: doors slamming, angry voices, her father and her mother yelling, and then the image of a pretty woman with curly light brown hair coming in focus through the haze of memories. *Who is she? What is she doing in my house?* Natalie saw the woman turn toward her four-year-old self and smile, only one side of her mouth curling up in a devilish smile and her hair bouncing like a thousand little snakes.

Natalie had to sit down on the bare floor, her mouth opened in shock, her head spinning. Lizzie reminded her of the woman her mother had found in her bed that one day Natalie and Ginette came back earlier than expected from a visit to Maman Amélie. Natalie had forgotten the incident. Now she remembered she had thought that the woman with snake hair was a witch who had put a bad spell on her family.

As if a heavy curtain had been pulled up, she could finally see the truth about herself. She already knew that she had trust issues because of her parents' divorce. What she didn't know until now was how deeply it had affected her love life and the choice of her partners. She had kept restricting the access to her heart out of fear. *What am I so afraid of?* Until now she had only selected men she had evaluated as "safe," meaning with whom she could control her feelings. And it explained her heavy resistance to Jerry.

Knowing her motivations didn't remove the fear. It was like being afraid to fly, a visceral fear that defied explanation.

She closed the folder. She wouldn't speculate on the photo of Lizzie. Natalie realized that she had always seen Jerry through the tinted glasses of preconceived ideas. Could she let go of them?

Jerry called just as she was opening the door to Peggy's apartment.

"I shouldn't have left like that. I'm sorry," he said as soon as she picked up.

"I'm sorry too," Natalie said after a pause.

"Let's talk about it over lunch. I'll pick you up in an hour, okay? Be ready." He hung up before she could answer.

Natalie lingered in the shower until her fingers wrinkled, dreading the few chilly seconds between the time she would cut off the soothing warm water and reach for her towel. After blow-drying her hair, she changed the nail polish on her toes to pearly white, put on white trousers with a fitted caramel tunic that matched her sandals, and took extra care with her makeup. Her desire to look good probably came from some type of female self-preservation instinct, or maybe it was her mother's motto coming back to her mind: When you don't feel too good, make sure you look good.

Jerry knocked at the door just as she finished applying a last layer of mascara on her lashes. He looked like he had just showered. His hair, still wet, dripped on his white shirt.

"Hey," he said almost shyly, and then taking the time to look at her, "you look stunning."

"Thank you." She didn't know what to think anymore, except that she had to make an effort to open up and let go of her defenses.

"I'm starving, let's just go right away," Jerry said.

His blue Harley was parked right in front of the building.

"Where are we going?" Natalie remembered the last time she had ridden with Jerry to go to that Mount Olympus party.

"To Malibu."

"Oh!" She hadn't been there yet. It reminded her that she had come to Los Angeles to have fun. In her mind, Malibu was the name of a brand of liquor that she liked, and a place where movie stars lived. She tried to suppress the smile that came to her lips, but Jerry must have noticed since he smiled back expectantly, displaying his dimples. She ignored his smile and climbed up behind him as seriously as if she were going to a business meeting. She wouldn't acknowledge how excited she was by the prospect of the motorcycle trip.

Jerry took Ocean Avenue all the way to the Santa Monica Pier, and then made a left onto Pacific Coast Highway. Natalie was getting used to the stares from both pedestrians and motorists. That was the effect of a Harley-Davidson. She enjoyed the view and the feeling of freedom as they wove through traffic along the coast. White sand on one side, rocky cliffs on the other; the scenery reminded her of the northern West Coast of Martinique in a grander scale. How would Jerry like Martinique? How would it affect his painting? He didn't talk for most of the ride, except to ask her how she felt. She regretted their fight this morning. This could have been such a romantic ride.

The road sometimes gave way to impressive entrances to hidden properties. Jerry made a left turn on a dirt road. It ended on a small beach with a large restaurant flanked by a full parking lot. He gently drove the Harley close to the entrance of the restaurant and parked it by a short fence. The humming and clicking sounds of the motorcycle drew looks of curiosity from customers eating outside under large umbrellas. Some of them smiled and gave a thumbs-up after watching the midnight blue Harley ride by.

"Is it always like that when you drive this motorcycle?" Natalie asked.

"Yep! I'm used to it now."

"You're a little bit of a showoff, aren't you?" Natalie declared.

"You think I like to show off?" Jerry smiled. "I always thought that I didn't like attention, but you could be right. I just love to ride this bike, that's all. I don't mind the looks."

Inside, the restaurant was buzzing. It looked like a Hawaiian fisherman's bar with old black and white photographs of men showing their catch and women in old-fashioned bathing suits. Barrels full of peanuts stood in the waiting area. The crowd consisted of clean-cut, middle-age people, and families with kids playing in the sand–not exactly Jerry's style.

"My friend Harry loved coming here. They have good seafood. And it's a nice walk on the beach. I thought you might like it here."

Natalie nodded her approval. "I like it. It's a great view. I hope that we can find a table outside or near the window."

There was no table available outside, but a pretty waitress with platinum blond locks, blue eyes and a wide smile found them a table by the large window. If it weren't for her black shorts and white polo, the girl would look like an actress from the 1950s. She couldn't keep her eyes off Jerry. She left with their order for drinks after some shameless flirting and simpering.

"Are you going to paint this one, too?" Natalie asked. She regretted it immediately.

Jerry raised an eyebrow and looked at her intensely. "What is that supposed to mean? Why did you say that?"

"I'm sorry! I shouldn't have said that. It was uncalled for." Natalie waved a hand to dismiss the whole thing. She had to change her way of seeing Jerry.

"No, I want to address this. It may have something to do with the fact that you don't want to keep seeing me. You think that I use my painting to pick up girls?"

"I think that you obviously like to paint women."

"So?"

Natalie thought a moment before she offered, "So your interest for one particular woman may not last that long when there are so many beautiful and probably interesting women to know and paint."

As if to prove her point, the waitress came back with their drinks and a huge smile directed only to Jerry. He, however, kept looking at Natalie as if to try to decipher the meaning of her sentence.

"Thank you," Natalie said politely to the waitress.

"You're welcome; are you guys ready to order?"

Jerry ignored her, and then she looked at Natalie with an interrogative look.

"We haven't looked at the menu yet, can you give us a few minutes?" Natalie said.

"Sure." The waitress left with her lips tight.

"Are you suffering from low self-esteem?" Jerry asked.

"Me? I don't think so," Natalie replied.

"So why can't you understand that just because I painted you doesn't mean I want to paint every woman I meet. You obviously have a very negative idea of me. Why? What did I do for you to see me as a womanizer?" Jerry looked straight into her eyes and

Natalie squirmed.

"The fact that so many women compete for your attention makes me uncomfortable. I wonder how long your interest in me will last. I don't want to be making choices that I may regret."

"You're very attractive and I know for a fact that there are plenty of men who want to get to know you. Does it mean that you cannot be trusted?" There was no anger in Jerry's voice this time. He had a point.

"It's not quite the same thing," Natalie protested.

"It's exactly the same thing, Natalie. You're scared, that's all. You have to know that."

She knew it, but she couldn't help but still object. She looked away. "What should I be scared of?"

"I didn't say that you should be scared of anything, but you're scared of living out of the ordinary. You're scared of losing control, you're scared of love, and you're scared of life. I know because I've been there."

Natalie couldn't find anything to say. He was right. She was afraid that when he left her for another woman, which she believed he would do sooner or later, it would hurt too much. And then she would end up wounded like her mother. She remembered her mother after her divorce, curled up in her bed, her eyes empty.

"Look at me, Nat," Jerry said, lifting her chin with his index finger. "What do you see?"

She painfully raised her eyes to meet his and a strange mix of emotions filled her chest.

"I love everything about you," he said softly, "all that you show me and all that you try to hide. You are amazing, and you don't know it, and I love that about you also."

Natalie felt her eyes tearing.

"Hmm! Are you guys ready to order now?" The waitress was standing right there and she must have heard some of their conversation because she was now looking at Natalie with what seemed to be interest tinged with respect.

"Do you want to try their seafood platter?" Jerry asked. "It's really good."

"Sounds great," Nat agreed. The waitress nodded and left quickly.

Jerry looked at Natalie's lips as if he wanted to kiss her.

"Who is Lizzie?" Natalie asked.

Jerry's gaze came back to her eyes. "Why do you ask?"

"When you left this morning I saw your project folder on the table in the foyer and there was her picture in it. I recognized her from your gallery opening and she was all over you."

Jerry sat back in his chair. "So that's what it is. You started to be different that night because of Lizzie?"

"She reminds me of someone from Martinique," Natalie said with some hesitation. She didn't want to sound jealous but she had to know. "I saw her at the opening and I also saw her later at the Blue Light, and after that you were acting strange. I'm very sensitive to mood changes. I could see that something was going on."

"There's nothing going on now, babe," Jerry said with an amused smile. "Lizzie is a model. I met her on my last trip in New York. That was before I met you. She's starting to make some money modeling and she wants to get into acting. She knows that I know a few producers like Bill, and she asked me if I could pass her picture along. That's it. I have no intention of painting her."

"But did you sleep with her?" Natalie said, ignoring his

amusement.

"Not really," Jerry said after a short hesitation.

"Not really? Either you did or you didn't."

"I'm not involved with her and I didn't see her after you left. If it's what you want to know," Jerry said, now sounding mildly exasperated. "You know what, Nat? I'm an artist and I'm in contact with lots of women. I actually like my life the way it is now and I have to stay creative. If you don't trust me at all, we won't make it."

Silence set in between them but the restaurant sounded very noisy with clicking sounds, bits of conversation and children's piercing voices. Something inside her told her that there was much more than he admitted between Lizzie and him. Jerry was saying that he sort of but not really had sex with the girl some time ago. Could she believe him? And did it matter? She'd never been the jealous or possessive type, and she wouldn't allow herself to become that.

"I'm sorry, Jerry. I do have trust issues, you're right about that, but mostly, I'm scared of starting a new relationship now because I need to concentrate on myself. I want to be creative and self-sufficient."

"It's fine to be willing to make changes in your life, Natalie. But the fears, difficulty trusting, all that is bullshit. You need to let that go. Those are excuses. You are already creative and self-sufficient. No one can take that from you, no matter what you do. It's already built-in there." He pointed to her head as if he were aiming a gun.

The waitress chose that moment to bring the huge arrangement of lobster tail, shrimp, and clams and set the platter on the table between them. She managed this time not to stare at either of them. "Enjoy your meal," she said very professionally.

Natalie and Jerry still stared at each other above the plate of seafood, neither of them hungry.

Jerry appeared quite dejected and Natalie felt a pinch of remorse. She had told herself that she valued her freedom more than love, but now she knew that she was just afraid to let herself love Jerry. She tried to imagine never seeing him again and her heart thumped loudly, making breathing difficult.

"What if you break my heart and disappear? It took my mother decades to recover when my father left. I don't want that to happen to me." The room seemed to spin slowly around her. Jerry got up to sit beside her and hugged her.

"We can't always control everything, Nat. You want to be an artist, but real artists don't play it safe. They dive deep into their feelings, even if it hurts and they come back with something beautiful that they can paint on their canvasses or express in their writing or acting or singing. And they never feel sorry because they followed their passions and it's always worth it. This is what life's about. Enjoy it, feel it, accept it. Life's much too precious to play games. When it's over, you don't get a replay."

Jerry's words felt true and they hurt. Tears formed in the corners of Natalie's eyes.

"Don't cry, baby." Jerry took her hand and kissed it. "I want you to be happy."

Suddenly the similarity between Jean-Marc, Michael, and Jerry struck her. They all said the same thing. They loved her and they were ready to let her go if that would make her happy. And there she was with her desire to live fully and passionately, but too afraid to get hurt, to give herself totally to anyone, and to see them as they really were. She loved all three men and she didn't want to hurt any of them.

She was probably making a mess of her makeup, and the thought of her face smeared with mascara stopped the tears. How could she be so shallow? And then she was overtaken by laughter. Jerry smiled affectionately and picked up a shrimp that he dipped into the red sauce.

"Let's eat, this is good stuff."

They ate without making any further reference to their relationship.

"The first time I came here with Harry," Jerry said, "I was so high that I felt as if the food kept popping back on the table as soon as I ate it, forever regenerating. Harry really saved me. If it wasn't for him I could go a day or two without food, only doing drugs and drinking. I refused to get a regular job, so there were some tough days."

"What kind of drugs did you do?" Natalie asked.

"I smoked pot mostly, and I did experiment with cocaine, but I never did any of the hard stuff. No needles. I didn't want to end up like Basquiat or my friend Marcel. My big problem was alcohol."

"What about your mother? Couldn't she help you?"

Jerry sneered. "I'd rather die from starvation than ask her for anything. And at the time, she was married to the most obnoxious rich man she could find."

"That's very hard. Why?"

Jerry sighed. "That's a long story. I used to hate her. Now I actually have compassion for her."

"What happened?"

"I don't feel like talking about it."

"Come on, Jerry, I really want to know. How will I ever get to know you if you don't tell me about you? It's important."

"Why do you want to know?"

"Because I care about you. I want to know you." They had finished eating and the waitress came back to pick up their plates. They ordered mango sorbets for desserts. Jerry still hadn't said a word and Natalie waited for him to speak.

"She killed my father," Jerry finally said in a matter-of-fact tone, looking in the distance. "She didn't use a gun, but she destroyed him slowly, with her words. She filled his brain with poison. She told him that he was a 'has-been' and a 'loser.' The more she pounded him with her venom, the more he drank and used drugs. She wouldn't yell or argue; she would tell him all that trash in the sweetest, almost concerned voice. I saw how she was eating up his confidence. He left several times, but he was concerned for me and he always came back. He loved her; God only knows why. They met when he was touring and she was a hostess in a fancy joint in Chicago. He was doing extremely well then. He was touring with the biggest names of jazz and putting together his own combo. She left Chicago to follow him to New York, and I guess everything was okay until I was accidentally conceived and then he married her. When things didn't turn out the way she expected, she made his life a living hell. I remember the day he died. That was the day after my twelfth birthday." Jerry stopped talking for a moment, deep creases in his forehead.

"My parents weren't living together anymore," he continued, his head bowing down. "We were renting two rooms in a motel in

Hollywood, my mother and I. My mother was working again as a waitress and she was pissed off because her mother in Chicago was sick and couldn't keep me anymore. My father came to get me so I could come live with him. They had an argument. She told him how pathetic he was and how he had ruined his chance to be something. She said some horrible things: how she never loved him, how his touch disgusted her. I was pretending to be asleep in the bed in the other room. And at some point I thought he could've killed her. But he calmed down and came in my room." Jerry stopped and swallowed hard. "He tried to wake me up so I could come with him. But I was upset about the way he'd let her treat him and I had waited for him the whole day. I tensed up and turned away from him. So he patted my back and said that he would come back to get me. They found him dead the next morning in his hotel's pool. He had drowned, but he had an almost a lethal mix of drugs and alcohol in his system." Jerry didn't look at her, but Natalie could see that he was struggling to keep his emotion from showing.

"Jerry, I'm so sorry," she said taking his hand in hers.

"It's the past," Jerry said, squeezing her hand back. "My mother finally found a rich guy who was stupid enough to marry her, and she got the level of luxury she always wanted. I left home as soon as I was old enough. She found me again when my paintings started to sell. I didn't want anything to do with her, but she kept showing up. After I cleaned up my act a few years ago I realized that she was also a victim of her own past. Now I just don't let her affect me that much."

"It's amazing that you became who you are with all that trauma!" Natalie said.

"Oh! I made a lot of mistakes and unfortunately I made other people pay for my mother. I've done things in the past that I'm not proud of. You probably heard about some of it, and that's why you don't trust me. But I changed all that a few years ago when Harry died…"

"Harry's dead?" Natalie exclaimed. "You said that he had moved to London."

"Well, his ashes moved to London with Sid, his boyfriend. Harry was almost a father figure for me. He treated me like a son. And he taught me a lot about painting. Without him, I don't think that I would have reached this level of success. He showed me how to let go and be sincere, especially in my art. When he passed away I had some reflective time. I saw what was still wrong in my life, and I changed a lot of things."

"Like what?"

"I stopped drinking and using drugs, for one thing. That changed my way of life. I'm not the deranged person I used to be." Jerry looked deep into her eyes. "A few years ago, I would have let you go and numbed the pain with drugs and another pretty face. But now I know better. I understand what you're going through. You want freedom; so do I. But don't dive into the trap of avoiding love because you're scared. Freedom then becomes an excuse to stay within your comfort zone. Do you know what I mean? When you're an artist there's no comfortable place if you give it your all. You have to confront your fears and transcend them."

Natalie felt the impulse to reach out to him. She extended her arm and caressed his cheek with the back of her hand. He closed his eyes, seeming to enjoy her touch, but reopened them right away.

"I don't want your pity."

"It's not pity. I..." She wanted to say that she loved him. Jerry looked at her expectantly. The waitress appeared with the bill before she had time to finish her sentence. "Whenever you're ready. Take your time." She smiled to both of them and left quickly.

"I don't want this to affect our lives in a way that either of us has to give up too much," Natalie said.

"Nat, you're trying to play God. Why not take it day by day?"

Natalie smiled. "Okay! Day by day, but I'm leaving next Saturday."

Jerry smiled sadly. "Yes, I know."

They walked on the beach, hand in hand, holding their shoes, until they found a little crest shielding them from the rest of the beachgoers. They sat on the dry sand and watched the waves crash on the shore. And Natalie decided that she would enjoy every instant of this day without thinking about the future.

"I'd like us to be in Martinique right now on my favorite beach," Natalie said.

"I would love that, tell me about it."

"The breeze is warm, the water is turquoise. There are no palm trees, only coconut trees and bushes with heart-shaped leaves. What else? The sky is a different shade of blue; it's crisper and you can see little white clouds moving quickly above. You have been in the Caribbean, you know how it is."

"It looks like you miss it," Jerry said.

"I think there's a part of me that still lives there," Natalie answered.

He looked at her and his eyes softened. "You look so beautiful right now. Stay like that for a minute." He brushed the sand in front of him with his palm to make it flat and used his finger to draw her profile.

"Let me see," Natalie said when his hand stopped moving. "Oh! I wish I could take it home." Her cell phone rang in her handbag. She recognized Simone's number. For a moment she considered calling her back later, but then she remembered that she owed Simone this moment. Without her friend she'd never have met Jerry.

"Hey girl, I need your help," Simone said. "I was shopping on Main and my car let me down, it isn't starting. I have to call a mechanic but I may need a lift home afterwards."

"Sure, right now I'm in Malibu with Jerry…"

"Jerry's back? Girl, I thought you were through with him. Actually, he may be able to help me; he's pretty good with mechanical stuff. Let me talk to him." Natalie handed the phone to Jerry who lifted an eyebrow but took the call.

"Simone, where are you exactly? Okay, we should be there in thirty to forty-five minutes." He handed back the phone to Natalie.

"I guess we have to go rescue my crazy cousin," he said.

Natalie didn't want to leave Malibu yet. She felt alive sitting on the beach with Jerry.

"I wish I could keep that drawing in the sand." She pulled out her cell phone and took a picture of it.

It was one of those rare moments when she felt that they could talk without restraint. Why did Simone's car have to break down right now?

Jerry helped her to her feet and hugged her firmly. She nudged her face in his neck, breathing him in deeply. She always liked his scent, clean and masculine, and with the sun heating his skin he smelled like warm bread. Time seemed suspended for a while, the ocean making a soothing sound that seemed to say *shush* to the crying seagulls. They kissed for the longest time, a passionate, sweet kiss they ended with regret before walking back to the restaurant.

Now there were five Harleys, different in color and style, lined up next to Jerry's. A few middle-aged men in leather motorcycle jackets were sitting at the outside tables and they waved at Jerry.

"That's how I imagined Harley-Davidson owners," Natalie said.

"Only God knows how devious your imagination can be," Jerry said with a mocking voice. Natalie made a move to punch him. He laughed and started the engine. On the way back, Natalie didn't look at the landscape. All she could see was Jerry's copper hands gripping the motorcycle handles. Sometimes they quickly cranked the gear, and bluish veins swelled and disappeared. Those hands created spectacular art; she loved the shape of his square fingers and the way he kept his nails short and clean. His hands suggested strength and inner beauty. She sighed. Only one week left with him.

"Hey guys! Did you have fun in Malibu?" Simone had been waiting at the corner of Main Street and Rose. "Sorry I interrupted your afternoon."

"Don't worry about it," Natalie said as Jerry parked the motorcycle by the curb. She removed her helmet to hug her friend. Simone led them to the nearby parking lot where she had left her car. She gave Jerry the car keys.

"It could be the battery," Jerry said after he tried the key in the ignition to no avail. "We need to get some jumper cables."

"You guys need help?" The red-haired waiter of the Boardwalk Café got out of the car parked beside Simone.

"I have some cables in my trunk," he said.

It took a few minutes to hook up the cables to the battery but with no results. They thanked him for his help and let him go.

"It could be something else, like the alternator," Jerry said. "I have a mechanic friend who can help; he's not too far from here."

Simone blanched. "Oh my God! But it's so late! I have to be in Hollywood at five. I'm never going to make it!"

"I'll get my car and we can drive you there," Jerry said.

"We're never going to make it on time with the afternoon traffic. I called this meeting with my agents, and I insisted that it be today. Now I have to call them to tell I may not make it? Oh crap! And Steve is leaving for New York tomorrow morning." Her face crunched up with worry then suddenly lightened. "Maybe we can beat the traffic with your motorcycle. Jerry, can you drive me there?"

"I don't want to leave Natalie. You're asking me to drive you to your agent so you can get on his case. I don't know about that."

"That's okay, I'll walk home. It's not that far and it's beautiful out." Natalie was secretly pleased that Jerry didn't want to leave her, but they couldn't let Simone down. "I'll see you all a little later."

"Are you sure?" Jerry asked

"Yep! I'll be fine, I swear," Natalie replied.

"Thank you, Nat. I love you," Simone said hugging her.

"See you in a few, baby." Jerry planted a wet kiss on her lips, a look of regret on his face, and cranked the motorcycle while Simone winked at her.

They disappeared, Simone wearing Natalie's helmet. Natalie found herself alone in the parking lot reflecting on what a difference a minute made. Now that she had done the gracious thing she felt short-changed. How did she end up exchanging a great afternoon with Jerry for some solitary hours of shopping?

She sighed. She was already missing him. How was she supposed to just forget about him after next week?

It took Natalie an hour and a half to get back home. Her feet were sore but she was happy with her shopping. On Main Street, she'd bought a pretty white dress and a pair of silver stilettos to go with it. She'd also found presents for her friends in Paris.

The afternoon in Malibu with Jerry had helped her understand him better and erase the bad taste of their fight in the morning. She wanted to enjoy the evening with him. There were so many things that they hadn't done together and so little time left.

CHAPTER TWENTY-ONE

Natalie smiled to her reflection in the mirror. She couldn't wait to show Jerry her new dress. But what was taking him so long?

At 8 o'clock, she turned on the little TV sitting on the dresser in the bedroom and climbed on the bed to watch whatever was on, but she felt restless. Did Simone and Jerry go for a drink afterwards without calling her? That would piss her off.

Then her cell phone finally rang and Simone's number flashed on the little screen.

"Nat, I have some bad news." Natalie's heart sank in her stomach and her arms went limp. "Jerry had a motorcycle accident after he dropped me off, but he's alive."

"Is he hurt badly?" Natalie didn't recognize her own voice. A jab of fear ran through her body. *Please God, no!*

"He lost consciousness for a moment, but he came back. They are about to operate on his leg. I'm at the hospital. I don't know much more." Simone voice turned into sobs.

"What's the name of hospital?"

"Cedars Sinai, behind the Beverly center. Oh gosh! I have to call Aunt May. I'll call you back later."

"I'm on my way," Natalie said. Her hands were shaking. How could that be? She couldn't conceive Jerry unconscious in a hospital bed. She tried to collect her thoughts but only felt panic. *Calm down! Breathe!* Her practical self took charge. What was the quickest route to Cedars Sinai?

Michael would know. Without an extra thought Natalie dialed Michael's cell phone. Then she hung up before he picked up. It wouldn't be right to involve Michael, not after what had happened between them this morning. How could she be so thoughtless? She could get directions online. Her cell phone rung again and it was Michael calling back.

"Hey Nat, did you try to call me? I was just thinking about you," Michael said. Natalie regretted her impulsive phone call. She didn't want to hurt Michael's feelings. But now it was too late.

"Michael, Simone just told me that Jerry had a motorcycle accident, he's in surgery right now. Could you tell me how to get to Cedars Sinai as quickly as possible?"

"Jerry? I thought he was in New York..."

"He came back this morning, unexpectedly." There was a short silence and Natalie's stomach ached.

"I'm sorry to hear that... I mean I'm sorry he had an accident. Listen, I'm just a few minutes away from home. I can just pick you up and drive you there."

"I don't want to bother you..."

"It's okay. I'll be there in less than five minutes. Wait for me downstairs."

The situation was awkward but it was the fastest way to the hospital. Natalie's heart beat erratically. She took a few deep breaths to calm down, and then grabbed her handbag and stormed out the door.

Michael arrived as soon as Natalie stepped outside. She saw

the look of appreciation on his face and she remembered that she was still wearing the dress she had just purchased.

"Any more news?" he asked.

"No, nothing else."

Michael opened the door of the passenger side for her to get in.

"Do you know what happened?" Michael said as they drove off.

"I don't have any details. Simone's car broke down on Main, and she asked Jerry to take her to Hollywood so she could be on time for a meeting with her agents. Jerry was driving his Harley. He had an accident after he dropped her off. Apparently his legs have been injured. I don't know anything else. Simone was in a state of shock."

Michael looked at her as if to try to decipher her feelings, but Natalie had learned not to show her emotions. She had seen many victims of accidents and a part of her was detached, making different diagnostics and prognosis: Broken femurs or tibia healed fairly well, but a fracture of the thighbone was potentially life threatening. She refused to let the worst possible outcome take hold in her mind.

Without Michael she would have lost her way. She didn't pay attention to how they reached the hospital. She just let him lead the way, her mind in a twilight zone, amazed to be back in the familiar setting of a hospital, but this time in a different role. Like in any French hospital, the front desk displayed calm detachment, patients looked worried or scared and everyone wearing scrubs looked busy.

They found the waiting room where Simone sat chewing

her nails, her face distorted with anguish and her eyes rimmed with red. She jumped up when she saw them and ran toward them.

"Nat, Mike, oh my God! I'm glad you're here."

"How's Jerry?" Natalie asked.

"He's still in surgery," Simone replied. "His right femur is broken. He got a concussion, but he was wearing his helmet and they don't think it's serious. The doctor said that all his vital organs are intact."

Natalie breathed deeply, somewhat relieved, but her heart still ached at the thought of Jerry's wounds.

"What happened?" Michael asked putting his arm around Simone's shoulders. She held on to him as if he were a life buoy.

"Oh Mike it's awful. I forced Jerry to drive me to Steve's office because my car broke down. And he was really sweet about it. He went with me and, of course, Steve was happy to talk with him. We had a great meeting. After that Jerry took me home and left. And then I heard a horrible crash." Simone's eyes opened wide as she relived the moment. "Somebody said that the truck ran a red light…"

"That's okay, Simone, you don't have to talk about it," Michael said.

"I feel so guilty. Jerry flew from New York this morning and he was probably tired, and I forced him to take me to that dumb meeting when all he wanted was to stay in Malibu with you, Nat…"

"How could you know? Don't worry, he'll be okay." Natalie hugged Simone while Michael patted her back. It was an awkward moment. Natalie was embarrassed. Now Michael knew that she had spent the afternoon with Jerry. She didn't want him to feel played. She avoided looking at him.

"Simone, dear, how is he?" They all raised their head to see Jerry's mother rush toward them, her manicured hand on her heart. She wore a chic black pantsuit and looked impeccable. Simone got up and walked toward her.

"He's in surgery for his leg. I wasn't allowed to see him. But they say that his life isn't in danger."

May's face expressed relief and she exhaled. At least she looked like she cared about her son. But she didn't acknowledge Natalie or Michael. Before Natalie had time to register the weirdness of the situation, she saw a blond woman in tears running toward the group.

Simone looked surprised "Brenda? How did you hear about it?"

"Amanda called me. Oh Simone, is he okay?" Brenda's face was scrunched into a web of worry lines.

"He's in surgery for his leg, but he'll be okay, dear," May answered, patting Brenda gently on her arm. Tears erupted from Brenda's eyes and she had to sit down on a chair. There was a silence and to Natalie's surprise, May sat down next to her, looking concerned.

"I'm sorry," Brenda finally said. "I can't help it. I love him so much."

Natalie felt herself blushing. She wasn't sure if it was from embarrassment or anger. She had already been embarrassed by May's rudeness. Now, with Brenda's confession, she wanted to crawl into a hole. Jerry had sworn that it was over between them. What was going on? And what about Amanda calling Brenda? They were both Jerry's exes and they were friends? Brenda looked up and attempted a smile.

"Hi, I'm sorry," she said, extending her hand to Natalie. "I'm Brenda, Jerry's fiancée."

Even May looked at her in shock. Simone's jaw dropped. Michael stepped forward.

"Hi, Brenda," he said. "I'm Michael and this is Natalie."

Natalie could do nothing. Her head felt as if it could burst and for a moment she worried about her blood pressure. Brenda didn't seem to notice and rummaged into her handbag to find a tissue.

Simone managed to close her mouth then snickered. "Come on, Brenda! You're not Jerry's fiancée. Who's going to believe that?"

"I'm not asking you to believe anything," Brenda shot back. She flicked her ring finger to Simone and flashed an expensive-looking diamond ring.

Simone looked unfazed. She shrugged. "Bullshit. You probably bought that zircon yourself." Brenda shrugged and dismissed Simone with a gesture of her hand.

Disturbed, Natalie left them to sit far away from Brenda and May. Michael followed her and sat beside her.

"Are you okay?" he said, watching her intently.

"Yes! I'm okay." But she looked toward the door as if she wanted to bolt out.

Simone joined them. "I'm sorry, Nat, Amanda called me and I told her about Jerry's accident, but I had no idea that she would call Brenda. I didn't even know that Brenda was still in town."

Natalie looked at May, now talking with Brenda. "So Jerry and Brenda are engaged?"

"Don't listen to her, Nat. I'm sure she's lying."

Michael looked uncomfortable. "I'm going to get some coffee. You guys want something to drink?"

"I wouldn't mind some tea, thank you, Mike," Simone answered. Natalie declined. They both watched Michael as he went down the hallway.

"I was so happy when Jerry went to that meeting with me," Simone sighed. "I even left there with a script and a new appointment... It's my fault, I'm so selfish."

"It was an accident, Simone. It's not your fault. It could have happened anywhere at any time. Jerry's alive, that's what counts."

"Thanks Nat. I'm glad you're here with me."

Natalie took her hand. It was cold and moist. "I want you to relax, Simone, take a deep breath, stay calm. Jerry will be fine."

Simone shoulders dropped down and she inhaled as instructed. She closed her eyes for two seconds then popped them back open.

"I can't believe Brenda. She must be making an act for you."

"She doesn't know me."

"Amanda must have told her."

"Does Amanda know about Jerry and me?" Natalie asked, looking at Simone with suspicion.

"She saw you guys at Bill's party. She's the one who told me about it."

"Oh..." Natalie remembered Brenda's visit to Jerry that same night and understood that it might not have been a coincidence.

"Jerry's mother seems to like Brenda," Natalie said. It felt like another dismissal from Jerry's mother. She wondered what she was doing there. "I can't stay here any longer. This situation is too weird." She rose.

"Don't leave, Nat." Simone said. "I'm sure that the only person Jerry would want to see is you. He told me that he's in love with you. I've never seen him like this. It made *me* jealous."

"Come on!" Natalie felt her cheeks getting warm.

"It's true. I'm serious. Don't believe Brenda."

"The last thing Jerry needs is a fight over him," Natalie said. "He needs to heal and be at peace. Just tell him that I was here and I'll be back tomorrow to see him."

"Here's Dr. Green!" Simone jumped up and ran toward a surgeon coming down the hallway. Time seemed to stop for a moment. Natalie's heart jumped in her chest then sped up. May and Brenda rushed to join Simone. Michael reappeared at that moment, a Styrofoam cup in both hands.

"The operation went well... he's awake... we have to run more tests ... should be fine."

Natalie was bracing herself for the worst, and now she felt her shoulders relax and the knot in her throat loosen as the surgeon's words sank in. The relief was visible in everyone's posture and Simone's face regained some color. May's eyebrows arched exactly like Jerry's when he was defensive.

"Can we see him?" Simone asked. The surgeon hesitated.

"He's awake but he's still drowsy. You should come back tomorrow morning."

"I'm Jerry's mother. I really need to see him." May flashed her most charming smile and Dr. Green, a stocky man in his forties, turned his tired eyes toward her. He gave her a double take and probably out of weariness, gave in.

"Okay, but only you then."

"I'm his fiancée," Brenda chipped in.

Blood rushed to Natalie's face again. She resisted the impulse to add: *And I'm the woman he slept with this morning.*

"I'm his cousin, I came in with him," Simone said.

"Only for five minutes, then he has to rest."

Brenda and May followed the doctor.

"Give my love to Jerry. I'm going back home," Natalie told Simone, who nodded.

"You sure you don't want to see him?" Michael asked as Natalie turned around to join him. "You could have told the doctor that you are also a surgeon. He probably would have let you in."

"No! That's okay. It's better like this. Let's just go now."

Natalie would've liked to know what was on Michael's mind, but his expression was indecipherable. She shouldn't have involved him, but there was nothing she could do about it now. They walked back to the parking lot in silence.

"Jerry's mother's a trip," Michael said as they drove away.

"That's an understatement," Natalie quipped.

"Last night you said that you didn't know where you were at with Jerry." Michael continued after a pause. "Do you know now?"

Natalie sighed. "Last night I didn't know. And then he came back early and we spent the afternoon together." Natalie couldn't find the words to express her confused state of mind.

"You don't have to say more. I understand." Their eyes locked for a short second before Michael focused again on the road. Natalie felt a surge of appreciation for him. A voice within her suggested that he was probably a better match for her than Jerry.

"I feel bad for my man Jerry," Michael said after a few minutes of silence. "Can you imagine waking up from an operation and having those three nuts waiting around your bed?"

Natalie smiled. She would've liked to say something to exonerate Simone from being one of the three nuts, but Michael kept going.

"I bet you one hundred dollars that Jerry sleeps the whole time they visit. That's what I would do. Act as if I were unconscious."

"I'm sure that he'd want to see his fiancée," Natalie added, unable to resist sarcasm.

"Oh come on! As much as I would love for him to have a fiancée so you could forget about him, I didn't buy it."

"No?"

"Jerry's not the kind to have fiancées, sorry to have to break it to you," Michael said.

"How do you know?" Natalie asked.

"I know him enough for that. I was there a few months ago when Simone tried to convince him to come to one of her agents' engagement party. He told her that engagements were stupid and engagement parties a waste of time."

Natalie tried to collect her thoughts. Michael was trying to make her feel better about the whole thing with Brenda and that was noble of him, but she realized that Jerry could have died tonight and none of this would've mattered. It could all have ended tonight. She was so grateful that he had been spared. It didn't change the fact that she had to leave in a week. She didn't want to live a life revolving around Jerry, no matter if it was in Los Angeles or in New York. She didn't know a soul in New York and she would be a foreigner forever. In France or in Martinique, she was at the top of her game, she understood the subtleties of the language, and she had friends and family. Here she would have to start from scratch. The more she thought about it, the more she knew that Jerry and her would never work.

What about Michael? She got along so well with him, she couldn't ignore that she cared about him. But Michael was an actor. At this stage of his career it was important that he stay free and unattached. Natalie had heard enough of Simone's complaints to understand how focused actors had to be in order to break through. She would be a distraction for Michael. It wouldn't work with him, either.

She was ready to go back to Paris. She started to miss her apartment. She missed Moustique, the neighbor's cat that came to visit her sometimes, and their conversations, her talking and him meowing. The café across the street produced espressos that no coffee shop in Los Angeles would ever duplicate. And what about her fresh baguette and *pain au chocolat* every day from the bakery two doors down?

She pushed back the memories of life in Paris with Jean-Marc and sighed. No love could stay perfect and untouched by domestic concerns, jealousy, time, or the mundane. Sooner or later, the flaws were revealed, passion wore off, and people stayed together because of the memory of beautiful moments they had in the past. She ignored the little voice telling her that it was a rather pessimistic thought. She didn't want to see the day when Jerry stopped loving her. That would hurt. It was safer to end their story at the end of her vacation.

Safe! How could she still use that word when Jerry was recovering from a terrible accident? How selfish of her! A few hours ago, he was full of passion, holding her on the beach, telling her that he loved her. But now he was lying alone in pain, metal pins mending his broken bones. She wanted to be with him, to soothe him and kiss him and reassure him. But she had missed the occasion to be there for him.

What if she went back there tonight and played the doctor card? They might let her see him. She couldn't ask Michael to take her back, but maybe she could go back after he dropped her off.

She came back to the present to realize that a heavy silence now lingered between Michael and her.

"I'm sorry, Michael, I got lost in my thoughts, but thank you so much for coming with me. I'm extremely grateful. I know it was strange for you."

"Don't worry about it. I told you. I'm there for you." Michael said with a reassuring voice.

Natalie smiled sadly. Michael didn't even look upset with her. He had to be disappointed with the turn of events. She admired his self-control. Somewhere, in an alternate universe, he would have been the perfect man for her. Someone who could calm down her angst and help her find her way. She was grateful to have him as a friend. At the same time, a small part of her remembered, with some regret, that he could have been more.

A man was sitting on the steps leading to the front door when Michael and Natalie arrived at the apartment building on Thornton. The night was dark and the meek light above the glass door revealed only a silhouette.

"Who is that?" Natalie asked.

"I don't know. Looks like he's waiting for someone."

The man stood up when he saw the car approaching and

Natalie, alarmed by his presence on their doorsteps at such a late hour, cocked her head to get a good look at him.

"Oh my God," she gasped in shock. "It's Jean-Marc."

CHAPTER TWENTY-TWO

"Who's Jean-Marc? Your ex from Paris?" Michael asked. Natalie could only nod. Michael shook his head. "What a day for you, huh?"

Natalie was panic-stricken. What was Jean-Marc doing here? Had she dreamed that they had broken up? Michael stopped in front of the building and she got out of the car. Jean-Marc came down the stairs, his eyebrows joined into a tight knot. They stood a few feet from each other, their eyes locked. She attempted a smile, but she just felt her lips tremble instead. Her legs wobbled when she stepped forward.

"*Mais oui, c'est moi.* You don't look too happy to see me," Jean-Marc said as he stared at her, a look of reproach on his face.

"It's quite a surprise," Natalie said cautiously. "I don't know what to think."

Jean-Marc eyes detached from hers and tensed up as he looked at Michael getting out of the car.

"*C'est qui ça?*" Jean-Marc asked, his voice somber.

Michael came around the car and planted himself at Natalie's side as if he were ready to protect her. His voice was calm and polite when he addressed Jean-Marc.

"*Bonjour, je m'appelle* Michael," he said in a strong American accent as if he was dusting off the only French sentence he remembered from high school. The look on Jean-Marc's face said that he wanted nothing more than to throw a punch at Michael.

Natalie recovered her presence of mind. "Michael is my friend," she said. "He lives in the same building and gave me a ride back home from the hospital because Simone's cousin had an accident." The two men kept staring at each other, both assuming a guarded stance. Natalie had never seen Jean-Marc look menacing; she was mortified to put both men in such an awkward situation– and Michael twice in one night.

"Thank you, Michael. Don't worry, I'll be fine," she said, turning to him.

"I'm her boyfriend. She's with me now," Jean-Marc said. He almost sounded American. Natalie remembered that he'd spent many months training as a pilot in Miami.

"Ex-boyfriend, from what I've heard," Michael said, his eyes still on Jean-Marc.

Jean-Marc took a step forward. "And I say you can leave now."

Natalie couldn't believe this was happening. She hated this kind of drama. What had happened to her life? She felt brave moving between them. "Please, let's stay civilized. Michael, don't worry about me, I'm perfectly okay. I'm sorry for all this." She turned toward Jean-Marc and pleaded, "Jean-Marc, there's nothing to fight about here. Michael and I are just friends."

Jean-Marc looked at Natalie, then Michael, and took a breath. "I'm sorry, man," he told Michael. "It was a long flight."

"That's okay, man, I understand," Michael answered. Natalie nodded to reassure him that she could handle the situation and she led Jean-Marc inside the building, leaving Michael to park his car.

Jean-Marc only had a small carry-on bag. "Can I come in?" he said. There was sadness and disappointment in his eyes.

Natalie was crushed. Part of her was happy to see him and wanted to hug him and make everything okay, but after the events of the day, his presence was just too much to deal with. And now she would have to confess about Jerry. "Of course," she said. "Let's go upstairs." Her heart heavy, she led the way.

She unlocked the door to the apartment and let Jean-Marc in. He dropped his bag in the foyer beside the door as if he wasn't sure he would stay. Natalie turned on the lights and looked at him.

"How come you're here?" she said. "I thought that you didn't want to see me anymore."

"Your brother called me and he said that you were going through a crisis and that you wanted to quit your career." He stepped toward her but she stepped back and crossed her arms on her chest.

"Does it really surprise you?" she said.

"Yes. Nat, why didn't you tell me?"

Natalie looked straight into Jean-Marc's eyes. "I thought I just needed a vacation. But once I got here, I felt like my life was handed back to me."

"I wasn't there for you," Jean-Marc said, walking to her. "I didn't understand what you were going through. I'm sorry. I want to make it up to you. That's why I'm here." He embraced her. She smelled the faint scent of his cologne and tears filled her eyes. His body felt familiar and strong, and she couldn't help but hug him. *Why did you have to let me go in the first place?*

"I have to go back to Paris tomorrow morning. Come back with me, love. Let's forget all the craziness and let's go back home together," he said in a tender voice.

Natalie felt as if a tennis ball were stuck in her throat, keeping her from articulating a word. Tears rolled down her cheeks. How could she explain to Jean-Marc that too much had happened since his last phone call for them to go back to Paris together?

Jean-Marc covered her face with kisses. "I missed you, Nat. It made me crazy to think that you were meeting other guys. But now I don't care; it's too painful without you. And I found our apartment."

Natalie stepped back and looked at him incredulously. "What?"

"Yes! You remember Eric, the co-pilot I used to work with? He called me yesterday and guess what? He's moving to Germany and he needs someone to take over his lease. It's a two bedroom near Porte d'Orléans. It's bright and spacious. There's a huge kitchen. You'll love it." There was so much hope in his eyes that Natalie wanted to disappear.

"Oh Jean-Marc! How can we act as if nothing ever happened?"

"Why can't we?" he answered a look of incomprehension on his face.

It was more than Natalie could take. She choked, unable to produce another sound.

"I see. There's someone else, right?" The look in Jean-Marc eyes became hard.

"You were so angry. I thought that you didn't want me anymore, I thought... I was devastated at first and I moved on," Natalie said, pleading.

Jean-Marc let out a moan. "It has only been two weeks,

Natalie!"

"I thought it was over between us."

"Is it this damned Michael I met tonight?"

"No."

"You called me Jerry last time. It's him, right?"

Natalie nodded. Jean-Marc seemed to struggle with the information; he stepped back and gave Natalie a wounded look.

"Did you ever love me?" he finally said.

"I still do."

"Why then, Natalie?"

"I also have feelings for him, even though I don't know what's going to happen between him and me."

"And what about us? What about our plans, our life together? Did you think about that when you were screwing this guy?"

Natalie felt offended by his tone of voice. "You don't need to be rude. I can't change the past."

"So you're going to spend a few more days with him and that's it?" Jean-Marc looked incredulous.

"Right now he's in a hospital bed with a broken leg. He had a motorcycle accident," Natalie said, realizing that none of it made sense.

"I don't think I can forgive this, Natalie."

"I'm sorry," Natalie said her head down.

"I'm going back to the airport. I can't stay here. I have to call a cab."

"Stay here until the morning," she pleaded. How could she let him go back like that?

Jean-Marc seemed to ponder what the offer meant.

"Is it over between us?" he asked.

"Yes," she answered. She didn't want to mislead him.

"So I need to go now." Jean-Marc seemed determined.

"Let me drive you then," she offered. There was nothing else she could do.

The atmosphere in the car on the way to the airport was charged with sorrow. The air felt too heavy to breathe. Natalie's eyelids were heavy, her face a mask of sadness. Jean-Marc stayed silent.

"What time is your flight?" Natalie asked.

"It's at 9:30 a.m.," Jean-Marc said after a moment, as if he didn't want to talk to her anymore.

"You're going to wait there for eight hours?"

"I'll hang in the first-class lounge. They have comfortable sofas in there." He looked away.

He had traveled thirteen hours to spend an evening with her and take her back with him. In other circumstances Natalie would have found the gesture so romantic. She wanted to hold him and soothe him, and ask him to forgive her for whatever hurt and disappointment she had created, but the words were stuck in her throat. She was afraid to create more damage.

She stopped in front of the Air France terminal. They looked at each other. She was crying and he looked drained.

"You can still come with me," he finally said.

"I can't."

Jean-Marc had a sad smile. He got out of the car without adding anything.

Natalie watched his tall silhouette disappear into the brightly lit terminal. She knew that she had stayed true to herself and had been honest with her feelings, but she cried all the way back to the apartment.

By the time she reached the building on Thornton she made the decision that she had shed enough tears. When she got back inside, she lay down on the couch and fell asleep in her wrinkled new dress.

CHAPTER TWENTY-THREE

Three days later, Jerry was ready to go home. Natalie had tried to convince him to stay until the hospital officially released him but he'd declared that he wouldn't survive another day at the hospital, so she had no choice but to come pick him up.

He was painfully sitting up on his hospital bed when she came in, and he greeted her with a relieved sigh. The bluish-green bruises on his nose and the cut on his right eyebrow, an injury caused when his sunglasses smashed into his face, made him look like he'd been in a street fight. His fractured right femur had been mended with metal pins, and he had large bluish bruises on his leg and torso. His right thigh was wrapped with rolled gauze to protect the raw flesh underneath. He also had a broken rib.

"Hey gorgeous," he said. "It's good to see you." Natalie could see that even smiling seemed painful. "Dr. Green just came by to convince me to stay another day, but I feel fine now," he continued. She gave him a kiss on the lips and handed him the clothes she had brought for him. He had been moved to a room with an unobstructed view of the city. She noticed white tulips that weren't there the morning before, displayed on the windowsill. According to Simone, his mother had come to see him every day; so had Brenda and plenty of other acquaintances. Natalie had managed to avoid them all by showing up first thing in the morning. She hadn't mentioned Brenda and wouldn't until he felt much better. But it was on the tip of her tongue.

"You should stay a few more days, you know," she said even though she knew it was hopeless. "They are still monitoring your concussion. In Paris, we would have kept you for a minimum of ten days."

Jerry rolled his eyes. "Ten days! I'm glad I'm not in Paris. The worst part is that my mother's delighted to see me stuck in a bed where I can't avoid her, and she comes here every day. I can't take it anymore. I signed a release; I'm free to go."

"Jerry, that's crazy. You should stay at least until tomorrow. You need to stay off your leg and rest."

"Too late," Jerry said with a smug smile. "Now if I don't go they'll probably kick me out. I told them that my girlfriend was a doctor and that she would make sure that everything's healing nicely. I'll come back on Monday for a follow-up."

It took two male nurses to help move Jerry from the hospital wheelchair into Natalie's car. They finally managed to sit him in the backseat, his bad leg stretched out, and his back resting on the door.

Natalie tried her best to avoid bumps in the streets, but through her rearview mirror she could see sweat dripping from his forehead, and he was grimacing. She would have to examine him as soon as they got home. She made a stop at a pharmacy and purchased a stethoscope, thermometer, and blood pressure monitor to check his vital signs. The hospital had already provided him with antibiotics and painkillers.

"I don't know how you do it," Jerry said when she got back to the car. "I can't stand hospitals."

"I can't blame you," Natalie replied.

"But I like it that you're a doctor, a doctor and an artist...That makes you even more special," he said with a little smile.

"I never thought of myself as special. On the contrary," she said, observing his face to detect his level of comfort.

"But you are, believe me," he added softly.

It took a huge effort to get Jerry out of the car. He was pale even though he didn't complain, and his shirt was dappled with sweat. Natalie regretted not dissuading him from leaving the hospital so early. But once they got inside, Jerry relaxed. He took a deep breath, lay down on the sofa and closed his eyes. Natalie propped up his broken leg with pillows to keep it elevated.

He would have to sleep downstairs in the living room. Climbing up stairs was out of question in his present state. Fortunately, the sofa downstairs could be converted into a bed and there was a second bathroom downstairs.

After she checked Jerry's vitals, Natalie moved some clothes and toiletries downstairs.

"I feel bad to make you work so much," Jerry said, looking at her busying herself.

"Don't worry about it, I'm happy to help you," Natalie said with a reassuring smile.

"Thank you, babe. I don't know what I'd do without you," he said gently.

"Well! I'm sure that Brenda would be very happy to do the same." The minute she said it, she regretted it. She didn't want to mention Brenda, at least not yet.

"What was that about?" Jerry said, looking like he had a sudden headache.

"Sorry, it came out before I could stop myself. I met Brenda

in the waiting room the day of the accident and she introduced herself as your fiancée…"

"What? That's hard to believe."

"Ask Simone or Michael," Natalie said, shrugging.

"I don't think that you're lying, I just can't believe it. Why
would she say something like that?" Jerry looked puzzled.

"You tell me."

"Brenda came to visit me but as a friend. She was concerned
but that's it. I don't understand."

"It could be that she has a double personality, or maybe she
had sort of memory loss and forgot that you broke up?" Natalie
said.

Jerry gave Natalie a sideways glance. "Even if she forgot, we
were never engaged. I don't believe in engagements. If you want to
get married you just do it. She knows what I think about it."

Natalie couldn't let go of the sarcasm. "Okay, let's say that it
was temporary insanity then," she added.

Jerry shook his head. "Sorry you had to deal with that," he
said.

"That didn't bother me too much, actually. What bothered me
more was the way your mother ignored me. She didn't even say
hello."

"I can't defend her," Jerry answered. "She's not the sanest
person." He became pensive as if he was trying to imagine the
scene. "I'm sorry about all that. That must have been hard for
you."

Natalie didn't want to keep talking about Brenda and May
and she wanted to give al her attention to Jerry getting better. "The
most important thing is that you recover quickly," she said. "It

hurts me to see you with all those bruises and wounds."

"Don't worry. I'll be fine. I'll miss my motorcycle, though," Jerry said with a sad smile.

"Won't you be a little apprehensive on a motorcycle from now on?" Natalie asked, feeling uneasy at the idea of him riding a motorcycle again.

Jerry looked at her and patted the place beside him, motioning for her to sit closer. She came near and sat down beside him.

"Are you worrying about me, babe?" he said, wrapping an arm around her.

"I wouldn't want anything bad to happen to you."

She gave him a light kiss on the lips, but he held her close and gave her a real kiss. Natalie moved closer but her weight on his chest made him cry out in pain.

"Oh! I'm so sorry," she said. "You need to rest now."

"There are some things we can do that won't hurt," he said, looking hopeful.

"Get some rest. Doctor's orders," she said with a wink. She went to the kitchen and opened the fridge. "I have to get some groceries," she yelled from the kitchen.

"You sure? You don't need to do that. We can order some food," he yelled back.

"You need the basics: bread, milk, cereals, eggs, and some TV dinners would help."

"My wallet is in my jacket pocket," he said.

"Don't worry about it!" she called back.

"Natalie! Don't forget to take your key," she heard him say as she was about to close the door. *Your key!* She officially had a key to his house.

"I got it." She came back just to give him another kiss.

"I love you," he said softly.

Moi aussi, je t'aime, she thought. He closed his eyes as she caressed his face. "Try to get some sleep."

When Natalie came back with groceries and sandwiches, Jerry was on the phone. She overheard him saying that it could be a month before he could make it back to New York. The accident would obviously change his plans but it could have been worse. As she put the groceries away he hung up but the phone rang again.

"Yeah! I'm fine," she heard him say. "I decided to go home earlier. I couldn't stand the hospital anymore... Sorry you came to the hospital for nothing. No, I don't need you there. Natalie's here with me... You met her at the hospital the day of the accident. No, he's a friend also. Yes! I told you about her. She's a physician. I'll be fine. Thank you for your concern, don't worry. I'm okay. When are you moving back to New York? Oh! No, I won't be able to go back anytime soon. Yeah sure, see you later... So do I. Bye."

No doubt in Natalie's mind, it was Brenda. The phone didn't stop ringing and Jerry talked to different friends checking on him.

Natalie brought him a sandwich and a glass of apple juice while he was on the phone and mouthed that she had to go home and would be back later.

He didn't seem happy to see her go but she left anyway.

Natalie left Jerry's house and drove back to her apartment. She didn't want to sit and listen to Jerry's conversations, and there was no space to retreat to. She needed a moment by herself to exhale.

She remembered that Jean-Marc had hoped they could live together and the memory of his impromptu trip to Los Angeles brought back new tears to her eyes, but she forbade herself to cry anymore. She hadn't wanted to hurt Jean-Marc but she had done it anyway. Now she had to let it go and try to forgive herself.

Her thoughts came back to Jerry. It would be wise to find a nurse to take care of him later.

She couldn't believe that by the end of the week she would be back in Paris alone and all of this would be a memory. The thought saddened her but she promised herself that it would be different now. She would make it her duty to finally enjoy what Paris had to offer.

A feeling of peace came upon her as she opened the door of her sublet. Peggy's green plants seemed to quiver and welcome her.

That's when Michael called her. He had checked on her the day after Jean-Marc left, but she hadn't seen him the last few days.

"Natalie, how are you?"

She smiled at the sound of his voice. "I'm good, thank you. Jerry left the hospital this morning and I drove him back home."

"Already?" Michael asked.

"He didn't want to stay any longer so he had to sign a release. He'll need some special care at home," Natalie answered.

"I guess that you'll be the caretaker?" There was a hint of sarcasm in Michael's voice.

"Yes. But not for long though," Natalie said. "I'm leaving Saturday."

"You aren't postponing your trip?" Michael sounded genuinely surprised.

"I can't really afford to," Natalie said. "I've been away a long time and I have things to take care of in Paris."

"Well, I'm leaving tonight for Thailand. I wanted to make sure I said goodbye before I leave."

"Oh no! I'll miss you, Michael."

"I'll miss you even more. What about coming upstairs for a drink?"

"Okay, I'll be right up."

Natalie had never seen Michael's apartment. He'd always come down to hers. She had been curious about it but not enough to come up.

A minute later she was knocking at his door. He wore jeans and a white shirt and there was not one hair left on his face. His head and face were completely shaved. He laughed at Natalie's surprised look.

"The character I'll be playing is bald," he said. "Besides, that will be the easiest thing to maintain in Thailand. I don't think they have any barbers who can hook up a brother with a haircut over there, and sometimes set hairdressers don't know what to do with my hair. I'm the only black man in the movie."

"Well, I hope that you won't have to be the first one to die. That's always what happens to lone black guys in those action movies," Natalie teased.

Michael had a big laugh. "I don't have to die at all. That's what I like the most with the movie. Actually, I'm one of the only two characters who survive."

"Wonderful! That means you're going to be a star. Let me know when you meet the hot superstar guys." Natalie winked at him.

"Why would I do such a thing?" Michael answered seriously, his eyebrows raised.

"Oh come on! You can hook up a girl, no?" she said, laughing. "Anyway, you look good bald."

"There you go. You can come in." Natalie stepped in the living room and looked around. The place seemed a little smaller than Peggy's apartment, but it could be because of the huge TV dominating the living room. The windows opened onto the same wondrous view on the beach, only from a higher angle. An impressive collection of well-organized DVDs rested on the shelves covering the walls.

"Now I know how you spend your lonely evenings," Natalie said.

"That's right. It's part of my research," Michael answered. "I do spend a lot of time watching movies."

"It seems to work for you," Natalie added with an appreciative look. She sat on a dark gray sofa by the window.

"Are you packed?" she asked.

"Pretty much, I just have one bag. I always travel light. If I need something I just buy it."

"I envy you. It must be exciting to go to such an unusual destination for a movie," she said.

"It's not like I'm going there for a vacation. But yeah! It's exciting."

There was a pause and Michael seemed to be traveling in his mind. Natalie had vivid images of him running through a muddy jungle in army fatigues, a machine gun in each hand like a black Rambo. The thought made her smile.

"Natalie, there's something I want to tell you." He paused and Natalie waited for him to keep going. "You should be proud of yourself for everything you've accomplished," he said, taking the time to think through his words. "I was impressed when I met you, to know that you were a surgeon. You can add drawing to your talents, but don't underestimate your profession. Hospitals need caring physicians like you."

Natalie was touched by Michael's concern.

"Thank you, Mike. I will take a break from the hospital, though. All that suffering, all that misery... it's really hard!"

"I know," Michael said in a soft voice. "Just be assured that you alleviate a lot of that suffering. You are a blessing to all those people because you care about them. Give yourself more credit." Michael put an arm around her and pulled her to him. "Just make sure that whatever you do isn't a reaction but that it comes from deep down. I really want you to be happy."

Natalie threw her arms around his neck in an impulsive embrace. "I will miss you!"

"I'll miss you too, Nat." They hugged for a while.

"Let me give you all my numbers in Paris, and my mother's number in Martinique so you will always know where to reach me."

They exchanged numbers and even though everything was said, Natalie still couldn't leave.

"I may want that drink after all," she said. Michael picked up two beers from his fridge and they sat in front of the open window sipping slowly. Natalie noticed a guitar resting in a corner of the room.

"Can you play the guitar?" she asked.

"A little bit," he answered.

"Oh please, can you play something for me?"

Michael sat on a chair while Natalie stayed on the sofa by

the window. He struck a few chords, and then played a mellow ballad that she had never heard before. Natalie listened, eyes half closed. Was it the beer or the melody? It was a magical moment, where her heart seemed to expand and overflow with love. Like in the fairy tale of the magic cauldron, her love for Jean-Marc, Jerry, and Michael, seemed to spill all over the room, through the window, all the way to the ocean.

When Michael stopped she emerged from a sweet dream-like state.

"That was lovely." The sun had begun to descend and the daylight had dimmed. She got up. "I should go now. Thank you for everything," she said.

He got up, too, and they embraced once more. She could feel his body in full contact with hers. She responded to his embrace with the same loving energy.

"It was my pleasure," he said. The longing and regret in his voice were obvious.

Natalie disengaged herself from his arms, but they still held hands.

"Let's set up a date," she said. "If you are not shooting a movie or living a beautiful love story and if we are both free, let's say a year from now, we can meet… on the Eiffel Tower."

Michael laughed. "Dr. Dorel, I think that you watch too many movies."

"Oh come on! Let's do it. It'll be fun!"

"Yeah, but in the movies there's usually only one who shows up and gets brokenhearted. And that probably will be me."

"Let's do even better. Valentine's Day on the Eiffel Tower, no matter if we are free or not."

"Hmmm! I don't know." Michael was still holding her hands as he looked at her, and the desire that she could read in his eyes moved her deeply.

He pulled her closer and bent to kiss her cheek, close to her lips.

"I love you more than you'll ever know," he said.

Natalie didn't know what to say. The emotion in his voice weakened her. Her legs felt wobbly. She felt the temptation to give in and make him happy.

Michael seemed to sense her turmoil. "Stay with me," he pleaded as he kissed her face and her neck.

"You're leaving tonight."

"Yeah! No! I mean… I can miss that plane."

"No, you can't."

"For you, I'll miss it," he whispered.

"But I would hate myself for that, and there's Jerry, you know that."

"Do you love him?" Michael took a step away from her, looking deep in her eyes.

She nodded. Her love for Jerry was a feeling she couldn't explain or do anything about. A peculiar thought came to her mind. She remembered reading about people in China called the Na. In this society, marriage didn't exist because men and women were free to choose as many partners that they wanted without being judged in any way. If she were a Na from China there would be no problem. She would have three men to love.

"But you're going back to Paris alone?" Michael insisted, interrupting her reverie.

"Yes, I'm going back to Paris alone and I don't know what

will happen in the future."

"Give me a real kiss then," he pleaded.

Natalie hesitated. She was tempted. Part of her wanted to know how it would feel to kiss him. The other part didn't want to get confused.

"If you don't kiss me..."

"What if I don't?"

He sighed. "I might die."

Natalie smiled, remembering that Michael was an actor. But she felt sorry for both of them. There was no doubt in her mind that she could love Michael, but that love never found its timing. Jean-Marc, Jerry, and now Michael? The joke was that she was ending up with none of them.

Michael saw her eyes misting. "I don't want you to cry." He kissed her face but waves of sadness engulfed her.

"It's okay. It's okay... I'm sorry. I put you in a hard position..." Michael was now comforting her, caressing her hair. If she stayed one minute longer she would probably end up making a bigger mess of their lives.

"Maybe in another life," she said, extracting herself out of his arms. She left without looking back.

CHAPTER TWENTY-FOUR

Natalie didn't go to her apartment for fear that Michael would come knocking at her door. She ran down the stairs and left the building. The sun was setting its magical glow on the board-walk. The crowd was now dispersing, children shivering in their wet bathing suits, dragging their feet to follow their parents. Only those belonging to the area still hung around. Her steps took her back to Jerry's house. She took a deep breath and opened the door to find him sitting on the sofa, his injured leg stretched in front of him, a large block of paper propped on his bent good leg. He was working furiously with charcoal pencils, putting them down some-times to use his fingers. He looked so focused that Natalie considered closing the door again to let him work. But he heard her and without lifting his head, greeted her.

"Hey, baby! I thought you'd be back earlier."

"You're working, I can come back later."

"No, stay! I'm almost done anyway." He stopped and looked at her. "If you don't mind, I mean."

"No, of course not. Take your time. I'm going upstairs," she said.

He returned to his work and she walked up the spiral stair-case. She splashed cool water on her face then lay down on the bed. When she felt calmer she got out of bed and went down to the kitchen to prepare dinner. It took her only a few minutes to fix a colorful salad with the roasted chicken and vegetables she had purchased earlier. She also heated and added some spices to a ready-made lentil soup. Nothing fancy but it should do.

Jerry had stopped drawing. His eyes closed, he was now lying down on the sofa facing her. He looked pale. Natalie sat next to him and checked his pulse. It was a little fast but not alarming. Jerry opened his eyes.

"Hi, doc," he said with a faint smile.

"How are you feeling?" she asked.

"Tired and sore, but I'm okay."

"Did you eat the sandwich I left you?" she inquired.

"Yes ma'am."

"What about your pills? You were supposed to take the anti-inflammatory and the antibiotics with your meal."

"Oops!"

Natalie sighed, "Jerry, if you don't want to go back to the hospital, you have to follow the prescription to the letter. You're not strong enough to skip anything. I also think that you should rest more. It's too early for all that work. Just lie down for a few days; keep your leg up. Let me check your blood pressure and temperature and I will clean up the wounds."

"Can't I just take the medicine now?"

"You can't double up the doses. That would be dangerous. But you have to take the normal dose for tonight with your dinner."

"Yes, doctor. Do I get candy if I'm good?" Jerry asked in a mock little kid voice.

"You haven't been too good. No candy for you today."

"I'll be good, I promise."

Natalie smiled. She checked his temperature with the oral thermometer she'd purchased earlier. His temperature and blood pressure were normal and it reassured her. There were no signs of swelling or abnormal erythema. She helped him out of his pants and slowly removed the dressing. Most of the skin on his thigh was gone and she couldn't help but wince at the sight of the long scar from his surgery. At least there was no sign of infection and the wound looked neatly closed. In a flash, she saw his bruised body lifeless in the hospital morgue. Her eyes widened and she stifled a scream.

His life had been spared. There was still a soul in this body and she felt grateful to the whole universe. After she was done, Natalie went back to the kitchen.

"I fixed some soup and a chicken salad; you should eat now," she announced.

"Heaven," Jerry said with a smile, but he looked tired.

Natalie brought him his dinner on a tray and he sat up to eat.

"You did all that for me?" He looked touched. "I don't remember anybody ever cooking for me."

"Are you serious?" Natalie asked, surprised.

"Very serious. None of my previous relationships were the cooking type."

"I don't think that I'm the cooking type either, but I don't mind. Besides, I don't call this cooking."

"Baby, don't take it the wrong way," Jerry said. "I'm very thankful and appreciative. It smells good." He took a sip of the soup. "It tastes good, too, thank you." He ate with good appetite, but when the last bite on his plate was gone, he turned reflective.

"I feel that I have imposed on you. I didn't realize how much work it would be…" Jerry said while she returned the trays to the kitchen.

"It's nothing. I'm happy to do it, believe me. But we'll have to find you a nurse who will take care of you when I leave." It obviously pleased him to be nurtured, but at the same time he felt shy about it. That touched Natalie. She could see the boy in him who didn't get enough love.

"Nat, I appreciate all that you have done today, but I don't want you to spend your last days in L.A. stuck taking care of me. I just want to enjoy your presence when you feel like it. I've made arrangements for a nurse to come twice a day. The housekeeper will take care of the errands."

"Is this nurse certified? Does she have experience?" Natalie asked.

"Oh yeah! I met her after I had a car accident when she worked at St. John Hospital. That was just before I went into rehab. Now she only makes house calls." Jerry said that in a matter-of-fact tone, as if it was the most banal story one could hear. Natalie raised her eyebrows. Why did he stay in touch with this nurse? She thought of asking him if she was an ex-girlfriend, and then realized that she didn't want to know. He changed the subject.

"I love to see you being your doctor self. That turns me on." There was a spark of desire in his eyes. She took his hand and pressed it to her cheek. His hands had sustained only minor scratches and that too was a miracle.

"I'm not going to be a surgeon anymore," she said as if speaking to herself.

Jerry paused shortly, his eyes full of surprise. "Are you

sure? You don't want to make a decision you may regret later."

Natalie shrugged. "I don't think I'll regret it," she said. But she wasn't so sure.

"Oh! Baby, I'm sorry. Do I have something to do with it?"

"In a sense, yes. You make me want to live my passions."

"That's all right then." He squeezed her hand and kissed it but he looked strained and she noticed dark bluish circles under his eyes.

"Are you still going to practice medicine?"

"I'll have to find another way to practice. But we'll talk about it another time. You should rest now."

"Only if you lie down with me," he said closing his eyes.

"I should go back home," Natalie answered. "I haven't brought anything to stay overnight."

"Please stay!" he pleaded. "I have an extra new toothbrush. I need you with me tonight."

Natalie obeyed and lay down by his side. They held hands until his breathing became regular, then Natalie freed her hand and got up to turn off the lamps. She wondered if she shouldn't sleep upstairs in his bed, which would be more comfortable for both of them. But what if he needed something during the night? Besides, there would be enough solitary nights for her in Paris.

She went back to the sofa, removed her jeans and slid beside Jerry under the light cover.

"Hospitals would get a better rap if all physicians were like you. Too bad they're losing you." Natalie was brushing her teeth when Jerry, in much better shape than the day before, made this remark.

She spat out the toothpaste and rinsed her mouth. Jerry

stood by the bathroom door, a crutch in each hand.

"That's what Michael said," she sighed.

"What Michael?" Jerry asked.

"Michael, Simone's friend." Natalie answered.

"The actor? I didn't know that you knew him that well," Jerry said, looking surprised.

"He's the one that hooked me up with Peggy's apartment," Natalie replied. "He lives upstairs, remember?"

"Yes, but how come you talked to him about it before you talked to me?" Jerry insisted.

"We're good friends. You should know what that means; you have hundreds of women friends."

"Yeah! My best friends are women," Jerry admitted.

"Well, I have also a few good male friends and Michael's one of them," Natalie said.   "I don't know why I don't like the sound of that," Jerry said, looking at her as if he were trying to read her mind.

"Probably because you have double standards," Natalie answered, amused.

"I just don't see how any straight single man could resist you. So I would have to assume that Michael is somehow interested in you in a more than friendly way."

Natalie looked at Jerry, her hands on her hips.

"You understand exactly how I feel then, when I have doubts about all your female friends."

"To be honest, some of them are ex-girlfriends. But there's no more sexual attraction between us."

"So you say," Natalie remarked.

"Okay. You don't believe me. Now I have a question."

Jerry's tone became more serious. "Is there something more than friendship going on between you and Michael? I just want to know."

Natalie hesitated. "Not really," she finally said.

"Not really? But a little bit?" Jerry asked.

Natalie sighed. "We're just friends. Let's leave it at that."

Jerry looked at her, unconvinced, but he didn't insist. A silence followed. Natalie wasn't sure what to make of their exchange. Did it mean Jerry felt as insecure about their relationship as she did? The conversation was moving on slippery terrain.

"If you're not going back to the hospital why don't you just stay in L.A. then?" Jerry said.

Natalie knew that the delicate subject of the future of their relationship would come back up. She thought about what awaited her in Paris. Her longsuffering Ficus tree that Madame Dos Santos, the "concierge" of the building, had promised to water weekly, visits from Moustique the cat that had adopted her, bills to pay and her part-time job at the clinic. She had to go back and deal with all that. She didn't know how she would handle her life after quitting the hospital.

What would life be like in Paris with Jerry? She just couldn't imagine him in her little one-bedroom apartment. They would have to move somewhere else. Paris would be a whole different experience with Jerry and probably a very interesting one. For a second she saw herself walking along the *Quais de la Seine* or visiting *le musée du Louvres* with Jerry. But she shook up the image; something was wrong with the idea, as if she was betraying Jean-Marc again. She couldn't let Jerry into her life before she set her own priorities. Plus it was hard to reconcile such different worlds.

How long would Jerry last with her in Paris?

"I can't stay any longer, Jerry." She recited to him the list of things she had to take care of but her reasons didn't seem strong even to her own ears and it bothered her.

"Sometimes your views seem so limited. You're no fun, you know that?" Jerry's tone had an edge that surprised her. "Just be honest with yourself and if you don't want this relationship, just say so. You always have excuses for every suggestion I make. You know what? You are not honest with me, or even with yourself."

"What do you mean, I'm not honest?" she said defiantly, her hands on her hips.

"You want to fly but you are afraid to jump. You can't even love without setting up conditions and restrictions. You wouldn't be able to recognize true love if it jumped in your face. You're afraid of everything. You're such a coward!" Jerry spat the last words, and he had an angry expression on his face.

His last sentence resonated in her head, making her feel small and vulnerable. Her eyes stung but she refused to cry. She stomached the blow and felt a little disoriented. Jerry was frowning and his lips made a hard line, but his expression softened when he saw that she was hit hard.

She tried to speak but couldn't articulate a sound. She was afraid and ashamed that he had seen through her. Then anger took over. Natalie dropped her toothbrush in the garbage can and, passing Jerry, walked toward the front door. She picked up her handbag and, on the way out, removed his key from her key ring and left it on the kitchen counter.

She looked back and saw him still standing in the same place with his crutches, his head down. Her anger deflated but she had already made her decision.

"Goodbye, Jerry," she said softly, almost to herself as she closed the front door behind her.

Natalie followed the boardwalk to go back home. A thin man with sparse blond hair practicing golf on the peeled lawn called to get her attention and ran up to her.

"Excuse me, miss. Are you interested in working on a pilot for Fox Television?" And Natalie recognized him. He had stopped her before, a few weeks ago with the exact same line. He had the same phony yellow-toothed smile. Last time she had thought that he was a weird- looking producer; now she realized that he was probably a regular nutcase. She just shook her head no and the man went back to holding his golf club and practicing his swing.

And all of a sudden, Natalie considered the possibility that every person on the beach, including herself, could be insane. Everyone could have lost it at some point without even noticing. She removed her sandals to feel the warmth of the sand between her toes and walked straight toward the ocean until she reached the shore. There she just sat on the tire tracks in the sand.

Jerry words had hurt her, probably because they were true. "You want to fly but you are afraid to jump... a coward." There was such harshness in his tone. She was hurting him, too, like she'd hurt Jean-Marc and Michael. Roger's wife told her once that love was the antidote to fear. What would happen if she really let herself fall in love? What if she stopped anticipating the worst? What if she just gave Jerry a chance? But it was too late. Now he had seen the real her, terrified and ugly, trying to gather barricades to protect herself.

Three men had come in and out of her life in a short period

of time. She had refused to commit to any of them. Everybody wanted to find love more than anything in the world. She had found three good men and managed to let them all go. What if God had only given her these three chances to be happy and no more? She'd wanted to be free to start over. Her wish had been granted. Her eyes watered but she held the tears in. She was done crying.

Natalie stood by the window, admiring the view for the last time. Her bags waited by the door. She had returned her rental car and scrubbed Peggy's apartment until the place sparkled. She hadn't stopped for a minute, forbidding herself to think about Jerry. Now it was time to go.

She heard a noise behind the front door and opened it before Simone had time to ring the doorbell. They hugged each other.

"I can't believe it. You're early!" Natalie said with a warm smile.

"That's part of my new resolutions. I'm changing all my bad habits," Simone quipped.

"Well, thank you for coming all the way from Hollywood to take me to the airport. I could have taken a cab, you know."

"What are you talking about? I would hate to see you take a cab. I'll miss you, Nat."

"I'll miss you, too. It has been a life-changing trip. Thanks for everything." Natalie felt nothing but love for her friend.

"It changed me, too, Nat. I think that after Jerry's accident, I finally realized how selfish I've been." Simone sighed. "*Mieux vaut tard que jamais*, like they say in France."

Natalie smiled. She would really miss Simone. Her eyes watered. "We should go now, I guess," she said, fighting her emotion.

She sent a last silent goodbye to Peggy's enchanted flat and left the keys on the kitchen counter on the top of her thank you note. The click of the door locking her out of the apartment for good was like a page turned on that part of her life.

With Simone's help she dragged her bags down the stairs and managed to stuff them into the trunk of Simone's car.

"I got the car back yesterday," Simone explained. "It cost me fifteen hundred dollars to get it fixed. Now I'm really poor."

Natalie got in. Before she started the car, Simone put a hand on her thigh.

"Jerry asked me to drop by on our way to the airport. He wants to say goodbye."

Natalie's heart jumped in her chest when she heard Jerry's name. "I don't know if we have time to stop," she said weakly.

"I take that for a yes." Simone answered, starting the car.

Natalie felt her heart racing during the few minutes it took to drive to Jerry's house.

"I'll wait for you in the car. You have at least thirty minutes. Take your time," Simone said with an encouraging smile.

Natalie nervously checked her reflection in the passenger mirror and got out of the car. She wasn't prepared to see Jerry. She took a few steps toward the house then turned back, but Simone signaled her to keep going.

The front door was ajar. Jerry was painting at his easel, bare-chested as usual. He stopped when she came in, pushed himself from the stool he was leaning on, and then grabbed his crutches. He had a two-day-old beard and his face looked a little thinner, but as usual when she saw him, her heart skipped a beat. She stopped a few feet from him.

"I have something for you." He limped to his working table and lifted a flat package wrapped in brown paper. She noticed that he used his crutches with more ease.

"For me? What is it?" Natalie asked, surprised.

"It's a small painting. You should be able to put it in your carry-on," he said, handing it to her.

"Thank you. I'm touched." She kept it pressed to her heart for a while. She wanted to open it right there but the package was so well wrapped, she decided to keep the surprise for later.

She looked at him. His eyelids were heavy and his eyes had a strange expression she couldn't decipher. On impulse, she threw her arms around his neck, pain tearing through her chest at the thought that she might never see him again.

He held her tight for a few moments then he released her.

"Take care of yourself," he said.

She turned around and headed toward the door, tears rolling down her cheeks, each step away from him causing her physical pain. She closed the front door behind her, aware that he could still see her through the tinted windows, and she walked to Simone's car.

Hours later, after she had said a teary goodbye to Simone, after she had embarked the plane, crying under her sunglasses until peace finally came, she remembered the painting and stood up to remove it from her carry-on in the luggage compartment above her head.

Back in her seat, she slowly opened the package to unveil an exquisite acrylic painting on a small canvas. She immediately recognized the little girl with the crimson dress blowing bubbles in Central Park, her face reflecting innocence and pleasure at the storm of bubbles around her. In the background a man and a woman were sitting on a bench arm in arm. Natalie recognized Jerry and her depicted as loving parents: her on the bench looking at the little girl with an expression of awe on her face and him looking at her, his eyes full of love and tenderness.

CHAPTER TWENTY-FIVE

Driving through miles of bumpy dirt road overlooking the ocean, Natalie crossed fields of yellow sunburned grass where cows and goats were left to graze peacefully. The road was sometimes so narrow that cars coming from the opposite direction would force her into the bushes or hedges of flowery fences.

She followed the handwritten sign, the shape of an arrow, pointing to the left, and then she drove into a large sandy clearing. Through the trees she could catch a glimpse of the turquoise water. She parked her car and lazily opened the driver's door, letting the breeze refresh her. She could hear the sound of the waves rolling on the shore, but she didn't have a full view of the beach yet. She let herself out of the car and removed her clothes until she was in her bathing suit.

This had become her daily routine since her arrival in Martinique. Picking up her beach bag, she locked the car and walked through a sandy path bordered by trees with large heart-shaped leaves, heavy with salty berries. And finally, the hidden beach revealed its wild splendor, with its coconut trees, white sand, and pools of greenish-blue water undulating under the always-present breeze. In the distance the waves broke on the coral reef in a white fluffy line. Each time she came there and looked at the ocean, her heart did a happy dance. She gave thanks for this piece of paradise.

The beach was almost deserted, except for a couple lounging

on the sand and a few kids frolicking in the water. Waves broke on the shore with an energy that sent their sparkly white foam up in the air. Natalie put down her beach bag and sat on her towel, facing the ocean, her legs in the lotus position. She came here to meditate almost every day.

After her swim, she sat back on her towel and retrieved a sketchpad from her beach bag. She had started experimenting with paint, delighting in her weekly painting classes in Fort-de-France, experiencing a mix of excitement and apprehension when she took risks with a bold stroke of her brush or an adventurous blend of colors. She had begun a series of paintings representing a woman emerging from tumultuous waters, her arms raised up in victory. She could recognize the influence of Jerry's surrealistic scenes in her own artwork, but she was willing to experiment with all styles and mediums.

The enthusiasm she felt waking up in the morning in Martinique with the song of roosters in the distance and familiar noises of the island was worth all the drama she'd been through since she had left L.A. When Natalie told her mother of her decision to abandon surgery, Ginette made her repeat it three times then fell silent for a while before hanging up. Roger didn't react much better. He wasn't silent though.

"What the hell, Natalie? All the-ass kissing I had to do to get you that position at Charité and you trash it like it's nothing. Have you lost your mind?"

"What will I tell people?" Ginette lamented when she finally called back her daughter days later. She had already told everyone that her daughter was a surgeon in one of the best hospitals in Paris.

"Roger thinks that I've lost my mind so tell them I'm insane," Natalie answered. She was being cynical, but her mother's reaction made her realize that it was exactly what she was thinking. In fact, the family began to treat her as if she had really lost it. But Natalie never felt so sane and so brave. She walked taller and breathed better. The heaviness in her heart had disappeared. Resisting her family, instead of depressing her, woke her warrior instinct. It was as if she had discovered a hidden reservoir of energy.

It did hurt when Jean-Marc refused to talk to her. He didn't answer when she called to ask what he wanted her to do with the things he had left at her place. He sent his cousin to pick them up. Some of their friends also gave her the cold shoulder. Jean-Marc's open hostility was one of the reasons Natalie left Paris. She presented her thesis only because it was ready, packed up Moustique the cat with the neighbor's blessings, rented her apartment and flew to Martinique.

That was three months ago. Even now, the family was careful with her, treating her as if she were recovering from a nervous breakdown. For weeks, her mother still gave her anxious looks, her forehead creased with worry.

Because there was no way she could stay at her mother's house under those conditions, Natalie rented a small house in the south of the island, close to her favorite beach, where she spent most of her free time. Then she started practicing medicine again. Even though it wasn't surgery, the family breathed a collective sigh of relief.

Natalie's mornings were spent taking care of elderly patients at a little retirement center, which gave her real satisfaction. The setting was quite different from the Parisian hospitals she had fled.

In this small center, every room had a view, some opening to the marina with its fleet of sailboats, others looking over roofs and fruit trees. Doors stayed open. When she made her rounds Natalie felt like a relative dropping by to visit old uncles or aunts. She had always enjoyed the company of seniors. A little bit of compassion, a warm smile or a compliment meant so much to them. Natalie felt rewarded when she revived a spark of life and appreciation in old eyes glazed with sadness and loss. She took the time to hold distorted hands, swollen by arthritis, to listen to the long list of ailments, to remember the personal stories. It wasn't very long before she had gained her patients' trust. She gave them the same attention and care she would give her own family members. "Yes, doctor," they said to everything she recommended with touching obedience and respect.

"Doctor is sooooo kind," Natalie overheard one of her patients, a ninety-six-year-old woman, tell her niece who had come visit. Sometimes the patients' family members brought her presents, ripe mangoes or oranges from their backyards, homemade coconut liquors. The love and appreciation she got back from taking good care of her senior patients put a balm on her heart.

Natalie took a deep breath and exhaled. Her body was in its element. She felt fit, healthy, centered. But she would be lying if she didn't admit that sometimes she questioned her choices. She missed her friends and she missed Jerry.

Michael had emailed to say that he was shooting a movie in Canada. Two weeks after he came back from Thailand he booked another movie and flew to Toronto. The tone of his email was friendly. Natalie was glad she hadn't interfered with his dreams.

One night a phone call from Simone woke Natalie up. "Oh

my God, I freaking got it. I just can't believe it. I finally did it."
She had just booked a good part in a promising motion picture
shooting in Rome. They talked for an hour, Natalie rejoicing as if
Simone's victory were her own. It meant that perseverance paid
off. She wanted to ask about Jerry–she hadn't heard from him–but
she didn't find the courage. It would hurt to hear that he was going
out with someone or that he was back with Brenda.

Still, Natalie was at peace with herself. She enjoyed every
ray of sunshine, every drop of rain, every blade of grass as if she
had just been born. Once again, she gave thanks for those precious
moments doing what she enjoyed.

Her cell phone rang in her bag, interrupting her thoughts. She
almost passed out when she saw Jerry's name appearing on the
digital screen.

"Hey gorgeous, what are you doing right now?" he said as if
they had just seen each other a few hours ago.

Natalie closed her eyes and smiled to the heavens. Jerry. She
had never stopped thinking about him. When she landed in Paris,
she had to exercise all the self-control she was capable of to not
take the next flight back to him. "I'm so happy to hear your voice,"
she said, her hand on her heart to keep it from beating so fast. "I'm
on my favorite beach watching the waves. What about you?"

"I'm watching you watching the waves."

She turned around to see Jerry's silhouette in the distance
walking toward her. She wondered if she were dreaming. He had
come for her. He had found her. The sky spun above her head. Her
heart pounded in her chest with so much strength, she wondered if
it could take it.

Jerry was there, as amazingly handsome as ever. While she

had felt occasional regrets thinking about Michael and Jean-Marc, she had thought about Jerry every day, remembering every detail of their story, wondering if she would ever be able to forget him, wondering if the freedom she had been so intent on obtaining hadn't made her pay too huge of a price. But there he was, in flesh and blood, coming toward her.

Natalie couldn't deny anymore the depth of what she felt for him. And so what if their story lasted only a few months or a few years? What if she just accepted this gift for what it was? What if she just trusted life?

And suddenly, as if the wall of a dam had opened up, her love ran free, a life force unable to be contained anymore. There was no more concern, only the clear knowledge that she wanted Jerry in her life for as long as the universe would allow it. She took a deep breath, stood up, and ran toward him, fear and doubt pouring out of her heart until there was only joy.

ABOUT THE AUTHOR

Born in Paris to a French literature teacher and a physician, Rafaële Désiré was raised on the French Caribbean island of Martinique.

An artistic child who loved reading above all, she chose science over literature when she moved back to France to become an orthodontist, but a trip to the United States radically changed her life.

She studied fine arts at Otis/Parsons, film production at NYU, and tried her hand at acting, modeling, and graphic design.

Rafaële Désiré is a painter, writer, and Tai Chi instructor, and she practices orthodontics in Los Angeles where she lives with her two daughters.

A published author in the dental field, she has written short stories, flash fiction, and poetry in English and French. *Paradise Bound* is her first novel.

www.ingramcontent.com/pod-product-compliance
Lightning Source LLC
Chambersburg PA
CBHW020558260626
47157CB00003B/760